SEM

CORA ROSE

CREDITS

Editor: Angela O'Connell

Copyright © 2023 by Cora Rose

All rights reserved.

No part of this book may be reproduced in any form or by any electronic or mechanical means, including information storage and retrieval systems, without written permission from the author, except for the use of brief quotations in a book review.

To my brothers who inspired the stupid stuff the van Beek boys do.

For all of you doubting that these kinds of people exist...I assure you, they do. I grew up with them.

And of course to my sister, who helped me bail our brothers out of way too many shady situations.

PREFACE

Sem and Magnus were a lot of fun to write, although very different from Caleb and Whit. They're two totally different people in the way they interact with each other and the world around them. When reading this, I hope you can suspend reality just a little and roll with it.

I hope you enjoy them as much as I do.

Content Warning:
This story deals with bullying and contains some homophobic language.

CHAPTER ONE

The pulse of the loud music vibrates through my body as I move across the crowded house party. My best friend August invited me to this shitfest, and I haven't seen him since my arrival ten minutes ago. He's probably upstairs with some chick getting himself off. Horny bastard.

I remind myself I'm just jealous because it's been a while.

Almost a year, to be exact.

My sex life isn't very exhilarating. It's more like a series of lousy hookups paired with the occasional minor disappointment.

I stand on my tiptoes and strain my neck to look over everyone, but it's useless. If August is somewhere down here, I can't see him over the people crowding around me. I'm not exactly the tallest person in the building. I'm probably more like the shortest, which is ridiculous considering my entire family is well over six feet. I'm one hundred percent sure I'm adopted. My mom decries this, but I don't really believe her.

I run my hands down my midriff shirt and then duck

under a guy reaching for someone else. I question why I decided to come here in the first place, but then I remember August's puppy dog eyes, and how I couldn't resist. He knows I have a hard time saying no to him when he looks at me like that.

Conniving bastard.

I squeeze past a couple making out, and slide along the wall. My size makes it easy to scurry around people. I eventually make my way to the corner of the large living room and stand on top of an end table to see if I can find my best friend.

My eyes skim across the throbbing, mostly drunk crowd, and through the haze of the lights and smoke, I see *him*.

Oh, mother of all that's holy. I groan. Not again.

How is he *everywhere* I am? I should've never accepted that ride home with him that one night. Ever since, he's been borderline obsessed with me.

I narrow my gaze at Sem van Beek who's looming across the dimly lit room. He's impossible to miss. He stands out in a place like this, full of dude bros and sorority sisters. Oh, how does he stand out, you ask?

Let me count the ways.

First, he towers over everyone, and the muscles on his arms and abdomen are clearly defined through the grey t-shirt he's wearing. You don't get muscles like that from working out in a gym. No, you get that from lifting heavy shit all day long. Second, he looks like he just rolled in from a hard day of manual labor, all scuffed up and calloused. His jeans are worn and torn at the knees but his long, shoulder-length wavy blond hair looks freshly washed.

I'm sure most people here haven't worked a day in their lives. Or if they have it's been in an office or maybe a coffee shop. Sem works in a scrapyard, and I've heard that he enjoys building off-road vehicles from the ground up on the weekends. Most people here don't even remember to get oil changes in their luxury sedans. And third, he just looks rugged, like a guy who enjoys guns and gasoline and blowing shit up.

Speaking of which, I've heard he likes to set things on fire. I should probably stay away from this pyro.

Very far away. Should probably move my eyes away from him right this second. Yep.

Spoiler alert, I don't.

I notice a few girls standing around him, craning their necks up to gaze at him and giggle. And I admit, he's good-looking... if you like a guy who looks like a fucking goliath Viking.

And I don't. I most definitely *do not*.

No, my tastes run more refined. And Sem is just too...rough.

You, I mouth, pointing at Sem and then slashing my finger to the space in front of me. *Come here.*

Sem cocks his head like the psychopath he is, those bright blue eyes flashing, and then he strides forward. He's so large that everyone moves aside for him. Like Moses parting the Red Sea.

Ridiculous, obnoxious man.

When he finally stops in front of me, he meets my eyes. We're literally the same height right now because I haven't moved from my perch on the table. It makes me feel like a pharaoh or a king for some reason, and it goes to my head. I just ordered Sem over here, and he came. What kind of black magic fuckery is this?

"What are you doing here?" I ask sharply.

Sem reaches out and flicks the bracelet on my wrist. "I was invited."

"By who?" I ask, not believing him. Because I know he doesn't live nearby, and he definitely didn't go to college here because I would have noticed someone like him hulking around campus.

Hold on, did he even go to college? Come to think of it, I hardly know anything about him. Just heard a lot of stories from his cousin, Caleb. I make a mental note to inquire more about him.

For purely educational reasons.

"Do I need to tell you who invited me?" he asks, those deep blue eyes squinting as he watches me.

"Yes. Yes, you do."

"Nah, I don't," he says, and I want to wrap my hands around that thick neck and squeeze. I doubt I'd be able to span its circumference, but I'd sure as hell try. I'm nothing if not an overachiever.

He folds those thick arms of his across his chest and steps slightly closer to me. My back hits the wall, and the table wobbles underneath me. His hands dart out to grip my arms, steadying me. The contact burns my exposed skin and I swat his hands away.

"Careful," he grumbles.

"I'm fine. Just don't...don't crowd me. I'm here with friends, and I don't need you scaring people away from me."

He fiddles with the edge of my shirt sleeve and I glower at him.

"Hands to yourself."

"Your shirt is pink."

"Duh."

"And short."

"Your eyesight is intact. Good to know. Now go away, Sem. I'm serious. Or else, I'm going to have to call your mother and tell her that you're doing it again."

Sem's jaw tightens at that, and he takes a step back.

"Why you talking to my ma?"

"Because Sem, your mother gave me her number when you started *stalking* me."

"I don't stalk."

"Oh, then what would you call this?"

Sem shrugs. "We happen to be at the same party. Big fucking deal. I'm not here for you anyway," he says, pulling that blond hair back into a loose ponytail. A wayward strand falls across his temple, and he tucks it behind his ear. He shoves his hands into the pockets of his worn jeans, and he lifts an eyebrow at me, causing me to bristle.

"Oh, is that right?" I scoff. "And who are you here for, if it's not me?"

Sem nods to the right, and I glance over but don't see anyone, in particular, waiting for him. Though there is still a gaggle of girls watching him talk to me.

"You're such a liar," I reply. "And a bad one at that."

"Don't be pissed that I'm not as obsessed with you as you think."

I roll my eyes to the ceiling and sigh. "You're obviously obsessed with *me*. You're everywhere I am."

"Nah, you just happen to be everywhere *I am*."

Okay, this conversation is getting me nowhere. If I continue like this, I'll be here all night. I'm turning into one of my kindergartners. I hop down from the table and wave my hand in front of me.

"Shoo. Back to your cave," I hiss, and Sem works his jaw back and forth before moving back to the other side of the room. Even though I can't see him anymore, I can feel his eyes on me.

Asshole.

"There you are!" a familiar voice says to my right, and I jump slightly, dramatically placing a hand over my chest.

"August! Where have you been? I've been looking for you for ages."

My best friend licks his lips and shrugs, causing me to sigh. "Gross. Did you at least wash your hands? Gargle with mouthwash? Vaginas are icky."

August chuckles and nudges me. "Yeah, that's your opinion, man, but I did. Don't worry. Wouldn't want to offend your delicate sensibilities."

His eyes flick across the crowded room, and I follow his gaze and see a dark-haired, tattooed guy sitting on the couch, making out with two girls.

"Why's Emery here?" I ask, and August huffs in irritation.

"My mom asked me to lug him around."

"Don't you guys like, not get along?"

August runs a hand through his hair and sighs. "Yeah, well, what am I supposed to do? Tell her no? It would break her heart. She wants us to be friends. At least he's occupied and leaving me the hell alone."

I eye Emery and watch as he slants his head and licks into one girl's mouth. It's kind of obscene what he's doing with those lips of his.

"Oh Jesus, stop looking," August grumbles and tugs me away. "Let's not talk about him or ogle him. He's not what I want to be focusing on."

"And what do you want to focus on?"

"How about the fact that I saw your Viking here."

"He's not my Viking, and don't remind me," I groan and

slap a hand onto my forehead. "He's everywhere. Everywhere! I should have never accepted that ride home from him. That was a huge mistake. I'm never going to escape him now. I'm going to be ninety years old, and Sem will be lurking around the backyard of my senior care facility."

August chuckles and ruffles my hair.

"Excuse me," I say with irritation. "My hair is a masterpiece. Took ages to get it perfect. Do not ruin it any further."

"Colin isn't even here, so why do you care what you look like?" August asks with a sly smile. "You trying to impress Sem now, huh?" He waggles his eyebrows at me, and I flick his nipple.

He hisses.

"Of course not! And Colin isn't here because he's a single dad. He wouldn't be at a stupid college frat party at ten at night. He has more important matters to deal with, like his son. Or working on some important lecture for class. And you know what? I'm jealous of him right now. Why are we here again? I never liked frat parties, they remind me too much of my brothers."

I shudder at the thought of making out with someone who even vaguely resembles them.

"You're here because you love me. And tell me again why you're so into that guy, Colin? Because he doesn't even notice you."

"Whatever. He will. All in good time."

August snorts. "Sure, Mag. Whatever you say. You're like the least patient person I know, but hey, maybe tomorrow in yoga, the man of your dreams will finally turn your way. You'll meet his eyes and end up barefoot and pregnant."

I arch an eyebrow at my best friend. "Maybe I will. But the better question is will *you* be there tomorrow morning after tonight? Because you look like you imbibed a little too much."

"Sure will," he says and then presses a hand to the small of his back. "My back's still killing me since the accident. Gotta work out the kinks so I can keep on playing ball, and you know...fucking all the hotties."

"You better not be lying to me," I say, poking him in the chest.

"I swear on our friendship that I'll be there no matter what I get myself into tonight. Or *who* I get myself into."

I press my fingers into my ears and shake my head. I do not need to know about any of his sexual exploits. Nope. No, thank you.

August and I met each other freshman year after being placed in the same dorm room. We hit it off, despite being different in so many ways. He's straight; I'm gay. He's tall; I'm short. He's a jock; I'm a geek. But the one area we intersect is the two of us are elementary education majors. We just finished up our senior year of college last month, and next year we will complete our teaching credentials. In the meantime, we both work at a daycare and are currently facilitating our own classes for summer camp. I'm in a classroom with the kindergartners, and he's with the third graders.

And despite being extremely good-looking in that boy-next-door way, I have zero interest in him. Nada. Zilch.

"Hey, I know. Maybe tomorrow, if we show up early to yoga class, we can get a spot right in front of Colin, and he'll have the perfect view of your tiny ass. You can show him how bendy you are. Might actually notice you exist after seeing how you can fold yourself in half."

I roll my eyes. "You are a *terrible* friend. Why do I even like you?"

"Nah, I'm the bestest friend you've ever had."

I sigh, and then a tiny smile lifts the corners of my mouth. "Yeah, you are. God, I hate you."

August slings an arm around my shoulders and presses a kiss to the top of my head.

"Alright, how about we grab you a beer and hang out on the porch. Maybe you can find yourself someone to get under tonight. Yeah?"

"Pfft, maybe. I'm holding out for Colin, though. He's my perfect man."

"He doesn't even know you exist, Mag. Let's find you a placeholder instead."

"Whatever," I say and see Sem watching me from across the room. "But drinks first. Lots of them."

———

"Oh my god, my head," I groan softly as I stumble into the yoga studio and slap my mat onto the floor. Colin hasn't arrived yet, but I'm not in the mood for him to notice me today anyway. I'm so hungover from last night I feel like I'm going to pass out. I don't know what happened or what provoked me, but I drank *way too much*.

No, actually, I *do know* what happened.

"I hate him," I mutter as August rolls his mat out next to mine.

"Who?"

"Sem. The manipulative bastard."

August snorts and sits down on the mat and stretches his long legs out in front of him. He looks fantastic despite leaving the party after me, drinking far more than me, and probably fucking away half the night between some girl's legs.

His dirty blond hair is combed nicely to the side, and his green eyes actually sparkle. Damn him.

I, on the other hand, look like I just rolled out of bed. All I did was brush my teeth before I staggered to the car.

"I don't think Sem forced you to down all those shots. That was all you, my friend."

"Yes, he did. Inadvertently. He was watching me the entire time, August. I couldn't escape his eyes. They're always on me, following me around. Drinking was the only way to get through last night without committing murder."

Hazy visions of last evening assault me as I stretch out my aching muscles.

Sem on the couch, a woman straddling his lap, his tongue plundering her mouth, and his eyes closed. Those long lashes casting shadows on his flushed cheeks.

His eyes snapping open and catching my gaze, letting them slide up my body as I moved on the dance floor.

Licking his tongue up that girl's neck, those blazing blue eyes on me the entire time.

Me lifting my shirt a little, running my hands across my stomach, teasing him, playing with fire.

His eyes flashing as he grinds up into that girl like he was fucking into me.

It was obscene and uncomfortable.

I hated it.

"Did he also inadvertently make you loudly proclaim to anyone within ten miles that you like big dicks?" August asks, just as the door to the studio opens and Colin strides through.

Perfect, unattainable Colin. With his lithe, trim body, perfectly coiffed hair, and that delectable sleeve of tattoos on his right arm. From my internet sleuthing, I know he's in his thirties, a history professor at a community college, and part of a book club. He also likes red wine, walks on the beach, and cycling. He's like a dream come true.

Colin glances over at us, the word *dicks* lingering in the air, and I blush from head to toe.

Gah, of course, *now* he notices me.

I expect Colin to ignore me, but instead, he offers me a small smile and then moves to the front of the room and places his own mat down.

When I'm sure he's not paying any attention to us, I reach over and pinch August.

"Ouch," he hisses, rubbing his arm. "You have strong fingers for such a little guy. What was that for?"

"You're an ass. The biggest one ever. Bigger than my brother Mitch and we both know that's hard to come by."

"Hey, don't be mean now. Mitch is the devil's spawn. Don't compare me to him."

"Fine," I huff.

"And don't hate. Colin noticed you, yeah?"

"Yeah, because you basically advertised that I like big dicks in my butt!" I hiss.

August chuckles at that as the door to the classroom opens again, and more people filter in.

"It's not a secret, is it? You told everyone last night about your preferences. Shouted it. Even Sem heard. He stopped dry humping that girl for a minute when those words left your mouth. He started panting. Think he came in his pants a little."

I groan at that image because it's *disgusting* and move into Child's Pose to hide my twitching dick. This is all Sem's fault. If he would just leave me alone, none of this crap would be happening to me right now. I peek up at Colin, who is typing on his phone before class officially starts. Our eyes meet in the mirror that runs along the front of the room and the corner of his mouth turns up. I look away quickly and am thankful when the instructor moves her way to the front of the room, distracting everyone.

Because, despite it being true, I'm still mortified he heard all that. That is not how I want him to remember me. No, I am sophisticated Magnus who likes teaching children and deep philosophical discussions.

When class is over, August forces me into a sweaty hug despite my squeals of protest, and then I head back home to shower. As I wash the grime of last night and this morning away under the warm water, my mind flashes to the small looks Colin gave me throughout class. I try not to overthink it, but I wonder if maybe he's intrigued now. I wonder if he likes what he sees. Or maybe likes what he heard. Perhaps this is the beginning of something new between us.

One can only hope.

Stepping out of the shower, I pull on a pair of small yellow track shorts and pad out to the kitchen to grab a cup of coffee when I see a shape lounging on the couch.

More like a person.

My heart thunders in my chest, and without thinking, I swipe a book sitting on the shelf nearest me and launch it at the intruder. It thumps against the cushion, missing my target by a mile.

Sem looks up at me, utterly unbothered by the fact that he just scared the shit out of me. Or by the fact that he's in my apartment uninvited.

"Jesus, Sem!" I shout and launch another book at him, but it misses again. I have terrible aim. Need to work on that, apparently. Should probably make more of an effort to play catch with August when he asks.

Sem just looks at the two books on the couch and then at me.

His brows furrow in confusion. "What was that for?"

"Um. Hello. You broke into my house!" I nearly shout, walking over to him and grabbing the photo album he has open on his lap. I snap it shut and set it back on the end table.

"What's the big deal? I let myself in. You didn't answer the door."

"I was in the shower," I reply, throwing my hands up in exasperation and then slapping them onto my naked hips. My eyes narrow at him, but his eyes don't meet mine. No, they're sliding across my mostly bare body, stopping momentarily on my crotch.

I'm pretty sure he can see the outline of my dick in these thin shorts, but whatever. He invaded my space. He can't be offended by what he walks in on.

"You can't just break into people's homes and go through their things. That's not what normal people do!"

"Who said I was normal? And sure, I can," he says, leaning back on the couch and stretching his thick thighs out in front of him.

I do not notice how strong his legs look under the fabric of his worn jeans. Nope. I notice no such thing.

"What do you want?" I grind out, standing in front of him. Too close, much too close.

He swipes a finger out and fiddles with the end of my shorts.

"These are short. And tight."

"Of course they are. I wasn't planning on having any visitors." I smack his hand away, and he sets it on the couch, flexing his fingers.

"You're not wearing underwear."

"So?"

He blinks. "You have tiny nipples."

"They're proportionate to my body."

His eyes flit across my body once more. "You don't have any hair anywhere."

"I know. It's called maintenance."

"That's weird."

"For you, maybe."

He swipes a finger down the smooth skin of my leg, and I flick his finger away.

"Why are you so smooth?"

"I use lotion. What, do straight guys not moisturize?"

"Nah," he says, swiping a hand across his mouth. "That'd be... gay," he says with a smirk and a twinkle in his eye.

Now I'm really pissed.

"Okay, you know what? I'm *not* doing this with you right now. What do you want, Sem? It must be important since you usually just lurk and loom like a gargoyle but don't actually commit felonies like breaking and entering... Or, do you?" I narrow my eyes at him.

He rolls his lips between his teeth, and those blue eyes meet mine.

He ignores my question and says, "I heard you last night."

"And what did you *hear* exactly?" I ask, taking a step back and folding my arms across my chest.

"Heard you brag you could take anyone. Any size."

I roll my eyes. "Yeah, so?"

I'm being bratty, but he's annoying me, looking ridiculously large in this small apartment. He consumes way too much space. I'm finding it hard to breathe.

"I don't believe you."

I sniff and arch an eyebrow. "And why do I care what you *believe?*"

Oh, but I do care. No one underestimates me. I've dealt with that my whole life. People think that I can't do what they can because I'm smaller than most men. Fuck them all.

"You were lying. Why would you do that? For attention?"

"I was *not* lying!"

Sem rubs a hand across the couch cushion. "How could someone so small take someone so big? They'd tear you in half."

I scoff. "What do you know, straight boy? I can take what I want to take. I'm incredible."

I don't know why I'm arguing with him, but he brings out my competitive side. I would never behave this way with anyone else.

Apparently, all bets are off.

"Nah, don't believe you. You couldn't take me."

I place a hand on my hip and, with the other, gesture to his crotch. Now I'm getting angry. "Is that so? Well, go ahead then. Show me."

Sem cocks his head, puzzled.

"Show me your dick, Sem. Do I have to spell it out for you? D.I.C.K. Or maybe you're one of those big guys with a tiny little wiener hidden away down there. Too ashamed to show me what you're really working with, huh?"

Sem's cheeks are slightly pink, and I relish his discomfort.

He shifts on the couch. "I don't have a small dick."

"Yeah, well, I don't believe you. Guys like you—big trucks,

big muscles—have tiny dicks. Fact." I'm goading him now, spewing petty insults, and I'm not even entirely sure why.

Sem narrows his eyes at me, his jaw clenches, and then he arches his hips and tugs those jeans down to his thighs, underwear and all. His half-hard cock lies on his thigh, and I swallow roughly.

Because, oh shit.

No tiny dick here. He's massive. Of course he is, because life is just unfair.

I clear my throat, pretending like seeing him like this doesn't excite me. "Get it hard. I have to see what it really looks like to make my final determination. Right now, you're just average. Nothing I haven't already had."

Sem meets my gaze, and determination filters through those blue eyes. He grabs it and strokes himself into a fullblown erection within a few seconds. And I find that watching him do this makes my dick twitch in my very tiny shorts.

Bad. Bad. Very, very bad.

When he's fully hard, he stops stroking himself, sets his hands on the couch cushions, and stares at me. But I can't meet his eyes; I can't even look at his crotch. He's ginormous, the shaft is super thick with a vein running underside and the head is slick and pink and fucking perfect. While my mind is screaming *no way, fuck off,* my body wants to climb on top of him and sit on that big dick. My body is a slut and obviously can't be trusted.

This is unacceptable because I do *not* like this man. There is no way we are having sex. I'm not that desperate. I have standards.

"Tell me now that you can put *this* inside your tiny body," Sem says slightly gravelly, gesturing to his twitching cock.

I refuse to look at it.

"Can't even look at it, huh?" he huffs. "It scares you."

I peek over at it for a moment and then meet his eyes. "I'm not afraid of anything."

"You're afraid you can't take it."

"I can."

"Liar."

That word. It makes me see red. I take a step toward him. "*I can.*"

"Fine. Prove it."

By now, I'm so irritated that I reach into the end table and shuffle through it. I pull out an extra-large condom that I keep for special occasions and toss it at Sem. It hits his chest, and he picks it up, eyeing it.

"Put that on, asshole," I say and then toss a lube packet at him. "That too."

I blame it on the hangover and the copious amounts of alcohol I drank last night. It's why I'm not thinking clearly as I walk toward the bathroom and shout, "I'm going to go prep. Do not move, or you forfeit, and I win."

As I stand in the bathroom, my fingers up my ass, lubing myself up, I wonder if I've gone insane. But for some reason, I don't think I can turn back now. Something about Sem makes me irrational.

When I've stretched myself, and I'm satisfied he won't actually tear me apart, I grab a jockstrap from the hamper and pull it on. There's no need for him to see my dick during this. Some things are still private. This is nothing more than proving a point.

Sem's still on the couch when I exit the bathroom, his cock sheathed in the condom I'd given him. It's glossy from the lube he applied. His shirt is still on, but his pants are pushed down to his ankles. His hands grip the cushions beside him as he watches me approach, his nostrils flaring slightly as he takes me in.

"You sure about this?" I ask, wondering how he's okay with this. He's about to have sex with a man. I half expect him to run away, but he just swallows and nods.

"Not scared?"

"Nah," he breathes.

"Fine. I'm going to sit on you," I say, happy my voice doesn't betray my nerves. Because he's bigger than I've ever had. Not that I'll ever tell him that.

"This doesn't mean you get to touch me, so hands to yourself."

His hands curl into fists at his hips.

"Scoot down a bit."

Sem does as he's told until his ass is nearly hanging off the couch, and then I straddle those muscular legs.

"Ready to be proven wrong?" I ask. I push him back with the tips of my fingers so he's farther away from me, and then I grasp onto my thighs for leverage. I'm going to need all the help I can get.

Sem doesn't even nod, just gulps as I grab onto his dick and position it at my hole. And then, without warning, I sink down onto it, the thick head slipping inside of me.

Sem exhales sharply, and his eyes move from the spot where we connect back to my face.

I try to keep my voice even as I explain, "This lube is a miracle, really. Spent a fortune on it and I'm not disappointed." I sink down a little more as Sem bites down on his bottom lip.

Oh god, this is so satisfying, watching him try and control himself. His first time with a man, and he likes it more than he thought he would. I smirk at him as I take him a little deeper, his thick, long cock stretching me almost painfully.

"See? Easy," I say, my voice a little breathless.

"I'm not even a quarter of the way in," he mutters, and I sink down a little lower to spite him.

His nostrils flare, and I breathe through my nose and then bear down and take him almost to the hilt.

His eyes widen, and his mouth parts slightly as he pants. "Fuck," he mutters.

"Almost. There," I breathe and then, on an exhale, sit on him entirely.

Sem's chest heaves, and we just sit there, our eyes locked—my hazel to his ocean blue.

"Told you," I whisper, trying to sound smug, but I just sound turned on. Because he feels way too good inside of me, and despite my mind not wanting to like it, my dick really, really does. It's hard, straining against my jockstrap and leaking profusely. If I look, I can see a wet spot right there.

Oh dammit.

But if Sem notices my current state of arousal, he doesn't say anything. He just sits still, his eyes locked onto mine from his slumped position on the couch.

"I win," I add and then tell myself to move off him, but I don't. I just sit there until Sem arches his hips slightly. My breath catches in my throat, and my fingers clench my thighs so tightly that it's almost painful.

"So, you can take it," he concedes, his voice like gravel, and then adds, "But what about actually being fucked by it."

"You don't think I can be fucked by your massive dick?" I ask, wiggling slightly on top of him because it feels unnatural to be impaled by him and not move.

He hisses. "Exactly."

Instead of answering, I simply lift myself until I'm at the tip of his cock and then slowly slide back down.

"Jesus," he pants.

"Like that?"

Sem swallows and nods once.

"Oh, honey," I breathe, swiveling my hips. "You have no idea what I'm capable of."

And then I start moving, fucking myself on him. Slowly at first, and then picking up the pace as my body adjusts to his size. I'm enjoying this entire thing far more than I should. Watching Sem's pupils dilate, his cheeks redden, his lips open in a silent gasp as I work him closer to the edge. Witnessing him lose this little bet he thought for sure he'd win is almost better than an orgasm.

"How does it feel to fuck another man, hm?" I ask, and Sem's Adam's apple bobs. He doesn't respond.

I don't skimp. I make sure to take him all, lowering onto him fully and then dragging my hole right to the tip of his cock. Just to prove a point.

The entire time, we never touch. His hands stay clenched on the couch as mine grip tightly to my thighs. I just ride him, biting my lips to keep any sort of whimper at bay because *I am not enjoying this*. Not even a little. This is just a bet, a dare that I'm winning.

I'm a fucking winner.

Sem's hips, which were previously still, start to move. Just a fraction, but it's noticeable, and then his breathing grows erratic, and a small huff exits his mouth. His eyes slam shut, and I feel his hips moving jerkily underneath me until he suddenly stills.

And then it's over. There's just me sitting on his spent dick while mine is still painfully hard. Of course, that's *totally fine*. I didn't expect to get off from this. That's not what this was about. No, this was nothing more than a childish bet.

"I win," I say and then remove myself from him, slowly, inch by long inch, until I'm completely empty.

I can't help but glance down at the full condom and Sem's half-hard dick.

When I speak, I keep a little bite in my words. "You may be the biggest I've ever had, but you were a lousy lay."

Sem flushes crimson at that, and I turn away from him. I flick my hand up in a bratty wave.

"Make sure to toss that shit in the trash," I say, making sure my voice doesn't hitch. "And please, lock the door behind you."

I don't look back at him as I saunter into the bathroom, and once the door is locked, I sag against the wall, trembling slightly. I glance down and apologize to my very, very disappointed dick.

No, I will not get you off to thoughts of Sem. I have more dignity than that. Thank you very much.

And then, as I step into the shower for the second time today, I apologize to my future husband, Colin. Because, really, what the hell was I thinking doing that with the most infuriating man on the planet?

CHAPTER TWO

I don't tell anyone what I did with Sem. I'm a sealed vault. I'm embarrassed that I let my pride take over my common sense. I doubt he'll say anything to anyone because he's probably wondering why he went through with it in the first place. Straight men don't have sex with other men simply because of a silly bet. That's not a thing.

And I'm sure I would hear about it if he told anyone. Caleb, my friend and Sem's cousin, would blow up my phone if he knew what went down. He can't help but nose around like he always does. I'm sure his fiancé, Whit, would be doing something similar, yet more discreetly, like arching an eyebrow or sending me accusing looks with his eyes. He's really good at that. Caleb says it's like a superpower, and I'm inclined to agree.

Nope, it's been radio silence since that fateful morning. I haven't even seen Sem lurking about like he usually does. Ever since I left him sitting on my couch, he's been a ghost.

It's been nice.

Very nice.

I think.

"I haven't seen your shadow around," August says, leaning against my classroom door, and I sigh as I wipe a table down with some paper towels.

It's five o'clock, and I'm exhausted. Today at summer camp, we had a water day. Just trying to get kindergarteners to put on sunscreen was ridiculous. Managing them around the water was another thing entirely. It seems all children make it a point to try and die on a daily basis.

I'm ready for a glass of wine and a good documentary. Maybe I'll even daydream about Colin and how he smiled at me again in class this morning, those sweet eyes sweeping over me as I moved into the Cobra position. He was totally admiring my legs.

"It's been a week since he last showed up," August adds and then moves into the room to help me push in some wayward chairs.

"So? That's a good thing, right?"

"What happened?" August asks, eyeing me with curiosity. "What aren't you telling me?"

"Pfft," I say and then toss the paper towels into the trash. "*Nothing* happened. Why would you even think that? Nothing happened. Nada. Zip. Zilch."

My cheeks are flaming. I'm a terrible liar.

"Bro, you look guilty. You sound guilty." August steps in closer and lowers his voice. "Shit. Did you murder him?"

"Oh my god, no! That's the first thing that comes to your mind? Really?"

August shrugs and then says, "You're small, but I'm sure you could manage to get a knife in that thick chest of his. I'm just not sure you'd have the strength to dispose of the body. Unless, of course, you chopped him up into tiny pieces."

I grab my satchel and throw it over my shoulders. "You are crazy. Certifiable. No, I did not murder him, nor would I ever do that to someone. And really, could we just not. No more talk of him. I don't even want to *think* of him, okay?"

"Alright, if you say so," August says, holding up his hands. "Let's go then. Let's go hit some balls."

"Ugh. You know I suck at that. I'm not sporty. Not in the least. Why do you keep inviting me to my own personal hell? Do you enjoy torturing me?"

August laughs and ruffles my hair. "It's good for your coordination and upper body strength." He reaches over and squeezes my arm. "Too skinny."

"It's just how I'm made, okay? I have muscles. They're just hidden. They don't just pop out like they do on you."

Or Sem. He has a lot of muscles. More than anyone I know, actually.

August grins as if he's followed my train of thought. I quickly squash it, just in case he truly is telepathic. "Come on. No more complaining. Let's go."

I groan but follow my best friend out of the school, locking up behind me, because there's no saying no to him, apparently.

"You still hanging out with Emery?" I ask, and August glowers at me.

"It's bad enough that he's going to be my stepbrother in a few short months. Can we please not talk about him now? You're ruining my night just mentioning his name."

"Oh, so you can go on and on about Sem, but I can't ask a simple question about Emery?"

"Yeah, but man, Sem has a total crush on you."

"He does not."

"Yeah, bro, he does." He walks me to my car and says, "But Emery and I...he's just a...tool. I'm doing this for my mom, okay? I'm trying to be nice, but he's just a little shit." He glances at me and then arches an eyebrow. "Happy now?"

"Perhaps," I say and slide into my car to follow him to the batting cages.

When I arrive home two hours later, I could pass out. My entire body aches even more than it did after work. Hitting balls is no joke. My arms are screaming at me. Luckily, August fed me before he dropped me off because I was getting hangry and was close to disowning him as my best friend.

"Oh, shit on a stick!" I shout when I see Sem sitting at my desk, thumbing through some of my bills. My heart jumps in my chest and continues to pound erratically despite knowing I'm not in any danger. Sem may be a bit of a stalker, but deep down I know he's not dangerous.

My eyes slide over him as I lock the door. He's wearing torn jeans and a sleeveless grey shirt. On his right bicep is a large tattoo of an eagle in front of an American flag. It's utterly ridiculous and ostentatious. How had I never noticed that before?

I shake my head because why would I have noticed that? I try my best to *not* look at him. Even if he makes it impossible.

"What in the hell are you doing here?" I say and rush over, snatching the paperwork he's flipping through, and stuff it into a drawer. I'd lock it up, but it wouldn't matter. He'd just pick the lock open if he wanted to. "You can't just snoop around like this, Sem. That stuff is not your business. It's private."

He glances up at me and swivels around in the chair, disregarding my obvious anger.

"Where were you?" he asks.

My eyes roll so hard it hurts. "None of your business."

"I waited for you."

"Tough shit."

Sem fiddles with the button on the bottom of my shirt, and I step back.

"I thought I finally got rid of you. What are you doing here?"

Sem leans back in the chair, those massive hands of his grabbing onto its arms, and it creaks under his weight. The chair was not made for someone his size.

"You're going to break that chair in two. Get up. *Up*. It's not made for goliaths."

He doesn't budge, and I fist my hands so I don't reach out and strangle him. Perhaps I *am* capable of murder.

"I was doing some research," he says, ignoring me.

"Research on what?" I huff and set my bag down on the ground, not letting my eyes leave his even for a moment.

"Gay sex."

"Oh, sweet Jesus, Mary, and Joseph. I have not had enough wine for this," I mutter and then raise an eyebrow because, damn it all, I'm intrigued. "What about it?"

He shifts in his seat and then says, "The position we...." His words trail off like he can't even say it, and I suppress a laugh. This entire thing is so bizarre I couldn't have even imagined it. In what world do I have sex with Sem and then discuss gay sex? This is some fucking *Alice in Wonderland* shit.

"Oh, do you mean the position we had sex in? Where you stuck your big penis in my tiny hole, that one?"

His cheeks pinken, and I find that I'm delighted by the sight. Making Sem uncomfortable is the best thing that's happened all day. Even better than Colin checking out my legs.

"Yeah. That."

"What about it?" I ask—sort of, kind of curious where this whole thing is leading.

"I heard that it was the easiest."

"Oh, is it now?" I snark.

"I was thinking…."

I shake my head in disbelief. *Oh, hell no.*

"Nope. No. No way. I won that little weird-ass bet we made the other day, but I'm not doing that again."

"Why?"

"Because having sex with you once was more than enough for me."

My dick obviously disagrees because it's hardening between my legs, but I ignore it. It's pathetic, just like what Sem is trying to goad me into right now.

Sem shrugs his shoulders and looks away, his body stiff. "Fine."

Throwing my hands up in the air, I ask, "Fine? Seriously?"

"Yeah, fine. Because then I win."

"Oh no, you don't. That's not a thing."

"Yeah. I do, and it is."

"Oh, fuck you," I say and huff out a manic laugh. "You are seriously delusional. I mean, psychologists should study that brain of yours and create a new mental disorder in the DSM. If you think I'm going to bend over for you or some shit just to win another bet, you have another think coming."

Sem shrugs again, and I say sternly, "Stop that. Stop shrugging. This doesn't mean you *win*. You can't win. I already won."

I don't know what I'm saying. I'm rambling. But Sem

makes me irrational and irritated, and, quite frankly, impulsive. I'm reverting back to being a child. Is that a condition? I make a mental note to look it up later.

"Nah, I win this time. You forfeit," he says.

"*That is not a thing*," I grind out and then stomp to the end table and pull out a condom and lube packet. "And I do *not* forfeit. I cannot believe I'm saying this," I grind out, slapping them both onto his chest and pointing behind me. "Bedroom now. And no snooping."

Sem wraps those thick fingers around the small packages and stands up, crowding me. He looks down, and a slight, satisfied smile quirks up one corner of his mouth, and I want to swat it away.

Instead, I rush into the bathroom and lock the door behind me.

"What are you doing, idiot?" I ask myself as I grab the lube and uncap it.

"You have nothing to prove," I mutter as I work myself open.

"You gain nothing from this," I say as I place my jock strap on and then stare at my flushed cheeks in the mirror.

"Oh, fuck it all. I can't let him win this," I whisper as I move out of the bathroom and into the bedroom.

Sem is sitting on the end of the bed, entirely naked, his hard cock sheathed and ready. His muscles bunch and flex as I move toward him. His blue eyes fly over my nearly naked body, his cheeks and neck stained red with his flush.

"Okay, straight boy. What position were you researching?"

He clears his throat, and those eyes meet mine. "Hands and knees."

"Fine," I grumble and crawl onto the bed, exposing my ass to him. It's a vulnerable position, but I do it anyway. Sem's a lot of things, but I know he won't intentionally hurt me. He can apparently irritate me to death, though.

He snaps the back of my jockstrap, and I turn my face and glower at him over my shoulder. "Hands off."

"Why you wearing this again?"

"Because some things are still private, even though you'll be tunneling up my majestic ass soon."

Sem looks confused at my reasoning as he moves behind me in silence. He doesn't touch me, just rubs his hard cock against my crack.

"Can I grab your hips?" he asks after a moment.

"Fine. Nowhere else, though. This is not anything but a bet. That I'll win, by the way. I always win."

He doesn't reply, he just sets those massive paws against my skin, and they nearly span my entire waist. And despite not wanting it to, his touch does something to me. It burns a trail from my hips to my chest, lighting a fire within me. I place my face in a pillow and breathe deeply. I will not react to him. Will. Not.

"Just..." I begin to say, but before I can finish my sentence, he pushes forward quickly. "Christ on a cracker!" I shout as he sinks a quarter of the way in.

"Oh shit," I grunt, my ass aching. "Give me some warning, Sem!"

"Sorry," he grumbles and doesn't move a muscle. He's frozen behind me, his fingers flexing against my skin.

I turn my forehead into the pillow and breathe deeply. Oh, holy mother. It stings.

"You have to go in slow," I grit out, looking over my shoulder and seeing Sem glancing down where his dick disappears between my cheeks. His bottom lip is trapped between his teeth, and his nostrils flare as he breathes.

It is not hot. Not at all.

"Okay, just...you can move now. Just give me time to adjust to your size. You can't go barreling in. My ass is not the Wild West."

Sem nods, and when he doesn't move after a minute, I say, "Go!"

This seems to spur him into action because he slowly inches inside of me. So slowly, in fact, that it ends up becoming some kind of sweet torture. I have never in my entire life been fucked this slow. It's *agonizing*.

"Not that slow," I groan. "What are you? Part sloth?"

"You told me to be careful."

"Just don't stick the entire thing in me all at once, yeah? My ass is fantastic, but it can't work miracles."

"Fine," he mutters but continues to impale me one slow centimeter at a time. It's excruciating. And I can't slam my hips back because he has a death grip on them, holding me firmly in place.

Why did I agree to this again?

Oh yeah, because I have deep-seated psychological issues, apparently.

When he finally sinks all the way to the hilt, I breathe out a sigh of relief, and Sem exhales sharply.

"See," I pant, trying to sound smug but only end up sounding horny. "I win again."

"You don't win. Not yet."

I wiggle my hips, and Sem hisses.

"Oh right. That's because you need to *fuck me* until you get off," I say dryly. "Well, go on then. Do it. You still won't win. I'll take it like a champ like I always do."

I glance over my shoulder and see Sem swallow, and then without moving his hands from my hips, I feel those thumbs move down, spreading my cheeks apart so he can watch as he pulls all the way out and sinks *slowly* back in.

He does it a few more times until I'm literally sweating. It drips down the bridge of my nose onto the pillow. I never sweat during sex. I rarely sweat, period, but with Sem, things are annoyingly different.

"Oh, mother of god," I hiss. "Will you just get on with it?"

I hate that I'm begging, but I cannot stand the torment of it. My cock is rock hard and weeping for release, and Sem is taking his goddamn time. He has no consideration for me and the agony I'm in at the moment.

"Don't want to hurt you," Sem mutters, and I growl.

"Just *fuck me* and get it over with. I still have stuff to do, and I'm tired. I have work tomorrow."

It's mostly a lie. I'm horny and want to come, and this lazy thing he's doing with his cock is driving me insane.

"Fine," he mutters and then slowly pulls out and then slams into me. His skin smacks against mine loudly as my entire body scoots up the bed. I lose the ability to breathe as he does it repeatedly until I have to grab onto my headboard for dear life as he pummels me. He's grunting softly, and I *hate* that sound. Wish he'd just shut up.

"Shut up," I murmur. "Shut your mouth."

Sem probably doesn't hear me because he doesn't stop making those sounds. Instead, he does something I don't expect. He digs those fingers into my hips and lifts me off my knees. I'm fully impaled on him now, my hands scrambling for purchase as he tilts his hips at just the right angle until he's hitting *that spot* inside. He doesn't stop hitting it either.

I will not moan. I will not. *Will not.*

I stuff the pillow against my face to muffle my whimpers. I bite my cheeks so hard I taste blood, and then to my utter mortification, I feel myself nearing the edge, and there is nothing I can do to stop the freefall. My balls draw up, and no mental pep talk can curb the loud groan that spills out of my mouth as I come violently inside of my jockstrap.

And there's no hiding what just happened because my ass clenches around him dramatically. Then a heavy *fuuuuck* exits his mouth as his entire body shakes with his own release.

Then there's silence, except for our ragged breathing permeating the room, and I want to crawl inside a hole and die. I cannot believe I not only let him inside me again, but I found some kind of satisfaction from it. I need to see a therapist immediately.

"Put me down," I hiss and feel Sem's fingers release that tight grip he had on my hips.

My skin throbs where he was holding me, and I know I'll have fingertip-shaped bruises there tomorrow. It does not turn me on. Not in the least.

"Get out of me," I grunt, and slowly, Sem pulls out of my sore ass and I collapse onto the bed.

I refuse to move, to even look at him. But I hear him getting dressed, hear the condom being tossed into the trashcan.

"Guess you win this one," Sem grumbles, and I squeeze my eyes shut, not wanting to even look at him as he ties his boots.

And then he stands and watches me for a moment, but I turn my face away and refuse to acknowledge him. Apparently, I've sunk to an all-time low. Is this my rock bottom? Is there rehab for this?

The snick of the apartment door closing has me opening my eyes and staring at the wall.

"That will not happen ever again," I promise myself.

"You've got that faraway look again," August says, staring at me. He looks a little concerned. Well, he should be. I still haven't admitted what I did with Sem. *Twice*.

Oh god, kill me now.

"You're making me worry, bro. You okay?"

I sigh heavily and run a hand through my damp hair. The two of us are standing outside of the yoga studio drinking from our water bottles. I should be in my car, driving home, but August cornered me. I guess I have been acting shady lately. Guilt has a way of doing that to a person.

August has every right to be worried. He probably thinks my parents have been bullying me again. Or my brothers. He's seen how they can be.

In fact, just this morning, my dad texted me asking me if I wanted to play on a softball team with him and my brothers. I don't know why he asks when he knows I hate traditional sports. And before I could politely decline, my brothers sent memes with the sole purpose of teasing me. I swear there are days I just want to block them all.

"I'm fine, but Jesus...I...I cannot believe I am telling you this, and if I do, you cannot tell a soul," I mutter as I stare at the sky. "I had...IhadsexwithSem."

"What?"

"I had sex. With Sem."

August chokes on his sip of water, his face turning red as his eyes widen. "What the—"

"Twice."

His coughing increases until I'm slapping him on the back roughly. For a moment, I worry I'm going to have to call an ambulance.

"Calm yourself. You can't afford a ride to the hospital. Healthcare in this country is atrocious."

"Why—would you do that?" he asks, his eyes leaking.

He swipes at them, and I frown. "You know how I get."

"Oh, Jesus. Did he provoke you into some kind of competition?"

"Maybe," I admit, scuffing my shoe along the ground. I'm a child, apparently.

"You are freakishly competitive."

"I know. It's an issue."

"So, he provoked you into it? He didn't force you, did he?"

"Jesus, no. He didn't rape me. But he did irritate me into agreeing to it. He said…" I lower my voice so no one from the gym will overhear me and lean toward August. "He said I couldn't take all of him."

August's brown eyes widen, and a smile tilts up his lips. "Oh, did he now?"

"Yeah," I sniff. "So, obviously, I had to prove I could."

I stand taller for a few seconds and then shrink when I see August's stare. To him, I must look ridiculous. Having sex with Sem just to prove a stupid, silly point.

"And the second time?" August asks, and I sigh.

"Same thing. He just…" I throw up my hands and pull at my hair. "He *provokes* me. I want to strangle him whenever I see him. And I just can't help myself when he says stuff like that. Like he thinks I can't do something because of my size."

August rubs a hand along his jaw and then says, "Well?"

"Well, what?"

"Did you like it?"

"What? Of course not! It was awful. Terrible. Worst ever."

August studies me some more and then shakes his head. "Be careful, yeah? Sem's…different."

"I know. *I know*. Ugh. I'm so stupid. Why did I have to go and have sex with him? Twice?"

A voice clears behind me, and August and I quickly swivel around. My jaw unhinges, and my face is almost as bright as that strawberry smoothie I had for breakfast. Because this is just my motherfucking luck.

"Oh shoot," I mutter when I see Colin standing behind us, his lithe body shifting uncomfortably before us.

"Sorry to interrupt, but you...um...you left your keys," he holds out his hand, and I see the lanyard I use for the school in his palm.

"Oh. Thank you," I say, grasping onto them. "I can't believe I left those. I'm so scatterbrained today."

August chuckles next to me, and I bite back a scowl.

"No problem," Colin says, his soft brown eyes meeting mine. They look so kind and mature and so unlike Sem's bright blue, mischievous ones.

Gah! Don't think of Sem when Colin is right in front of you!

"I'm Colin, by the way. You are?"

He holds out his hand, and I slide mine inside his. His palms are smooth, unlike Sem's, which are calloused and rough.

No more thoughts of Sem!

"I'm Magnus. And this is my best friend, August."

"Nice to finally meet you. I've noticed you in class...."

"I've noticed you too," I say way too enthusiastic and then add on calmly, "And it's nice to finally meet you as well."

I pull my hand away first and fiddle with my water bottle, needing something to do with my fingers.

"Hey, um, Magnus. I was wondering...Do you mind if I..." he runs a hand through his light brown hair, musing it slightly.

He's properly adorable. "Do you work at a school? I saw the lanyard's logo and just assumed."

"Yeah. A summer camp, actually. Kindergarten facilitator. August is with the third graders. We're both finishing up our credentials for elementary education next year." Okay, this is way too much information. Calm the hell down. I clear my throat and ask, "Why?"

Colin's smile widens. "It's just...it's just a coincidence. I have a six-year-old at home."

"Is that so?" I say, and August subtly nudges me.

"I'd love to pick your brain, actually," Colin says, looking almost sheepish. "I'm considering creating an online vlog for teachers. Something along the lines of how to teach history to elementary aged children. Is that something you'd be interested in?"

"Absolutely!" I say, sounding much too cheery. "Anytime. Want my number?"

Colin bites down on his lip and nods. "Yeah. That would be great."

We exchange numbers and then wave goodbye, my eyes on his delectable ass until he disappears into his car.

"You are so screwed, Mag. What were you thinking getting involved with Sem when you've been pining after Colin for months?"

"I know," I groan and roll my neck. "Why does my brain short circuit when someone thinks I can't do something?"

"Probably your shitty parents. Or those asshole brothers of yours."

"It always comes back to them, doesn't it?"

August shrugs, but he has a point. If my brothers weren't so competitive and my parents so very disappointed in how I turned out, maybe I wouldn't feel the need to prove myself to everyone.

You're not tall enough.
You're not big enough.
You can't wear clothes like that.
Why can't you be like your brothers?
Why can't you stop being such a disappointment?
This is just a phase.
Grow up, Magnus.

Those phrases and questions were spoken to me so often as a child that somehow it warped my brain. Now, anytime anyone underestimates me, I go a little crazy, proving that I *can* do it. I might not be tall or strong, but I am intelligent and determined. I can do anything I set my mind to.

My phone buzzes in my pocket, and I see that Colin has already texted me. Nothing exciting, just a generic *nice to meet you* text.

I shoot him back a smiley face because I don't know how else to respond. Colin *is* my dream guy. Educated, smart, handsome, and a real family guy who loves children. He's everything I want in a man. I cannot blow this by continuing to engage with Sem.

No, I need to cut him out of my life entirely.

This may be problematic because he's a part of my inner circle. And getting rid of Sem has proven to be more challenging than I expected.

―――

"You told me he wasn't going to be here," I hiss at my friend Caleb as I try in vain to get my towel to settle on the sand. It just blows around in the wind and refuses to lie down flat.

My friend scratches a hand across his bare stomach and glances out at the ocean.

"He wasn't. He was supposed to be camping with friends. Changed his mind last minute, though. Wonder why?" Caleb turns to look over at me and smirks.

I use my finger to make a motion for him to turn back around and mind his own business. Then I glance over at the waves and watch as Sem rises from the surfboard and rides a wave before getting knocked over and tumbling into the ocean. A moment later, he reemerges from the water, those muscular arms grab onto his board, and he lifts himself onto it once more. He's nothing but determined. I'll give him that.

"He's gotten good, huh, babe?" Caleb tells Whit, who is brushing the sand from their little canopy. "Been coming out here with Mal a lot, I guess."

Whit hums a response, and Caleb turns to his fiancé and frowns. "Will you stop brushing the sand from the tent? We're at the beach. We're going to get dirty."

Whit sighs, pushing his dark hair behind his ears and biting down on his lip.

"I hate the beach."

"You love the beach."

"I love you," he mutters. "I came here to make you happy. The beach can go to hell."

Caleb grins widely and practically crawls into his fiancé's lap, pressing his mouth to Whit's and licking into it.

Okay, enough of that, I think as I turn my head away from the two lovebirds. I don't know why I even bothered coming here with them. They'll most likely end up under that stupid canopy making out the entire time. Ever since Caleb crawled into Whit's bed, they've been inseparable. Let's just say I *did not* see that coming.

I look out toward the ocean once more and see Sem crest another wave, the muscles in his chest flexing, the suit on his hips hanging seductively low. He has V-cut abs. I've never actually seen such definition in real life before. I thought that it was just a myth, like unicorns or the Loch Ness Monster. Damn him and his perfect body.

Nope. Not going there, I tell myself as I finally manage to right my towel and lower myself onto it.

I slather my fair skin with sunscreen and pull out my phone to read.

In the distance, I can hear the waves hitting the shore and Whit and Caleb chatting. I can't see their faces, but I can see them from the waist down, and Caleb's leg is thrown over Whit's as they cuddle out of the sun's harsh rays.

For a moment, I'm jealous of what they have.

Whit and I were together for a year. Not together, really. Just had sex whenever there was the urge. It was good sex too, and there was a time when I missed what we'd had, but I'm over it. Whit's so happy with Caleb that I can't help but be happy for him. The two of them are different in many ways, yet they work so well together.

I turn over on my stomach, continue reading, and occasionally lower my shades so I can watch Sem ride the waves. Because how can I not? He's hot. Objectively speaking. But he's not my type. Not really. I mean, I do like big guys that can throw me around a room, but not *that* big. He's too tall. Too muscular. Too much like the bullies at school who made my life hell. He's too much like my brothers. He's just too...much.

And yet you let him fuck you. Twice!

I squeeze my eyes shut, lower my forehead to my arms, and sigh. I'm such an idiot.

"What are you wearing?" a voice says above me, and I startle.

Craning my neck up, I see Sem standing over me, dripping wet, his retro-designed surfboard on the sand behind him. From here, I can see every wet muscle bulging from beneath his skin. It's not anything I'm interested in. Not really.

"It's a swimsuit."

"That's not a swimsuit," Sem says, his eyes moving across my back, ass, and legs.

I bristle. "It is."

"It's...too short."

I scoff and then grab my phone, pretending to read when I'm actually biting back a snarky retort. Of course, my swimsuit is short. It's also bright yellow because the intention was to come here and show myself off so hot guys would look at me. Check out my ass. Admire how cute I am. But the only one who seems to be paying me any attention is Sem, who's looming over me like a thunder cloud.

"You need to put sunscreen on."

"I'm fine."

He shifts in front of me. "You're turning red."

I sigh and then dig around in my bag for my sunscreen and then hold it up toward him.

"Fine, if you're so worried about me..."

Sem crouches down, those powerful thighs right in my vision, and I refuse to look at them. They're admirable, sure, but goddammit, I will not be lusting after this man. Instead, I rest my face on my forearms and close my eyes.

I hear the top of the cap pop open, and Sem's large hands start moving across my shoulders and then across my back. Those rough, calloused hands.

"When did you learn to surf?" I ask, trying to distract myself from the feel of him touching me.

"Tried it last summer with Mal. It came easy," he says, continuing to rub the skin of my back. It feels like he's being incredibly thorough. I guess skin health *is* important.

"You're good at it."

"You were watching me?" he asks, his hands pausing right above my lower back.

"Not really," I mutter and then bite my lip as he squirts some more sunscreen in his paws and moves them down the back of my thighs. It's not necessary, I can put sunscreen on my legs, but I let him do it anyway.

"You should try it," he says.

"I'm not a great swimmer."

"Would you drown if you go out there?" he asks, his fingers brushing up under my shorts. Dangerously close to my balls.

"Watch your hands," I say sternly, and Sem's hands move down my legs instead. "And no, I wouldn't drown. I can swim, but if I end up out there, I'd probably just flail about and then have a panic attack because there is an excellent chance I'll be mauled by a shark."

"Nah, no shark sightings today."

"How reassuring."

"Come on. Come out with me. We can bodyboard back in. We don't even need to stand up."

"No, thank you," I say when he removes his hands from me and leans back on his heels. I turn my head to look at him and realize I can see right up his shorts. I glance away quickly.

I will not look.

"Why not? Scared?"

I lean up on my elbows and remind myself that I will not be provoked into doing something stupid.

"I'm not scared."

"Prove it," he says, and I narrow my gaze at him.

I slowly push myself up into a seated position and begin reapplying my sunscreen to my front, trying to remind myself to be rational. To not act without thinking. But the way he's watching me...ugh. Those eyes are tracking my hands as the sunscreen is spread across my torso and limbs, and there's a challenge in those depths. Something within me roars to life. Standing up, I place my hands on my hips.

"Fine. I'll go out there. Because I'm not afraid. Of anything."

Sem's mouth turns up in a wicked smile, and he reaches for his surfboard and tucks it under his arm.

"Let's go, Maggie."

I turn my head slightly and side-eye him. He's never called me *that* before, but the nickname makes my heart flutter in my chest.

Probably just nerves.

My dad insists on calling me Magnus because he thinks it sounds manly, even though I'm anything but. My friends call me Mag. But no one has ever called me Maggie. My family would hate how feminine it sounds. I should tell them that's my nickname next time I see them. Watch their heads explode. I mean, my dad wouldn't even let me join a dance class when I was younger because he thought I was effeminate enough. He put me in soccer instead. I got my ass beat by the other kids on the team. It was a *really great* experience. If I told my dad my so-called masculine name was shortened to Maggie, he would die.

I walk into the water with Sem and shiver, realizing how

cold it is despite the sun beating down on us. A wave crashes into my shins, and I almost topple over, but Sem reaches out and wraps a strong arm around me, pulling me into his side. And I let him because I don't want to be knowingly reckless.

We push forward, and when the water is at my chest, Sem gestures to the surfboard and says, "Hop on."

I try and launch myself onto it but end up just hanging onto the side of it like a weakling. Apparently, I don't have enough upper body strength to actually pull myself onto the board. Not that I'm surprised. I can bend myself into weird positions but forget a pull-up. That's not happening.

Sem chuckles at me and then reaches over, picks me up, and plops me right onto it as if I weigh nothing.

"Scoot up," he says, and I do as I'm told, grasping onto the tip of the board with white knuckles as Sem pulls himself on behind me. We're both now laying on the board and he spreads my legs slightly to fit between them. When I glance back, I see that *his face is right above my ass*.

Oh my god.

"You have a tiny butt," Sem says and then leans down and bites it.

He bites my ass.

A gasp leaves me, and I narrow my eyes at him.

"Keep your mouth away from my ass."

"Why?" he says, with a quirk of his eyebrow. "You let me stick my cock in it. Twice."

My mouth unhinges, and I contemplate rolling off the board and into the water, but then realize that I might get eaten if I do that. So instead, I face forward and tell myself that my face is hot because I'm a little sunburned. Not because he was teasing me. Was he flirting? Does Sem even know how to flirt? I imagine him just throwing someone over his shoulder caveman-style and then fucking them through a wall. He doesn't seem like the type to actually work for it.

We move farther out into the water, Sem occasionally touching my ass with his face as he paddles us forward, but I pretend to ignore it because acknowledging it will only make it worse.

Suddenly we are spinning around, and Sem says, "Come on, Maggie. Sit up. Look around." I glance back at Sem pushing his wet hair back, looking entirely too sexy to be real, and I inhale deeply.

"I don't think I can," I say, prying my fingers from the board's edge. They're practically glued to it.

"Nah, you can," he says, unnecessarily running his hands up the back of my thighs, gripping onto my hips, and pulling me up.

But he doesn't stop there. He slides me toward him, pulling my back to his front and keeping a steady grip on my waist. And I let him because it's dangerous out here, and he's my barrier between life and death. It's totally a safety thing.

My eyes wander the blue horizon, and I see a few other surfers nearby paddling toward a cresting wave closer to shore.

"This is insane," I say, grasping onto the edge of the board and willing myself not to think about what lurks beneath. "I can see why you like this. Sort of."

"Yeah. It's fun. I've always been into extreme sports. Surfing just made sense."

I glance over my shoulder at him, and he cocks his head as he watches me. Our lips are much too close, and I have to look away. Much too risky to do that.

"You look good in the water," I say, needing to compliment him. "Like you belong here."

"Feels like I do too."

"Kind of like Aquaman."

"You think he's sexy?"

"Pfft. Duh."

We sit in silence for a moment before he asks, "Want to bodyboard in now?"

"God, do we have to? I think I've changed my mind."

Sem's fingers flex against my hips, and he says softly. "I've gotchu. Don't worry."

I shudder slightly at how those words sink into me and then nod. "Fine. Okay. But if I die, I will haunt your sorry ass."

Sem lets go of me and points to the front of the board. "Nah. I'll keep you safe. Now, lie down. I'll paddle us up there, and we'll ride in."

I do as he says, and then, once again, his face is hovering over my ass. I am slightly disappointed he doesn't bite it again, which is ridiculous. Because I really don't want him to do that.

But my thoughts are interrupted when Sem says, "Hold on," and suddenly, a wave rises up beneath us. My eyes widen, and I let out a little shriek as we're propelled forward.

"Holy shit!" I squeal and hear Sem laughing behind me as he places his hands farther up the board near my waist, almost as if to shield me from tumbling off.

We ride that wave all the way to the shore. When the board stops, I don't even move, just turn and glance at Sem, who meets my gaze.

A smile splits my face. "Fuck that was fun. Can we do it again?"

"Sure thing, Maggie," he says, and that flutter in my chest

happens again. I'll have to go to the doctor and see if I have some kind of heart condition. Might be genetic.

"Okay. You can come in. But only because you saved my life today. There are ground rules, though," I say, pushing the door open to my apartment and slinging my sandy beach bag onto the floor.

Sem had indeed saved my life earlier. While riding our fifth wave, I managed to somehow roll off the board and into the water. For a moment, I really thought it was the end of my life because I was upside down, and no matter how hard I'd kicked, I couldn't find my bearings. I'd inhaled a lungful of water and was basically regretting my life decisions until Sem reached down and pulled me back onto the board. He did it so effortlessly as if he could lift ten of me. And then he was on top of me, those strong arms paddling us to the shore with some kind of inhuman strength. The entire time he paddled, I just laid there coughing up a lungful of saltwater and listening to Sem swear.

When we made it to shore, I was immediately lifted off the ground, Sem's surfboard discarded on the wet sand. He'd carried me to my towel and fussed over me like I was a child. His hands ran over my face, abdomen, and even my legs until he was satisfied that I wasn't hurt.

The entire thing was mortifying, but I let him do it because he looked so concerned. A few people were staring at us, pointing and texting on their phones. Probably because it's not every day that you see a behemoth of a man cradling another man in his arms like a princess. It also didn't help that

Whit was eyeing us with an amused expression, and Caleb was snickering.

Assholes.

Standing in my living room, I hold up a finger. "Ground rule number one. We are *not* having sex again."

Sem shrugs and flops down on the couch, spreading his thighs out. He's still wearing his swimsuit but had pulled on a loose tank top on our way home. I can see his nipples if he moves just the right way, not that I'm looking.

"All good. Don't want to do that anyway."

The casual way he says it makes me stiffen slightly, but then I remember I don't want to have sex with him again either.

"Good. Wonderful. Glad we are on the same page."

Sem throws his arms across the back of the couch and turns that blue gaze on me.

"What are the other ground rules?"

I think about it and then shrug. "That's the only one."

"Hm. Got it. You have fun today?"

"Yep."

He grins widely, and I have to look away because he looks so sexy when he does that, and I *do not* need to be lusting after him. Especially because I have Colin's number now, and we've been texting a little. It's kind of, sort of, flirtatious.

"How do you afford this place?" Sem asks, watching as I move to the fridge and grab a bottle of wine. I open it and pour a heaping cup full of it into a mug.

"Want a drink?" I ask him, and Sem shakes his head.

"Water's fine," he replies.

I hand him a bottle and then explain, "August's uncle owns this complex. Gave me a sweet deal on this place. Just for the year. And then I have to move out."

"Where will you go?"

"Dunno. Hopefully, I can get a job around here, but I'm not opposed to moving farther away for work."

Sem taps his fingers on the couch and says, "You got sunburned."

"Just a little," I reply with a shrug and then sit down on the couch facing Sem. Probably should change out of my swimsuit, but I'm tired from the sun and the beach. And I just want to sit for a minute and drink my wine before doing anything else.

"Should put something on that," Sem says, his eyes moving across my exposed skin.

"I'll be fine," I reply, letting my eyes drift over Sem's giant arms. I take a large mouthful of wine and swallow. "You got tan."

"Yep. I'm lucky, I guess. Never really burn."

I swallow some more wine and then nudge his thigh with my toes.

"Want to play a game?" I ask, feeling a little tipsy. Should have probably eaten something before I gulped down almost an entire mug of wine in ten seconds flat.

"What game?" he asks.

I begin to pull my foot away from him, but Sem grabs onto it and pulls it onto his lap. "You have purple toenails."

I wiggle them. "You secretly love them. Want me to paint yours?"

Sem doesn't respond, just digs his fingers into the sole of my foot and begins to give me a massage.

He's massaging my feet.

"Nah. You have pretty feet. It suits you."

I blush because I drank too much, and apparently, I haven't been complimented in ages. Why don't men get complimented more? It's a pandemic, really. We all secretly suffer from epically low self-esteem.

"Thank you. You have strong hands," I tell him, feeling the need to return the compliment.

"I know."

I roll my eyes as he continues to massage my foot. I tell myself that I need to remove it from his lap, to end this madness, but I end up just finishing off my wine like a lush and biting back the urge to moan. It's criminal how good he is at this.

Just when I think I'm finally going to put an end to it, he reaches down and pulls my other foot up onto his lap.

I'm helpless to do much else but allow myself to relax into it. Relaxing is not something I'd ever thought I'd do around Sem. He's always made me feel nervous and irritable and slightly off-kilter. But today has been...fun.

I can admit when I'm wrong. I'm an adult like that.

"We should play a game," I say drowsily. "That way, I can kick your ass. *Again*. I quite like winning, especially when I win against you."

Sem eyes the Xbox and then looks at me, "We can do that. But what do I get if I kick your ass instead?"

"I always win," I retort. "No one can beat me. So, there's no need to discuss this."

He pops the knuckle of one of my toes, and I hiss.

Sem chuckles. "Maybe today will be the day you lose."

I snort and then sit up, moving my feet from his lap and shaking my hands.

"Fine. If I win, I want..." I tap my lips with my fingers and then giggle almost evilly. "I want you to wear a plug. Up your ass. For half a day minimum."

Sem cocks his head, watching me for a moment, and then nods. "Deal. And if I win, I want to see your cock. Hard."

My eyes widen at that because he doesn't even think about it. Just blurts it out so confidently.

"I'm sorry. Are you gay, Sem?" I blurt back because, dammit, I'm curious. What kind of game is this to him? Is it even a game?

"I don't...I'm not sure."

"Um, okay, we'll be discussing this more later because it's important. But for now, let's table it and discuss the reason you want to see *my* dick."

"Just curious about it."

"Fine. But this is your funeral because you won't win. So be prepared to have something up your virgin asshole."

He runs a hand across his jaw and eyes me with a smirk. "We'll see, Maggie."

CHAPTER THREE

My controller hangs loosely in my hands, and I stare at the screen, feeling crestfallen and just a little flabbergasted.

"Impossible."

Sem smiles widely, blows on his fingernails, and wipes them smugly on his shirt. Like an asshole.

"I win."

I shake my head. "I don't believe it."

Sem gestures to the TV, and I see it. It's there in bold, red letters. I lost. I blame the wine and the foot massage. And Sem for just existing. He's throwing me off, just like he usually does.

"There must have been a glitch in the game."

"Or, I'm just better than you," Sem says and nudges me with his knee. "Admit it. I won. Be a man about it."

I scoff. *A man*. "Fine. I concede. You won."

Sem turns a little on the couch and then watches me

intently, and I swallow roughly. Because a deal's a deal. I never go back on my word.

"Just...before we get all crazy...and don't worry, I will follow through with this. But answer me this first. Why do you want to see it so bad?" I ask, curious as to his fascination with my dick.

He shrugs. "Want to see how small it is."

I bristle and feel my face flush red. "It's not *small*. It's perfectly proportioned to my body. If I had a dick the size of yours, I'd look ridiculous. I'd barely be able to walk around with that thing hanging between my legs."

"You feeling insecure?" Sem's blue eyes narrow, and I scoff.

"No. I have nothing to feel insecure about."

He leans back against the couch and gestures toward my shorts. "Go on then."

I huff, and try not to overthink it too much, because then I'd probably forfeit, and I'd never let myself live it down. I lift up my hips and tug my swim shorts all the way down my thighs. My cock sits limply between them, much smaller than Sem's, but then again, I'm half his size. It's nothing to be ashamed of.

Sem leans forward slightly and puffs out a breath.

"It *is* small."

"It's normal relative to me," I bite out.

"Show me it hard," Sem says, his eyes on my dick, his cheeks slightly pink.

"Whatever, perv. You just want to watch me jerk off. That it?"

When he doesn't respond, I just roll my eyes, wrap my hand around my dick, and stroke it until it's fully erect. I *do not* look at Sem at all while doing it, mind you. But Sem sure as shit looks at me the entire time. Like I'm some kind of weird science experiment.

"Happy now?" I ask, and Sem runs a hand over his mouth.

"We should...should probably compare it to mine. See how much bigger I am."

"You know you're bigger," I scoff. "It's blatantly obvious. All you need are functioning eyeballs to see it."

"It's okay if you're insecure...." Sem begins, which only makes me sit up straighter. My shoulders square, and I gesture at his boardshorts.

"Go on then. We can compare dicks all day long for all I care. No skin off my nose."

Sem hesitates for a moment before tugging his shorts off and kicking them onto the floor. His dick is half hard and resting on his thigh. He inhales deeply and then wraps a hand around it.

"I'll get it hard. That way, we can compare."

"For science," I mutter and sit up a little more.

I'm watching it all, not because I think it's hot. Nope. I'm just curious how much bigger he is than me. Really. This is a totally controlled scientific experiment. I'm a biologist now.

When he's fully hard, he glances at his dick and then mine.

"What do you think?" he says on an exhale.

"Probably should get a little closer to see," I mutter and then straddle his lap because how else can a person measure two dicks without sticking them side-by-side.

My dick bounces against his as I maneuver onto his lap, and Sem shakily inhales.

"Don't be scared, big guy. You already fucked me. Our cocks touching won't make you any less straight."

Sem reaches out and pulls me a little closer. "I'm not worried about that."

I eyeball him and then grab both our dicks and press them together. Sem exhales sharply, and his nostrils flare as I inadvertently stroke up and down. Just once because damn, it's been a while since I frotted with someone. And it makes my dick happy to be close to another dick. It's been lonely.

"You're bigger," I breathe. "See. Happy now?"

I don't let go of our cocks, just keep my hand wrapped around them and then bring my other hand into play because my fingers cannot fully wrap around the two of us.

"I think if we jacked off, I could last longer than you," Sem says gruffly, and my eyes flash up and meet his.

"No, you would not. I happen to have amazing self-control."

Sem cocks that head of his and shrugs. "Want to test that out?"

I narrow my eyes at him. "What do I get if I win?"

"A plug up my ass. And if I win, no jockstrap next time."

He doesn't need to explain what *next time* means. I know and yet I still don't call off this foolish plan. I probably shouldn't drink around him anymore. Apparently, I'm more liable to do crazy things...like yell *"deal"* and then reach over and grab some lube, dribbling it onto our connected cocks. Then I replace my hands with his because he only needs one to do this. Totally makes more sense this way.

His nostrils flare, and his cheeks darken as he begins to stroke us. Up. Down. Up. Down. The tip of his cock leaks profusely, mixing with the lubricant, and the sight drives me crazy. I lean back, my hands on his knees as he slowly works us toward the edge.

I can hear Sem breathing, his mouth open and panting.

His tongue flicks out at one point, and he wets his mouth, his eyes bouncing from our dicks, to my face and then back again. Our eyes meet at one point, and he holds my gaze, his pupils blown out. The blue of his eyes is barely visible. And I know. I know I'm going to win this. Because he's loving it.

Oh, Jesus. I'm going to enjoy spreading those muscular legs out, pushing his knees into his chest as I slip a finger into his tight hole. I'll watch his thick chest heave with each inhale as I work myself to the knuckle, stretching him for that plug.

Oh shit. Should probably stop thinking about that. That's a visual that I like too much. I'm way too close to orgasm.

Sem's hand picks up the pace, and I'm sweating, my nails digging into Sem's flesh and my hips thrusting gently, but he doesn't say anything. He just bites down on his lower lip and watches me.

"I'm going to so enjoy pushing that plug into your ass," I breathe, trying to take my mind off the filthy visuals I'm conjuring up.

"Not going to happen," he grunts.

"Yeah. It is. You're going to wear it so good."

"Nah, Maggie. You're going to wear me so good," Sem retaliates, his hand gripping tighter around us, moving faster. "My cock buried in that tight hole. Your dick out and begging for it. I'm going to love watching you come all over me."

Oh shit. Dirty talk is my kryptonite.

No.

Nononononono.

My balls draw up, and suddenly, I'm biting down hard on my lip to keep my whimper inside. But that's the only thing I'm able to control. Because I'm coming, shooting white ropes across Sem's hand and stomach. It slides down those tight abs and disappears into his happy trail.

He watches it all, eyes hooded as he continues to stroke that hand over my pulsing dick until he erupts right after with a long groan and a shudder. And I shouldn't look, but I do. It's magnificent. The way his dick pulses, the amount of cum that's released. There are buckets of it.

It takes everything within me not to lean down and suck him into my mouth. Just to get a quick taste.

Nope. Not going there. This was just a bet. Nothing more. I am not sucking on his cock.

"I win," he mutters, and I sigh loudly, my entire body tingling from the orgasm.

"Whatever."

He smirks and swipes a thumb over my cockhead, pressing into my slit, and I hiss.

"I like your dick," Sem says, and I refuse to blush. *Refuse*.

"So not too small?" I ask.

"It's...Nah, it's perfect."

My cheeks heat, and I bite my lip and turn away from him. I was not expecting compliments, but then again, Sem is nothing if not surprising.

His fingers release me, and I force myself to stand up.

"Well, you're welcome to use the shower before you go," I say, gesturing to the mess we both made on him.

He swipes a finger through it and rubs them together. Then he brings it up to his mouth and sucks that finger right in between his lips.

Oh my fucking god.

"Yeah. Probably a good idea," he says, licking his lips.

And I just stand there and gape as he pushes himself up and walks past me. And no, I do not check out his tight, round ass as he moves into the bathroom. I would never do that. Instead, I pour myself another glass of wine and gulp it down. Because, really, what's one more glass when I already let my stalker jack me off? What other kind of crazy shit could I possibly get into?

Goddammit.

I have no idea what I'm doing right now, but I can't quite seem to stop.

SEM

It's late. Too dark, with the moon just a sliver in the night sky. The fluorescent lights above me aren't bright enough, and my eyes ache. And yet I can't stop sketching. Papers litter my RV's small kitchenette table, and I scrub at my cheek, smearing charcoal across my skin. Since meeting Magnus months ago, I've drawn him a hundred times. My drawings have become more precise the more I've watched him. The way he postures when challenged, the clothes he wears, the slope of his cheeks, and the smooth curves of his body.

He's my muse.

That's what Anne says. She would know. She's an artist.

I'm sure that's all this is, this unhealthy obsession with him.

I glance down at my drawing and eye the naked planes of Maggie's body sprawled across the paper, and shift in my seat. My cock is hardening in my shorts, and I reach down and squeeze it. Something about the guy makes me unreasonably horny. I never thought I'd get with a guy, but it doesn't feel weird with Maggie. Not in the slightest.

Nah. It feels...right.

When I first laid eyes on him, something shifted inside

my brain. My neurons rearranged themselves. After driving Maggie home from the hospital the night Caleb hurt himself in an ATV accident, I parked on the street outside the campus, pulled out my sketchbook, and drew him. It was the beginning of a sickness that invaded my brain. I have stacks of sketches of him, one for each time I discovered a new part of him. I glance to my right and see a drawing of Maggie's torso staring up at me.

I drew that the first night I saw him in that short shirt. A midriff is what it's called. Who knew guys wore shit like that? I hadn't, but I'd liked it on him. I sat in my truck that night after the bonfire and sketched it, the way his ribs slightly protruded from his abdomen, the curve of his hips, that small belly button.

The evidence of my insanity is tucked away right here. If anyone saw this, they'd lock me up.

I rub at my face and inhale deeply. Fuck, I cannot stop envisioning him. And now that I've seen him naked, I can draw the hidden parts of him too. Before, I'd had to use my imagination, but now...I glance down at his dick on the paper and run a hand across my mouth. It doesn't look right. Not like how I remember.

Shit.

Before I overthink it, I fiddle with my phone and Face-Time him. It rings twice before the screen changes.

"What do you want?" Maggie grumbles, his face half shadowed by the lamp on his bedside table. He looks so damn pretty, half asleep.

"I need something," I say, feeling a little stupid for calling him. In fact, I usually feel dumb around this guy. He's so smart, so different than anyone I've ever met. Me, I've never been book-smart. Amazingly, I made it out of high school. If Maggie knew, he'd probably laugh at how dumb I really am.

"What do you need, Sem?" Maggie asks, sounding irritated.

I know I annoy him, but I can't quite seem to leave him alone. He intrigues me and confuses me. I don't know how to stay away from him without going out of my mind. Tried it once. Do not recommend.

"I need to see your dick again."

"Um. Excuse me?" he asks with a small laugh. "You won your bet this afternoon, but that reward only extends to the next time we fuck. Unless...are you calling for phone sex? I could work with that. I happen to have a way with words."

I swallow as my dick twitches at the thought of his pretty mouth spouting filth, and I move the phone away from my reddening face.

"Nah, just..." I swallow and then move the phone back. "Just having a hard time remembering what it looked like."

Maggie sits up in bed, showing me his bare torso, and I huff out a breath. God, he's so damn pretty. Makes my chest ache just looking at him.

"And why do you need to know what it looks like?" he asks, his pretty hazel eyes narrowing. He has really long eyelashes. Sometimes when he closes them, they cast shadows on his cheeks. I want to brush my fingertips across them, run my thumbs down those defined cheekbones, then slide one into his mouth, and watch him suck on it.

"No reason."

"There has to be a reason, Sem. You're calling me at eleven at night to see my dick," he says, and I shake my head before just hanging up on him. Because I don't know what the fuck

I'm doing. I've been wandering around in perpetual confusion for the past six months. I'm fucking exhausted.

My phone rings a second later, and I debate *not* answering it, but I do because I'm helpless when it comes to him. I press the green button and see Maggie's pretty face appear on the screen.

Why the hell is he so cute? He's pint-sized, petite, and feminine. The clothes he wears are slightly ridiculous. Those suspenders, silly bowties, and midriff shirts that show off too much of his flat, smooth stomach drive me crazy. And Jesus, his belly button is really small. I want to lick into it. And don't get me started on how he paints his nails and sometimes wears tinted ChapStick to make those lips even redder. Makes me want to eat his mouth.

And there's no hair on his body. Anywhere. What the fuck is up with that?

"Why did you hang up?" he asks.

I shrug and lie, "I had nothing else to say."

"You're a weird guy, you know that? You have to say goodbye. You can't just hang up without warning. It's rude."

I examine his face, my mind capturing each expression he wears. Then suddenly, the phone drops, and I hear a rustling, and then Maggie's face is back on the screen.

"Okay, I don't know why you need to see this, or why on god's green earth I'm even doing this, but I drank too much earlier, and I'm obviously not thinking clearly. You have one minute."

And then he's holding his phone over his dick, and I exhale shakily. Oh fuck. He's...he's....

I adjust myself and let my eyes take him in.

All of him.

"Why you hard?" I ask, my voice rough.

"None of your business," he says, and I bite down on my lip, remembering how good he looked on my lap earlier. Like a fucking dream. No, not a dream. I couldn't even dream that up.

"Have you seen enough?" he asks, and I shake my head before remembering that I need to actually speak.

"Nah, can you show me your...balls."

Maggie laughs nervously before spreading his legs and angling the phone, so I can get a good look at them. He rolls them in his palm, offering them up for my consumption, and I blink several times, snapping mental frames of him. As soon as we hang up, I'll be sketching this.

Memorializing it.

"Good?" he breathes, and I grunt out a strangled, *yeah,* and then Maggie's face appears on the screen.

"Will I get to know what that was all about? Because, not to kink shame, but it was a little random."

I lick my lips and shrug. "Maybe. One day."

His eyes narrow. "You got secrets, big guy? What are they?"

"No secrets," I lie and then reach down and squeeze my hard dick. Gotta keep it together. Just a few more minutes.

Maggie hums on the other end of the phone and then sighs. "Fine, well, I guess I'll have to be satisfied with finding out eventually. I've got to go to bed now. Work tomorrow."

He meets my gaze and smiles softly at me.

"See ya, Maggie," I say, my chest aching.

"Night, Sem."

The tender way he says my name does things to my insides. When we hang up, I set my phone down and cradle my head in my hands and breathe deeply for a few seconds before getting back to work.

My hard dick can wait. I've got to draw him before I forget.

A thump on the motorhome door wakes me up, and I startle from my position slumped over the table. I must have fallen asleep last night, sketching away like a maniac. Paper sticks to my cheek, and I peel it off. It's one of Maggie's face as he came last night. God, he looked good like that. I want to do that all over again.

And again.

I don't want to stop.

"Open up, asshole!" my brother Luke shouts from the other end of the door, and my stomach drops.

"Shit," I mutter, quickly gathering all of my drawings and stuffing them into a drawer. My brother knows I sketch, but he doesn't know what I've been drawing recently. He'd never let me live it down if he knew.

Although he does know about my obsession with Maggie, he doesn't realize how bad it really is.

"What the hell you want?" I grumble, wrenching the door to my RV open and glowering down at Luke, who looks all too smug.

He looks way too much like me. All our lives, people thought we were twins. We both have the same build and eyes, but his hair is cut shorter than mine. And personality-wise, he's a little more reckless than I am. Which is saying something.

"Ma wanted me to come check on you since you moved out this way and you haven't been home in a while."

"It's been two weeks. She can deal."

"Well, you know how she is. It's just me at home now, and she's having a mini-crisis. Thinks we've all flown the coop or some shit. Dad says she's having empty-nester syndrome," Luke says with a shrug and then roughly pushes past me and into my RV. He glances around and then looks at me.

"You got shit on your face," he says, and I swipe at my cheek, noticing the black smear across the back of my hand. "Drawing again, I see."

He lowers himself into the booth, and when something crunches under his ass, I internally groan.

"Do not look at that," I mutter, trying to grab it from Luke's hand, but it's too late. My brother's laughing loudly as he looks at my crumpled sketch.

"You've got it bad, bro," he says, showing me what he's holding in his hand. It's a picture of Maggie's face. One I'd sketched before I really perfected the art of him.

"I do not. He's just...unusual. That's all it is."

I swipe the drawing from his hand, and Luke says, "As your older brother...."

"You're only ten months older than me, asshole."

"As your *older* brother, I think your obsession with this guy is fucking weird. You like him, Sem?"

"He's fine," I mutter.

"I mean, do you *like* him, like Caleb likes Whit?"

I swallow roughly. "Nah."

My brother watches me intently, and I shift in my seat, wishing I was alone. Because while we're not twins, Luke has this special way of looking into my soul that I can't seem to escape.

"You're not gay?"

"Nah."

Fuck. Am I?

"I mean you could be a lot of different things. Bi, pan, demi…"

"What the hell, Luke. How do you know all this stuff?"

He shrugs. "Just did some research after Caleb and Whit. Was fascinating stuff."

I lean back in my seat and then rub a hand over my face. "I dunno, Luke. Maybe I'm bi. Maybe it's just Maggie. It's too fucking much to think about right now. My head is all twisted."

"Well, you moved out here, five miles from his place," Luke says and then smirks at me. "Whatever it is, it looks to me like you've got a little crush. On a tiny little dude. I guess you don't need to label it right now. Just let me know if you do."

"Yeah, man. I dunno. I just moved out here because it's closer to work. You know this."

"You've never lived close to work."

"I do now."

Luke eyeballs me and then smirks at me. "Goddammit. You've totally fucked him, haven't you?"

My face burns so hotly it hurts. "Shut the hell up."

He smacks the table loudly and then guffaws. "You sure fucking did, asshole! You can't lie to me. We might not have shared a womb, but I can read you like a book!"

My face is aching, and I rub at my jaw. "You don't know a fucking thing."

"I know when you're lying." He leans forward, his blue eyes meeting mine. "What was it like? How does it compare to pussy?"

I clench my jaw and turn away. "I'm not telling you shit."

Luke launches up and grabs onto the back of my neck,

pulling me toward him. I struggle under his strength as he laughs wildly and ruffles my hair.

"First Caleb and now you! Shit. What's going on around here? Is there something in the drinking water? Am I next?"

"That's not how it works," I grunt and finally pry his hands off of me. I plop down onto my seat and stare at my annoying brother with narrowed eyes. Both of our chests are heaving, and I bite back a smile. I will not let him think this is a fucking joke. I think I'm going insane. It's not fucking funny.

"Alright, man. You tell me when you come to terms with your sexuality, yeah? You know we're cool with it. Ma is like, beside herself with Caleb and Whit's wedding. Never seen her so happy."

"I know."

"And Mag seems cool." I send him a glower, and he holds his hands up in mock surrender. "I'm not into him, dude. Don't stress. I'm still just into chicks."

Satisfied with his answer, I ask, "What are you here for, besides annoying the shit out of me?"

"Just missed my brother. And ma wanted me to make sure you were okay. I have to report back like a good little soldier."

I snort. "I'm fine. I'll call her."

Luke shrugs. "Come out this weekend, and we can wheel, work on the Jeep a bit."

"Can't. I have a thing."

"What thing?"

"A thing."

He narrows his eyes at me. "And why was I not invited to this *thing*?"

"Because."

Luke huffs. "Whatever. Keep your secrets, asshole. I'll find out eventually. But you're not ditching on the Fourth of July. It's a family tradition. Bring Mag if you have to. Just don't bail. I bought like a shit ton of fireworks. We are going to blow shit up."

"I won't."

"You better not, or I'm going to hunt you down. Drag you kicking and screaming back home."

I crack a smile at that.

"Okay, fine. If you won't hang out with me this weekend, let's go do something crazy right now. I'm itching to do something stupid."

"Like what?" I ask, getting excited. Stupid shit is my middle name.

"Hm," Luke says thoughtfully and then says. "I have that thing in the back of my truck...The one we were working on last weekend...."

"Fuck yeah," I respond, my mind already conjuring up ways to make this epic. "Helmets?"

"Nah."

"Perfect."

CHAPTER FOUR

"Jesus, Sem! What happened to your face?" I ask when I see him sitting on my couch, shuffling through a book that I'd discarded on my end table. Apparently, I'm no longer shocked to see him inside my apartment uninvited. I *am* surprised to see the long, rough gash across his cheek, though. It looks like road rash? Does he have a motorcycle? Knowing him, if he did, he wouldn't wear a helmet.

Dangerous, reckless man.

It's been four days since I've last seen him. Not that I've been counting. That would be ridiculous. I don't care when I see Sem. He could disappear, and I'd never even notice.

"Nothing happened."

I glower at him and move to stand before him, grabbing onto his chin and tilting his face up toward me. A light stubble covers his jaw, and I resist the urge to brush my thumb across it.

"What did you do, Sem?"

Those blue eyes meet mine, and he shrugs. "Fell off a bike."

"A bike? Doing what?"

"Going down a hill."

"Do I even want to know?"

"Probably not."

I drop my hand and sigh heavily. "Fine. Don't tell me. What do you want? I'm assuming it's something important since you broke into my apartment. *Again*."

Sem shifts before me and runs a hand through his hair.

"Was just doing some more research...."

"And how do you do your research exactly? You don't exactly look like you hang out in libraries."

"Porn."

I raise an eyebrow at him, surprised at his blunt answer. "And what was your research about?"

"A new position."

My dick twitches in my shorts. Of course, it does. It's been feeling a little neglected since I've been refusing to jerk off to thoughts of Sem. Absolutely refusing.

"Ah, and what position is this?"

"Easier if I show you."

"Hm," I hum, pretending to think about it. I *really* shouldn't be considering this. Colin and I have been texting a bit throughout the week, and we have plans to meet up this weekend. It's not exactly a date but I'm going to meet his son. That's a big deal, and yet, for some unknown reason, I'm not ushering Sem out of my apartment.

Probably because I'm curious where this is going.

"Go on then. Show me. With clothes on, though. I'm not convinced we need to do this."

Sem stands up, walks to the bedroom, and lies down on his side.

"You go here," he says, pointing to the place right in front of him.

"Ah," I say and then crawl in next to him. He puts his hand on my hip and slides me closer to him. My ass presses against his crotch, and I can't help but wiggle against him a little. "This is a fun position."

I glance back at Sem and see him watching me intently.

"But I see no reason to do this with you. I've already proven I can take it."

"But not in this position."

"When you've done one, you've done them all."

Sem's brow furrows, and he tilts his head slightly. "But I won the last bet."

Shit. He's right. "So?"

"So...what's the point of winning if I don't get to collect?"

I chew on my bottom lip and then sigh. "Fine. *Fine*. But this is the last time. I'm serious, Sem. I have a sort-of date with someone this weekend, and I cannot be fucking you while I'm going out with my dream guy. That's not something I do. I have morals. Kind of. Most of the time."

Sem stiffens behind me.

"A date?"

"Yeah. I guess."

"With your dream guy?"

"Yeah."

I turn over and lean my head on my hand, staring at Sem's confused expression.

"What?"

He shakes his head and swallows. "Nothing."

"You sure?"

"Yep."

"Okay. So, are we going to do this or what? I need a few minutes to prep."

I sit up and pull my shirt off, a little too eager to get on with this. Not because I'm going to enjoy it but because I just always make good on my promises. Doing so really brings a sense of satisfaction to my soul.

This is a religious thing.

Sem looks conflicted for a moment, and then instead of stripping out of his clothes, he asks, "What makes a guy your dream guy?"

"Are you for real right now? Why do you care who my dream guy is?"

Sem doesn't respond. He just keeps watching me. "Just curious."

"Fine. Uh...my dream guy is someone educated, smart, witty, well-read, hot, *obviously*, and kind. Oh, and he has to like kids. I want like ten kids when I get married. A whole brood. If I was a woman and could get pregnant, I'd be popping out babies for years."

Sem looks away from me, fiddling with the button on my shorts. I contemplate slapping his hand away but decide against it. I'll just let him wander for a bit. He did save my life, after all.

"That's a long list."

"Yeah. Well, I have high expectations. And why shouldn't I? I'm not going to settle for some idiot. I'm not that desperate. I want what I want."

Sem's eyes flick up and meet mine. Something flashes within them, but I can't get a read on him. He's difficult to figure out.

"So, are we going to sit here and chat forever, or are we

going to get on with it? I have work tomorrow, and I need a full eight hours, or else I'm a monster. Plus, I have this deep-seated desire to win again since you kicked my ass *twice* last time. It's starting to hurt my fragile self-esteem."

Sem sighs and then runs a hand over his face. "Nah. You know what, I'm good. I'll let you get to sleep."

He sits up, and my face falls. "What? Why? When do you ever forfeit, Sem?"

Questions are shooting rapidly out of my mouth, but I can't help it. I'm confused.

"I'm not forfeiting, just decided I'd rather not right now."

He moves to stand up, but I latch onto his arm, and he stops moving.

"Are you for real right now?"

"Yeah, Maggie. I'm going home."

He glances down at my hand wrapped around his bicep, and I quickly let it go. Then his eyes flick to my bare chest, and he inhales deeply.

I bite down on my lip at the look he's giving me. Like he wants to stay and collect but something's making him want to leave.

"Fuck," he mutters, glancing away and running his hand through his hair. He breathes through his nose and then turns to peek at me again.

"It looks like you want to stay, Sem. You sure you want to go?" I ask softly, and he exhales roughly.

"No."

He's struggling with something, and I can't help but watch it unfold. When he doesn't move toward the bed or make a move to leave, I unbutton my shorts. His gaze snaps to the movement, and his chest heaves.

"What the fuck you playing at?" he grumbles, and I smirk.

"Nothing, just getting undressed after a *long* day at work. Going to take a shower, actually. You can show yourself out when you're ready. You've wasted enough of my time already."

I push myself up and kick off my shorts as I move toward the bathroom. Slowly, I close the door and start the water. My cheeks are flushed, knowing I'm playing with fire but not able to help it. Something deep inside of me craves how dangerous this is.

The room steams up as I strip out of my underwear and move under the water, running my hands through my hair. And that's when I hear it.

The bathroom door opens with a *snick*.

I blink through the haze of water in my eyes and see Sem approaching. He's a mirage of tan skin and bulging musculature. I swipe at the glass to get a better look. I am *not* disappointed.

"Thought you were leaving," I tell him as he opens the shower door and steps inside.

He's way too big for this space. He crowds against me, and I poke his chest. But it accomplishes nothing. It only seems to move him closer.

"This shower is not big enough for the two of us."

He doesn't move back, just stands there completely naked, water hitting his chest and sliding down those delicious abs.

I can't help but reach out and run my fingertips down them. There are literal grooves between them.

Heaven, help me.

Then something catches my eyes. "Sem, what is that?" I grab onto his hips and turn him slightly.

An enormous red scrape runs across his right side. It looks like it hurts.

"Nothing. Just from the bike accident."

"Jesus, Sem. How fast were you going to get literal road rash?" I ask, my eyes flashing up to meet his.

"Too fast."

I arch an eyebrow, and he reaches behind me for the shampoo. "The hill was steep, and there were no brakes," he explains, and I open my mouth to respond, but nothing comes out.

"Why were there no brakes?"

He shrugs. "It was Luke's idea." As if that explains anything.

He squirts way too much shampoo into my hair, but I don't say anything, just let those big hands run through my hair. It's all I can do not to moan at how his fingers massage my scalp. This is *not* how I expected this day to end. And yet here I am. Isn't that how it is with Sem? I end up doing the opposite of what I expect.

"Smells like..." he sniffs the air and shakes his head. "Smells like pie."

"Pie?" I giggle and then hiss, "Shit. Soap in my eye!" I turn my entire body to blink rapidly under the water, rinsing it out the best I can. "Fuck, that stings!"

"You okay?" Sem asks, his hands spanning my entire waist, his thumbs rubbing gentle circles against my skin. I can feel his cock pressed against my ass cheeks, and I can't help but press against it a little. Because apparently, my eyeball disintegrating doesn't deter me from wanting to have a dick in my ass.

"I'll be fine," I say after a moment. I turn my head to look at him with my red eyes, and he frowns when he sees them.

"Sorry," he says softly, and then he grabs the bar of soap and runs it along my stomach. "I don't know what the fuck I'm doing here with you."

"Me either," I admit candidly as he lathers me up.

"You told me to leave, but I ended up in here with you instead."

"Hey, that's not my problem. You made that decision. No one forced you in here."

"Nah, you have some weird-ass voodoo thing going on."

"A voodoo thing going on?" I ask with a small laugh, looking over my shoulder at him. "What does that even mean?"

"It means I don't do this shit. I don't stand in showers and wash dudes with fruit-scented soap." He brings the bar up and inhales. He wrinkles his nose and then goes back to washing me.

"And you don't normally fuck guys either, do you? But seems like that's all we've been doing when we see each other."

"I'm not fucking you right now."

I rinse off and then turn my body to face him. "No, we're not. Because you got scared and were about to run away for some reason. Can't quite figure out why. You seem fearless most of the time."

Sem frowns as I duck under his arm and step out of the shower, pulling on the fluffy floral robe that I bought off Etsy last year. Bending down, I toss Sem a towel and watch as he slowly dries himself off.

"I wasn't scared, I just..." he hisses when he rubs over the scrape on the side of his abdomen, and I wince. That had to hurt.

"Hold that thought. You need to put something on that. Did you even clean it after you got it?"

Sem glances down at it. "Ran some water over it. I think."

"Oh my god," I mutter and then reach under my sink for

my first aid kit. "How you ever lived to be this age is amazing. Your poor mother."

I pull out some gauze, cream, and a bottle of hydrogen peroxide. "Now, don't move. I'm going to disinfect it, put some cream on it, and then bandage it up."

Sem does as he's told as I slowly clean his wound and bandage him up. He doesn't even flinch when the hydrogen peroxide begins to bubble. Impressive.

When I'm done, I stand up straight and pat his chest. "That should help it heal."

"Yeah. Thanks."

"No problem."

I look up at him, and he swallows roughly. "You confuse me," he mutters.

It's said so softly that I tilt my head and say, "Excuse me?"

"You confuse me, Maggie. Seriously, if it isn't voodoo, then what is it? Why is it you?"

"I don't know."

"I don't like guys like this."

"So you've said."

"I've never had sex with another guy either."

"That's obvious."

"But you...something about you draws me to you."

"Why?"

"I don't know," he replies so earnestly that I run a hand along his arm in the act of comfort. The muscles bunch and flex beneath my touch, and I suddenly feel incredibly powerful, like I could ask this man to kneel for me, and he would.

"You must think I'm insane."

"Mostly," I tell him, and the corner of his mouth quirks up.

"You're just as bad, you know."

"I am not," I say with a small laugh. "I'm *nothing* like you. I am civilized."

"You are not. You're crazy. More subtly, but you are."

"Oh, whatever. Talk to the hand."

I hold my hand up, and he grabs onto it, pulling it to his mouth and nipping lightly at my fingers.

"You sat on me that first time," he tells me, his lips brushing against my fingertips. "What was that, if not insanity?"

I tug my hand away quickly and stare at him because he's right. I might not be riding down mountains on a bike with no brakes or blowing shit up, but I did go along with his crazy bet in the first place. I let him goad me into fucking him. I let him goad me into many things, if I'm honest about it.

"Fine. I'll admit I am a little crazy. At times. Sometimes. Not *all the time,* like you."

"What about your dream guy? Can he handle you when you go off the rails? When you crave something dangerous."

I sniff and move my gaze from Sem's. "I don't know him that well. I'll let you know when I find out."

Sem shifts on his feet, still gloriously naked in front of me. It's criminal how good he looks right now. He really should put some clothes on.

"Well, what's the plan now? Is that bet still on, or should I paint your nails instead? Ooh, I'm thinking bright pink. Ooh, maybe maroon!"

Sem's Adam's apple bobs, and he fiddles with the tie on my robe.

"How about this. If you win this one, then you can paint my nails."

"You know I'll win. My hole is fucking phenomenal," I say

and then point to the bed, and Sem moves toward it. "And when I win, I pick the color. No complaining."

I lie on Sem's naked chest and move the small brush over his blunt thumbnail. Cherry red. Looks absurd on him. But he's letting me do it anyways.

"You will look *so pretty* when I'm done with you," I say and smile up at Sem, whose eyes are closed.

"I never look pretty," he grumbles, and I snicker. He peeks out of one eye at me as I blow onto his wet nails.

"You looked pretty when you came earlier," I tease, and he frowns.

"Shut up. If anyone's pretty when they come, it's you."

My cheeks pinken at that, and I lift up his other hand, getting to work on painting those nails.

"You know, you're the first person to tell me I'm pretty."

I don't know why I blurted that out, but I'm just going to go with it.

His eyebrows rise at that bit of info. "That can't be true. Just look at you."

"Oh, well, I've gotten cute, sweet, tiny, but never pretty." I swipe the last bit of color on his nails and blow on them. "So, you're my first."

"Well, fuck everyone else. You are. Just stating the truth," he sighs, reaching up and tracing the shell of my ear and then resting his hand back on the mattress. We don't really touch. That's not our thing.

"My dad would die if he heard you call me that. He's so disappointed that I didn't turn out like my brothers. He's embarrassed by me. I'm much too feminine for him. He told me that way too often to believe he's just kidding."

"Fuck him."

"Not quite that simple, but he'd *love* you. All masculine. Tall. Athletic. A real man's man."

Sem leans up on his elbows and meets my eyes. "How about I kill him, hm? Shut him up for good."

"Jesus, Sem," I chuckle nervously. "I don't want him to *die*."

Sem shrugs and then lays his head back, and I wonder if he's serious for a moment. And then remember that he has a wide range of explosives and guns, and I'm pretty sure he could bury a body and get away with it.

"Seriously, Sem. Do not kill my parents. Or my brothers. Or anyone, really."

Sem huffs and looks put out, "Whatever you want."

And despite being a little concerned at how easy he said he'd end someone's life, I feel something blossom within my chest. *He'd kill for me.* How many people could say that about someone they know?

Apparently, I'm a psychopath because that turns me on a little bit.

I tamp that weird feeling down and move off Sem, slipping under the covers. I pull them up to my chin and force myself to stay on my side of the bed. Because for some reason, cuddling up against him is much too tempting.

"You can leave when you're ready," I say softly, but Sem's chest is moving up and down rhythmically, and instead of waking him up, I just turn on my side and close my eyes.

CHAPTER FIVE

When I wake up, Sem's gone. The sheets are cold to the touch, and I feel a hint of disappointment. I roll on my stomach and wince as my ass twinges from the fucking I took yesterday. That position was hot, but damn he went deep when he was inside of me.

And he took his goddamn time too. Sem seems to like to do everything fast and furious *except* when it comes to sex. Then he moves like he has all the time in the world. It's almost...as if he's memorizing it.

My cock twitches beneath me, and I turn over onto my back, conjuring up images from last night. How he grabbed onto my thigh and lifted it as he tunneled inside of me, his fingers flexing against the skin of my hips. How he buried his face in my neck as he rutted in and out of me, his groans vibrating throughout my body.

How he said, "So fucking pretty," as I came onto the sheets with a gasp.

I press the heels of my palms into my eyes and groan.

This time, fucking him was not really a bet. This time I did it because I *wanted to*. And I enjoyed it.

Motherfucker. What is happening to me?

I move a bit sluggishly throughout the day, my mind a jumbled mess. My kindergartners notice and seem to try and make up for it by being extra wild today. But they're not the only ones who take note that something is off. August can tell something's wrong because he eyes me from across the playground and shakes his head.

He knows I did it again.

I'm such a sucker. He's totally judging me.

"Shoo," I mouth and wave my hand to ward him away. It doesn't work. He just continues to judge me with his eyes.

I avoid him until he approaches me at lunch and says quietly, "You did it again, didn't you?"

"Why do you think that?"

"Because you look guilty."

I rest my face in my hands and groan. "Fine. I am, and I did."

"Damn, Mags. What were you thinking? What about Colin? You're seeing him tomorrow, yeah?"

"Yeah, that's the plan. I invited him to the thing at the park. We're meeting up toward the end of it."

August sighs and opens a bag of chips, crunching down on one as he thinks. "You've got yourself a dilemma."

"I know. Don't remind me."

"Do you like him?"

"Who, Colin? Of course, I do!"

"No. Sem."

I swallow and turn to face my best friend. "I don't know. He's...he offered to kill my dad for me."

August's eyes widen, and his mouth drops open.

"Jesus."

"I think he meant it too. And I...August, I *liked* it. That he'd do that for me. That he'd protect me like that. Does that make me a criminal? Oh god," I groan and smack my forehead twice. "I'm going to end up in jail because of this guy, aren't I?"

"Quite possibly," August muses, and I nudge him with my elbow.

"I need to...I don't know. Distance myself from him. Focus only on Colin. This whole thing with Sem is craziness anyways. Nothing good can come from it."

"Think he'll let you?"

"God, probably not."

And I'm right because on Saturday, as I'm helping Lisa set up for a day of fun in the park for the kids at the group home, Sem shows up. He's wearing board shorts, slung way too low on his hips, thank you very much, and a tank top that shows off his muscular arms and that eagle tattoo. His blond hair is pulled up in a ponytail, and those blue eyes twinkle when they see me. He looks like sex. If he was anyone else, I'd gobble him up. Like a snack.

Everyone else helping to set up seems to have the same idea too. They're all staring at him. Male. Female. It doesn't matter. He's like some kind of Norse god. No one can look away.

"What are you doing here?" I swallow as he helps me right a folding table that I was struggling with. The muscles in his arms bunch, and I resist the urge to rub against them.

"I'm volunteering."

"Why?"

"Because," he says with a shrug.

"Sem, you need to be fingerprinted and background-checked to volunteer today. You can't just show up to something like this."

"Did all of that weeks ago."

My eyebrows rise with that bit of information. "Seriously?"

"Yeah, heard August mention it. Thought I'd help out."

Even if he's truly only here to stare at me, my heart warms at that. Has Sem ever spent a day with kids in his life?

I slide a disposable tablecloth across the table and lean toward Sem, "You do know there will be kids here? Little kids..."

"So?"

"So...do you even like kids?"

"What's not to like. They're wild, aren't they? Crazy little fuckers."

"You cannot swear like that here," I say, and then my lips twitch. "And if you do happen to let one slip out, keep it down. Lisa will lose it if she thinks you're a bad influence."

He pretends to zip his lips and then moves to help me set up another table.

Hey, we need all the help we can get. As long as Lisa approved him, there's nothing I can say to get him to go away. And maybe the kids will like him. He is a little wild. Kids seem to be drawn to people like him.

"Okay, just remember...these kids...the things they've been through are mostly horrific. We're here just to have fun and let them be kids, yeah?"

"I can do fun," Sem says, looking offended. The large gash on his face is healing, and I reach up and tilt his face toward me.

"Looks better. How's your side?"

"Fine."

I arch an eyebrow at him. "I'll be checking that later."

"Whatever you want," he replies and then moves across the grass to help Lisa set up a few of the games. She's a forty-year-old woman with a husband and kids but blushes like a schoolgirl when Sem talks to her. It makes me a little jealous if I'm honest. He should save all that charm for me.

"You're not surprised to see him here, are you?" August says in my ear, making me jump a mile, and I press a hand to my chest.

"Jesus. Warn a guy."

August laughs and then cocks his head toward Sem, who's bent over to grab a stack of water bottles.

Look at that ass.

"Think he'll be okay with the kids?"

"I have no idea. I hope so." August turns to face me fully, and my eyes widen, "August, what happened to your face."

A dark purple bruise covers his right cheek. "Don't want to talk about it."

I tilt my head in frustration and place my hands on my hips. "Emery?"

"He's just a little shit. It's fine."

"I'll sic Sem on him. How about that? We can teach him a lesson."

August glances over at Sem, who is lifting a large bucket of water and carrying it across the lawn. It looks heavy, and he's carrying it like it weighs nothing.

"I doubt *you* could teach Emery anything. Sem could throw him around a little, but what would you do," he says with a smile. "Lecture him?"

"I'm great with words," I say and then poke him in the chest. "I could talk him to death."

August huffs a laugh. "Probably could, but hey, let's just focus on this afternoon. And make sure Sem behaves."

But apparently, neither of us has anything to worry about. As soon as the kids are offloaded from the vans, they make a beeline for Sem, shouting "Look! *A real-life giant!*" and start literally crawling all over him.

And Sem *lets* them. He's actually grinning.

They shimmy up him like little monkeys on a tree, and he just stands there, plucking them off of him, and hanging them upside down by their legs. I nearly have a heart attack when he throws some of them up into the air, but I can breathe again when he actually catches them. When he's not giving me a heart attack, he's trudging around the lawn with them clinging to his legs, torso, and arms. They take turns riding on his back like he's a horse.

The kids are having more fun with him than with any of the games we've set up for them. Most of them sit unused and ignored.

"Where did you find him?" Lisa asks me, her eyes wide as she watches Sem collapse onto the ground with children still attached to him. Then suddenly, he's rising up, jogging around as fast as he can while the kids squeal in delight. He looks like a Christmas tree with ornaments hanging off of it.

"He's a friend of a friend," I reply. Because how do I tell her that he stalks me, sort of. That he breaks into my apartment and waits for me to get home. That we dare each other to have sex in different positions. It sounds ludicrous.

Lisa smiles as Sem plops a little girl onto his shoulders. "He's really good with kids."

"Yeah," I say, rubbing at my chest. "He is."

Sem's puffing in the distance, his eyes filled with excitement as he holds a kid above a large tub of water.

"Hold your breath!" he shouts, and then the kid goes under before being yanked up and placed onto the ground. The kid shakes his head, droplets of water spraying everywhere, and then the kid launches himself back onto Sem.

The rest of the kids go wild seeing this, lining up for their chance to have Sem hold them headfirst over a bucket of water. Wonders never cease.

"Anyone would be lucky to have him. Imagine him as a dad," Lisa says, and I inhale shakily. Because yeah, Sem would be an incredible father. He'd be just wild enough.

The image of that.

Fuck me.

"Hey, Magnus," a voice says behind me, and I tear my eyes from Sem, who's dunking his own head into the bucket of water and shaking it at a group of squealing kids.

"Oh! Hi, Colin," I say, overly loud and clear my throat. I kinda, sorta forgot he was coming. I try not to look guilty for making heart-eyes at Sem across the field when Colin's standing right here in front of me.

Then my gaze is drawn down to a little boy near Colin's side. He has brown hair like Colin and the same sweet eyes.

"Hey there," I say, bending down and smiling at him. "You must be Daniel. I'm Magnus."

The little boy smiles shyly at me and then looks over my shoulder at what's happening behind me. I can hear Sem growling like a monster as kids squeal their delight.

"What's he doing?" Daniel asks, blinking rapidly.

"Being a crazy, silly man," I say with a laugh. "Want to join?"

"Yeah," he says and then looks up to his dad for approval. Colin nods once, and then Daniel is off like a shot, making a direct beeline for Sem, who is plucking another kid off the ground. Colin and I watch as Daniel taps Sem on the side. Sem turns to look at the new kid and glances over his shoulder, meeting my gaze. I smile at him, but his eyes flick to Colin, standing next to me, and those blue eyes narrow. Then he looks down at Daniel and hefts him up into his arms, turning him upside down and holding him over the tub of water. Daniel screams in delight as Sem dunks the top of his head into it, wetting just the tips of his hair.

"Who's that?" Colin asks with a laugh as Daniel is set back on the ground, his eyes wide with glee. Water drips down his cheeks and soaks his shirt. Then Daniel's clamoring onto Sem again, obviously as enamored with him as everyone else.

I feel ya, buddy.

"A friend," I tell him and then force myself to look away because I could watch Sem with kids all day when my focus should be on Colin. Colin, who made the trip over here to meet with me. The one who looks good in those athletic shorts and fitted tee. The dedicated father. The smart, well-read man of my dreams. He's a professor, for god's sake. Like, swoon.

"It's really great that you're doing this," he says as I hand out bags of chips and bottles of water to some hungry kids. They rip into the bags, spilling half of it on the ground, and then bend down to shove it in their mouths before I can tell them not to.

Oh well. We all made it out of childhood alive, right? What's a little dirt?

"Yeah, it's something August, and I do every year. Started doing it three years ago, actually, and it kind of, just stuck."

Colin bends down to help me distribute water to more kids, and I force myself to keep my eyes on him and not on Sem, who's chasing kids with water balloons.

"Watch your back, ladies!" Sem hollers, acting like this is World War III, as he ducks behind a tree. He pretends like a water balloon is a grenade, pulls the imaginary pin out of it with his teeth, and chucks it at an unsuspecting little girl.

It hits her on the back with a splash, and she screams in frustration.

"Gotchu!" he shouts and then jogs over to grab another large armful of balloons. They're cradled in the bottom of his shirt, and *everyone* watches him as he moves around the park. Probably because those damn unicorn abs are showing.

"Daniel was really excited to come, too," Colin says, pulling my eyes back to him. Shit. Must pay attention to *this* guy. Not *that* guy.

"Glad you all could make it."

"Me too. It's been a little chaotic since things ended with my ex, and I've found myself not making enough time for him."

"I'm glad I could provide something fun for him to do," I say with a flourish. "Anyways, this is almost over, and then we can head out."

Colin smiles softly at me, and then both our heads whip to the side when I hear a loud groan. Sem is bent over, clutching his crotch as a little girl lobs another water balloon at him. It smacks him right in the face, and Sem growls, standing up straight and grabbing the girl into his arms, tossing her into the air. She laughs so hard her breath comes out as a wheeze. I can't help the smile that erupts on my face.

"Wow, he has energy," Colin says in amazement. "I wish I had that."

"He sure does," I say as Sem laughs, grabs another water balloon from his stash, and chucks one at Daniel's back.

"Maybe I should hire him to babysit," Colin adds, and I

force myself to grin at him, lest I smack his face off. Colin will not be getting *anywhere* near Sem.

"I don't think he's much of a babysitter."

"No, probably not. A man like that...."

His words trail off, and I bite back my urge to ask what he meant. A man like what?

So," Colin says, turning towards me and reaching out to lightly touch my hand, diverting my thoughts from Sem back to him. "Tell me more about you, Magnus. I'd like to figure out what makes you tick."

SEM

I watch that fucker touch Maggie, and I want to rip his arm off. But of course, I don't because that would be, well, physically impossible. But I still envision it as I chase the kids around.

Me walking up and tugging dream guy's arms clean off.

Bashing his skull in with the bloody stump.

Throwing Maggie over my shoulder and carrying him home.

Fucking him against the wall.

It's better if I don't look at the two of them, and then I'll be fine. Won't go nuclear. But sometimes, my gaze slips, and I see how Maggie smiles at his dream guy. It's like he's looking at Jesus or something. He never fucking smiles like that for me.

Because I'm not who he wants.

I press my back against a tree and take a deep breath. Even if I wanted to be his, I couldn't be. I'm not smart enough, not witty enough. Not well-read. Nothing like the guy who's literally playing with Maggie's fingers as they stand side-by-side.

Fuck.

I just can't look at the two of them. It makes my chest hurt.

I manage to make it through the rest of the morning without losing my shit and then help Lisa clean up, the best I can, as Daniel clings to my legs. His dad hasn't spared him one single glance the entire time he's been with me. Even I know better than that. That's some lame parenting.

I toss Daniel around a few more times to make up for the fact that he has a shit-for-brains dad. And then force myself to act as normal as possible as I deposit dream guy's kid on the bench beside him.

"Here you go," I say, not meeting Maggie's eyes.

If I look at him, I'll do something irrational. Like, kiss him. Stake my claim or some barbarian shit.

That's not what this is.

"Hi there. Magnus was telling me all about you, Sem. You're really good with kids. I'm Colin," dream guy says kindly, holding out his hand.

I know I shouldn't, but I do it anyway. I crush his fingers beneath mine, and he hisses, pulling his hand away with a grimace.

"Sorry," I mutter even though I'm not fucking sorry.

"Sem," Maggie chastises, but I can't even look at him. Can't see him looking disappointed in me. I'm humiliated, fawning over another guy who doesn't even like me. A guy who will fuck me but would never even think about going on a date with me. Maggie's already mentally planning his wedding to the guy sitting across from him.

I don't even factor into this equation. Makes sense. I never was very good with math.

"Going home now. Later," I bite out and then stalk away.

The entire drive home, I stew over the whole morning. Colin looked fucking *nice*. Like a regular family guy with perfectly cut hair and those nice clothes. He had kind eyes, even when I crushed his hand in mine. He probably owns his own home with a white picket fence and a garden.

His motherfucking dream guy.

Asshole.

I walk into my RV and quickly grab a few stray sketches of Maggie littering the space and rip them in half, stuffing them in the bottom of the trashcan with a grunt. My chest is heaving as I stare at them, crumpled and torn. Kind of like my mind right now. I've completely cracked. First, the irrational obsession with another man and then letting myself actually like him. I tug on the ends of my hair, shout in frustration, and then bend down and gingerly pull the rumpled pages out, smoothing them the best I can. I even tape the torn fuckers together. Because I can't throw Maggie away. No matter how much I want to. Nah, I'm entirely too selfish.

My phone dings, and I glance at the screen.

Maggie: You didn't say goodbye.

Maggie: You were really good with the kids today. Daniel really liked you.

Maggie: Want to come hang out with us?

That one really pisses me off. I try to get it together, to calm the fuck down, but the more I think about Maggie with *him*, the angrier I get. Maggie seamlessly moving into their perfect little family. Forgetting all about me. What does he want me to do? Show up and babysit Daniel so they could fuck around? Is he letting that prick stick his cock inside of him? Does he let Colin actually touch him? Kiss him?

I work myself into such a state that I don't sleep at all, I just end up pacing and furiously sketching like a madman. When morning arrives, papers with Maggie sketched on them are strewn about the RV, and I hastily gather them up and stuff them into a drawer. Without thinking about it too much, I pull on some clean clothes and drive to his apartment. Because the fucking devil couldn't keep me away right now.

If I see Colin in there with him, I will full-on murder that asshole.

I pound so hard on Maggie's door that I almost put a hole in it. It shakes and rattles as I beat my fist against it.

I need some fucking closure to move on with my life.

That's what I need.

"What in the hell are you doing?" Maggie spits angrily as he yanks the door open. He glowers at me, with no smile in sight. Not that I expected him to give me one of those. No, those are for Colin.

But everything dies in my throat as my eyes slide over him.

"What the fuck are you wearing?" I roar, trying to process what I'm seeing. He's wearing some kind of ugly athletic shirt that's way too baggy on him and a pair of oversized jeans.

He looks *different*.

I hate it.

Is he wearing this for Colin? Is that asshole trying to change him already?

"I'm wearing clothes," he grumbles as I push my way inside his apartment. He stumbles back and huffs in annoyance as I slam the door shut and lock it. "You can't just barge in here."

"I do it all the time."

"What do you want?" he sighs. "I don't have time for this."

"What I want is for you to change your fucking clothes. You look like a clown."

He flings his hands up into the air and grumbles. "I know that, Sem, but I'm meeting my dad and older brother for breakfast and...."

I cock my head at him, and he sighs, his hands on his trim hips, "They don't know I'm gay, okay? I mean, it's not like I hide it, but they just think I'm effeminate. I wear this, so they just leave me alone, okay? If I don't, I'll never hear the end of it. They'll be on me about it for days. Next Christmas, they'll still bring it up. I just can't...."

"Do they make fun of how you dress?" I ask, my heart thumping angrily in my chest. First Colin and now Maggie's asshole family. I'm going to fucking erupt. Watch out, Chernobyl, I'm almost radioactive.

"Yes, they would, and they do. And I'm not in the mood for it. I just want the morning to pass peacefully without any comments about my clothes or my figure or the way I walk. And one of the ways that I can guarantee some peace is if I dress like this."

He gestures to his outfit, and I see red. Literally, I see it. It nearly blinds me.

Without even thinking, I reach, grab onto the neckline of his shirt, and yank the fabric apart.

It tears in half with an audible *riiiiiip*.

Maggie gasps, his eyes wide. "What the hell, Sem? Why'd you do that?"

"You're not wearing this shit," I bite out, balling up the ruined shirt and dropping it onto the floor. I'm going to burn it next weekend. Blow it the fuck up. Maybe shoot it first, too.

I move my hands to his pants and rip them open before he can move away. The zipper breaks, and the button flies across the room.

"Sem!" Maggie squeals, and I bend down, tugging his jeans to his ankles.

"You're not wearing this shit," I repeat. He exhales shakily and then steps out of them because what else can he do? I demolished them.

As soon as he's free of those ugly ass clothes, I shred them in my hands, tearing them right down the middle and feel better almost immediately.

"Oh my god," Maggie whispers, eyeing the heap of fabric on the floor. His cheeks are flushed, his hands shaking slightly. "I don't have any other straight guy clothes in my closet. I'm so screwed."

"Wear your normal fucking clothes."

Maggie's eyes flash up to meet mine, and he shakes his head. He looks so dejected. "I can't."

"You can," I say softly.

I move toward him and gently clasp his chin and force his wary gaze to meet mine. "Don't let those fuckers make you feel bad about yourself. You're perfect. Just the way you are."

He swallows roughly, and I can't help myself. I pick him up. I lift him into my arms as easily as those children I threw around yesterday. His legs automatically wrap around my waist, his arms tightening around my neck as I carry him to the bedroom. He clings to me, his face buried in my shoulder, and my chest expands with delight at how close he is to me.

I hold him with one arm and begin shuffling through the clothes hanging in his closet with my other hand.

"Wear this," I say, holding out a red midriff shirt I'm slightly obsessed with.

"No, not that. They will die if they see me in that."

I huff, "Good riddance then," and then pull out a button-up short-sleeved shirt with little pigs on it.

"Yeah, okay," Maggie says and then he slides off of me, grabbing the shirt and tugging it on. I move to his dresser and pick out a pair of shorts that I've seen him wear. They're my favorite, a little shorter than they should be. They show off a lot of leg. I toss them to him, and he pulls them on.

"Sem, will you…I know this isn't what we do, but…will you come with me?" he asks, looking so fucking small. He fiddles nervously with the buttons on his shirt, and I notice. I fucking *see* it.

"Yeah, I'll come, but first, you're painting your fucking nails. Why'd you take that shit off?"

"Because…" his voice trails off, and I grab onto his hand and pull him into the bathroom, roughly grabbing a drawer and yanking it opening. The glass bottles rattle and clink inside, and I pull out a color that will match his shirt.

"If you don't put this on, I'll do it. And it'll be a shit job. Don't make me."

Maggie laughs on a small sob and grabs the bottle from me. "Okay."

He swipes at his damp eyes and meets my gaze, and I brush a hand over his cheek.

"Don't let anyone make you feel small."

"It's hard."

"Then I'm glad I'll be there. I won't let them say shit to you," I tell him as he uncaps the nail polish and begins to paint his nails.

"Okay," he says softly, and I can't help myself. I rub my thumb across his pouty mouth, causing his breath to hitch.

I reluctantly pull my hand away, my fingers on fire. I lean against the wall and watch, his lip between his teeth as he finishes up his nails. Then he blows on them, and those hazel eyes meet mine.

"We should go. My dad hates it when I'm late. He's going to be upset."

"Let him," I say firmly and place my hand on the small of his back as we walk out of his apartment and down to the carport. He's shaking slightly, and I have to ball my hands into fists to resist picking him up and carrying him back inside. I'd keep him safe. I'd never let anyone hurt him.

"I'm right here," he says. Parked in his numbered space is a micromachine. What did I expect, though? He's pint-sized.

"This is a roller skate," I grumble, my eyes taking in the bright blue car. "I won't fit in it."

Maggie looks at me and then back at his car and giggles. "Oh my god," he says as his laugh becomes a full-on wheeze.

"Shut the fuck up," I mutter, but my lips twitch into a small smile. I'm damn pleased with myself for making him laugh when just seconds earlier, he was trembling.

"Okay, yeah. Sorry. That's just...the idea of you folding yourself inside is too good."

He presses a hand to his stomach and bends over, tears tracking down his cheeks as he laughs.

I just stand there and watch because those sounds he's making are causing my heart flutter uncomfortably in my chest.

Maggie clears his throat after a few more moments and then straightens, swiping at his cheeks. "Okay, I'm really sorry. I'm done. Promise. That was just...God, that was good. Felt good to laugh." He locks his car and then steps toward me. "Where's your car? You can drive. Does that work?"

Those eyes fucking twinkle when he looks up at me, and I can't help it. I just can't fucking resist. I walk over and pick him up, carrying him across the lot to my truck. People stare, but I couldn't give two shits. Let them look. And Maggie doesn't complain, doesn't smack me to put him down. He just buries his face into my neck and holds on.

No wonder Whit's always looking so content when Caleb does this to him. It's amazing.

With one hand, I unlock the door and yank it open with a loud creak.

"In you go," I say and set him down gently before buckling him in. I hop into the driver's seat and turn the key. The engine roars to life. I let it idle for a moment and then put the car in reverse.

"Thank you," Maggie says softly. He looks so tiny in the large cab, and I clench onto the steering wheel with both my hands. Because if I don't, I'm going to pull him over to me and do something crazy, like hold his hand. Considering everything we've done already, that shouldn't be a big deal, but it is. It feels like a very big deal.

We make it to the restaurant in fifteen minutes because I drive a lot slower than I should. His dad and brother can fucking wait. I already don't like them, and I haven't even met them. They sound like bullies and overall dickheads.

But when I see them, the way their eyes widen at the mere sight of Maggie, the disapproval lining their gazes, I really fucking hate them.

Making him feel less than makes me want to commit murder.

I stand tall, squaring my shoulders, and move behind

Maggie, narrowing my gaze at his dad and older brother. I can see the resemblance, even if Maggie is much shorter than both of them. They both have the same hazel eyes and the same narrow build. But his dad and brother are much more masculine in almost every way. I'm glad Maggie isn't like them. I want him just the way he is.

"Magnus, son, glad you could meet. It's been a while," his dad says as he clears his throat, leans over, and slaps him roughly on the back.

Maggie's entire body is jostled forward, and I clench my fists at my sides. No one should touch him like that. *No one.*

His older brother does the same, and I crack my neck, envisioning myself choking them.

"Been a while, Mag," his brother says and then looks up at me. As if he could fucking *miss* me. I'm at least five inches taller than him.

"Who's this?" his older brother asks.

"Sem. He's a...friend," Maggie says and bites down on his bottom lip, worrying it. I want to pull him into my side but resist. Because he's not out to his family. They've made him ashamed of who he is.

Assholes.

"Ah, nice to meet you, man," his brother says, "I'm Max, Magnus' older brother."

I don't even think about it. Just crush his hand in mine. His fingers pop, and I smirk a little when he fights off a wince and tugs his hand out of my grip.

Take a good look, buddy. I'll crush anyone who fucks with what's mine.

"He's told me a little about you," I say through gritted teeth and then eye his dad, who's watching me curiously. I let him look.

Yeah, asshole, I'm fucking your son. Sticking my big cock in that tiny hole. Come at me.

"Hopefully, all good," his dad says, looking at Maggie and then back up at me.

"Not really," I grind out, and his dad frowns and opens his mouth to say something else but is interrupted by the hostess who leads us to our booth.

His dad and brother slide in on one side, and Maggie and I slide in on the other. I make sure to sit really close just to irritate the two asswipes facing us. My thigh bumps Maggie's, and I place my arm on the back of the booth, cocooning him against me.

The waitress brings us water, and Maggie nervously gulps some of it down. His eyes flick from his dad to his brother to the table. He's just waiting for it. For the comments. For them to open their ugly mouths and tear him down.

"You doing that again?" his dad asks, gesturing to his hands at the nails I made him paint earlier. "Thought we talked about this, son. You can't be painting your nails...or wearing those clothes. People talk. They'll think you're gay."

I snort, and Maggie nudges me with his knee.

"Yeah," Maggie says softly, and I hate how insecure he sounds. Usually, he's spouting his mouth off, but he's cowering right now, and I despise it.

His dad leans forward, pretending to be concerned. "Remember how it was in high school? I just don't want to see you hurt...."

"It wasn't just the kids who bullied me, dad. It was you. And you too, Max. Same with Matt and Mitch," Maggie says, his hands trembling as he confronts them.

Makes me unreasonably proud.

"That's not how it is. You're being dramatic like usual. We

don't bully you. Don't be like..." his dad starts, but I interject. Because him just opening his mouth makes me feel like wrenching the table from the floor and squashing him with it.

"You know," I say. "I work at a scrapyard. Own it, actually." Maggie shifts next to me and gulps down some more water, his eyes on the wall behind his dad. He doesn't stop me, so I go full speed ahead. And why shouldn't I? I'm done with their bullshit. "There are miles of it. Things can get lost out there." I pause and let the silence fill the space between us. "You know what else I own?" I glance at the two of them before explaining, "I also own machines that crush things. They can grind metal to dust. One minute it's there, the next it's gone."

His brother eyes me warily. His dad still looks clueless. He's obviously not as smart as Maggie.

I lean forward and run my finger around the edge of my glass. "Imagine what those machines could do to humans?"

Maggie chokes on his water, and I turn to look at him, reaching out and swiping a thumb over his cheek. Tenderly. His eyelids flutter at my touch.

"Are you...are you threatening us?" his dad asks, sounding offended. He has no right when he just offended Maggie.

"I sure am."

His dad is trembling slightly. "Who *is* this guy, Magnus? Is he your..."?

He can't even fucking say it. Bigoted asshole.

I turn to the two of them and shoot them a serious, most likely crazed look. "I'm whatever he wants me to be. And if you talk shit about him, make him feel anything other than *fucking perfect*, I'll murder you both. No one will ever find the bodies. I guarantee it."

Truthfully, I've never murdered anyone before, but I would. If anyone lays a hand on Maggie, looks at him wrong, or even breathes weirdly in his direction. I'm capable of anything when it comes to him, apparently.

He's most likely more than a muse at this point.

His dad and brother stop breathing, their eyes wide. Silence permeates the table as they just stare at me. Both of them don't know what to do. Or what to say.

Good. Let them shut their fat mouths.

I glower at them and then slap the table roughly, making them both jump.

"Boo, motherfuckers!" I shout and then laugh maniacally. I sound like a psychopath, but you know what? Did I ever claim to be anything else? No. No, I did not.

"Why the fuck can't we all just get along? Huh? I don't want to have to kill you," I say with a toothy smile.

The two of them swallow roughly, and I pick up a menu and peruse it. "Let's order. I'm starving. What's good, Maggie? I'm thinking pie."

Maggie's hand snakes under the table and rests on my thigh. When it squeezes softly, I bite back a satisfied grin.

Worth it.

CHAPTER SIX

We walk to the truck in silence, my hands tucked into my pockets. The entire time we spent with my dad and brother, Sem didn't leave my side, not even to go to the bathroom. And for the first time in ages, they were *nice* to me. They didn't make their typical degrading comments. They didn't tease or mock me or make me feel like shit.

No, they were even fairly respectful.

They barely even glanced my way, actually. And for the first time in my entire life, I felt the dynamic of power shift in my favor. I felt like I had the upper hand.

And it was all because of Sem. Crazy, out-of-his-mind Sem.

After threatening them with murder, Sem was surprisingly calm. He sat back and ate his food, letting my dad, brother, and I talk. But if their comments even veered in a disrespectful direction, Sem would clench his fork like a weapon, and my dad and brother would clam up. It was the best thing I've ever experienced in my life. No one has ever done anything like that for me before. It was like my childhood dream of showing up to school with a superhero at my side and having him vanquish all the bullies.

Sem was my superhero today. He was remarkable.

When we reach his truck, Sem lifts me up and sets me on my seat. But before he can walk away, I reach out and grab onto his shirt.

"Sem," I say, fisting the fabric in my hand. I'm sitting higher up than I usually stand, so we're now eye to eye. I can see flecks of gold in his blue irises as he blinks slowly.

My other hand cups his neck, and I can feel his pulse throbbing wildly. He lowers his forehead to mine and exhales. "You're angry," he says roughly. "I shouldn't have threatened them. I...I know I went a little nuts in there but your family sucks ass. Please don't ask me to apologize. I can't do it. I won't do it."

A manic giggle escapes my lips, and I bite it back. But Sem hears it. He lifts his head and meets my gaze with a confused look on his face.

"No, Sem. I'm not mad, and I don't want you to apologize. I just...*thank you*. No one's ever stood up for me like that before," I say softly and then pull him into a tight hug.

I press my face against the skin of his neck and inhale deeply. He smells of motor oil and sage. It's addicting.

Sem freezes for a moment, and then his large hands wrap around my back, and he pulls me a little closer. My legs wrap around his waist, and I cling to him. I've never felt safer than I do at this moment.

"I want to just go somewhere and chill. Away from here."

"You could come back to my place," Sem says, and I lean back, my brows scrunched in question.

"Don't you live like an hour away?"

"Nah. Live pretty close to you, actually."

My eyebrow lifts, "Is that so?"

"Yeah."

"When did that happen?"

"Recently," he says, brushing a thumb over the pulse in my neck. He presses down on it lightly, and those blue eyes flick to mine. My heartbeat is betraying me in the most delicious way.

"Okay, let's go," I say, licking my lips.

His nostrils flare, and he exhales shakily before setting me down on the seat and buckling me in.

When he moves to the driver's side, he glances over at me, grumbles something under his breath, and then unhooks my seatbelt, and drags me right into the middle seat.

"Buckle up, Maggie. Gotta keep you safe."

I do as he says, and he puts the truck in drive and pulls out on the street. I probably shouldn't, but I lean into him. Actually, I full-on nuzzle myself under his arm until he has no choice but to wrap that heavy arm around my shoulders. He pulls me into his side, his hand rubbing small circles against the skin of my arm. And I like it, way more than I probably should.

My phone dings in my pocket, and I pull it out, sighing heavily when I see a long column of texts from my dad and brother. My mom sent one, too, and I roll my eyes.

"What is it?" Sem asks, and I just turn my phone off.

"Just texts from my family. Making sure I'm safe. They think you're a psychopath."

He huffs, and his grip tightens on my arm. "They shouldn't have been fucking with you then. Maybe if they were nicer, I'd be nicer. I can be nice."

I bite down on my lower lip and peek up at him. He glances down at me, and my heart flutters in my chest.

"Has it always been like that?" he asks, his one hand gripping the steering wheel tightly.

"Yeah. It has. It got worse when they realized I wouldn't be like them. They're not bad people, just stuck in their ways. They don't understand me. And it doesn't help I haven't officially come out to them. I probably should, but I don't know... I don't want to. Don't want to hear it. It will be incessant comments and nagging, and I'm just not ready for it."

"Well, they can fuck right off then. Trying to change you," he mutters and then adds, "I think you should stay away. Unless I can be there with you."

"To threaten them a painful death?" I ask with a laugh. "Oh my god, I cannot believe you did that! You said you'd grind them to dust."

Sem smirks down at me and leans over, pressing a small kiss to the top of my head. That does all sorts of things to my insides. Butterflies flap their wings and take flight in my stomach. I shift in my seat and nuzzle farther into his chest. I'm practically in his lap.

"I'd do pretty much anything you ask, Maggie."

I reach up and press a kiss to his cheek, and the tips of his ears turn pink. Fucking adorable. This big psychopath blushing because I *kissed* him.

"Almost there," he says, clearing his throat and turning down a road I've noticed before but paid very little attention to.

"You live in an RV park?" I ask, sitting up a little taller and staring out the windshield as we move past rows and rows of motorhomes.

"Yeah, like I said...moved here a few weeks ago. Made it easier to get to work," he says, as he pulls in front of an older class A motorhome. And yes, this gay boy knows the different motorhome classes. I grew up with a bunch of men obsessed with camping and "toughing it out". I spent my childhood vacations in tents dying for something comfortable to spend those dreary days in. I would have killed for something like this growing up.

"Very cool," I say as he shuts off the engine and jumps out of the truck. I scoot over, and shoulder open the passenger side door, but before I can hop down, he grabs onto my waist and picks me up, carrying me to his RV. Apparently, I'm getting used to being lugged around by him because I don't even protest. I just wrap my legs around his waist and tuck myself nicely against his broad chest.

We fit perfectly.

I can hear keys clanging as he opens the door to the RV. Then he's striding up and flipping on the lights.

"Oh my god, Sem," I gasp, looking around, still attached to his torso like an opossum. "This is amazing."

I unwrap my legs from his waist and slide down his muscular body until my feet hit the floor.

"This all looks brand new. Did you remodel this?" I ask, looking around at the sleek couch, the wood floors, the white subway tile backsplash, and the granite countertops.

"This is...beautiful." I look at him, and he blushes again.

I need to compliment this guy more often. He's amazing.

"Yeah," he says, running a hand through his hair and mussing it up. "Just a little project I started a while back and got a little carried away."

I move around the large space, marveling at how nice it is. "A little project? This must have been a lot of work. Did you..." I run my hands over the new cabinets and look at him. "Did you make these?"

He shrugs. "Yeah. The motorhome was in pretty bad

shape, but I got a good deal on it, so I bought it and rebuilt it."

"Just like that?" I ask, my fingertips trailing across the counter.

"Yeah."

"You're so talented, Sem. Not everyone could do this," I say and open a drawer and peek inside. Nothing exciting, just utensils. I want to find the good stuff. Everyone has at least one drawer filled with the filthy things they want to keep secret.

"Can I see the rest of it? And by that, I mean can I look *everywhere*?" I say, and Sem nods, following me as I open each drawer and cabinet. I even peer in the fridge and side-eye Sem when I see the amount of beer inside relative to food. Then we make our way to the bathroom, which has also been remodeled. When I look under the sink, I see a gun.

"Seriously?"

"Can never be too careful when you're taking a shit."

"Oh my god."

I close the door and step two feet into the bedroom.

"Are there guns in here too?"

"Yep. And some knives too."

I try to peek into a drawer by his bed, but he stands in front of it.

"Nah, not here, Maggie. This is off-limits."

"Ooh. Why? Now I'm intrigued." I rub my hands together and wet my lips.

He looks away from me, and I try to reach around him, but he just picks me up and sets me on the other side of the bed.

"I'm not ready for you to see."

"Damn."

"Patience, Maggie."

I smile at him and then run my hand across the dark grey comforter. "So, sans all the weapons hidden around here, this is…I can see why you live here. I think I like this better than my apartment. This is so cozy."

Sem leans against the doorway of the small room in the back of the RV.

"Glad you like it. I can make you one if you want."

I snort at that and then shake my head. "No way. I could never drive this thing. It's much too big. Maybe I'll just be your passenger. If you'll have me."

He rolls his lips between his teeth and then moves toward me, running a finger down the buttons of my shirt.

"You're always welcome to tag along." Sem pauses a moment and then says, "Can I…I want to sketch you."

My eyebrows rise at that. "Sketch me?"

"Yeah."

"You draw?" Because this guy could not get any more surprising.

"Yeah."

"Can I see your work?"

Sem unbuttons the first button of my top and then the second. "You can see the one I draw today. How 'bout that?"

I pretend to mull it over because I can't seem that excited. No one's ever wanted to draw me before…makes me feel special.

"Okay, fine. Where do you want me?"

Sem gestures to the bed. "Here."

I start to sit, but Sem stops me. "Nah. I want you naked."

He unbuttons the rest of my shirt and pushes it from my shoulders. It falls onto the mattress, and he runs a finger across my left nipple, and I force myself not to tremble. Jesus, but it's hard. His rough hands on me feel good. Why didn't I ever let him touch me before?

Oh, that's right, because it was just a game before.

It doesn't feel like that to me anymore.

He tugs my shorts off and then my underwear, and I'm left standing naked in front of him. My half-hard cock bobs in front of his face, and I have to look away. It's too much, seeing him on his knees.

"How do you want me?" I ask, and he swallows, standing up.

"On your back."

"K," I whisper and then lie down.

Sem stares at me for a moment before he turns around, reaches into a cabinet, and pulls out a piece of paper and charcoal pencil.

"You have to stay still for a while. Can you do that?"

I bite my bottom lip and nod. "Yeah. I can do that. I won't move a muscle."

But it's harder than I thought. Lying here. Watching him. Those fingers flying across the paper, smudging it. His eyes flicking over my body, the lines on his forehead wrinkling with concentration. A smudge of black has appeared on his cheek, and I want to lick it off. Sem has always been hot, but he's complete and utter sex right now.

I move my hand and tug on my hard cock, and Sem's eyes flash to it.

"Stop it," he grumbles and continues to sketch, but I can't help it. I run my hand over my cock again, and Sem's pencil screeches to a stop.

"I'm warning you," he says, his eyes meeting mine.

"I can't help it," I breathe. "Watching you watch me is making me horny."

Sem reaches out and grabs onto my hand, pulling it away from my straining dick and holding it to the mattress. So, I just use my other one. That's why God gave us two, right?

Sem huffs, and then my other hand is pressed to the mattress, and Sem is straddling me.

"You're a bad listener, Maggie. You keep squirming. Why are you so wiggly?" he mutters, and I arch my hips, trying to get some friction on it.

"Goddammit," I mutter when my efforts end in vain.

"I'm almost done, and you can't keep it together?" he says, and I hump the air again.

"Too long," I whine, and Sem watches me for a moment before his hands are suddenly digging into my sides.

Oh shit.

I hate being tickled.

"Oh, fuck!" I squeal and writhe beneath him. "I'm sorry! Stop!" I can't inhale quickly enough, my breath coming out a long wheeze while Sem's smiling above me. He's just loving this.

"Shit!" I'm laughing so hard now that my eyes are running, and my stomach aches from the strain of it. "Stop, *stop*, I'm begging...."

Sem's hands are suddenly still, and I catch my breath. "God...dammit, Sem. You're awful."

Sem traces a fingertip across my hip, leaving a black streak there, then meets my gaze.

"Caleb was right. You squeal like a girl when tickled."

"I'm going to kill him," I hiss, and Sem trails that finger down to my throbbing cock. And all is suddenly forgiven.

"Please," I whisper, and Sem's mouth opens slightly, his tongue flicking out, wetting his lips.

"Not until I'm done with my sketch," he says, and I reach

down to stroke myself, but Sem grabs me again. "You won't lie still, will you?"

"Can't," I groan, and Sem shakes his head before grabbing both my hands and pulling them roughly over my head.

My breath hitches. "What are you doing?"

He reaches over into a drawer, pulls out a double cuff zip tie, and slides it over my wrists, restraining me.

The shock of it stuns me momentarily. "Why the hell do you have zip ties in your bedroom, Sem?"

Sem ignores me and instead tightens the restraints and uses another to keep my hands locked above my head. It *shouldn't* be hot, but it *so is*. Apparently, I like being tied up. Who knew?

"Do you usually tie up the people you draw?"

"Never have," he says and then moves off of me, obviously satisfied when I can't move anymore. "Never drew anyone before I met you."

"You're evil," I mutter, and Sem reaches out and runs a finger across my belly button and then moves to the tip of my cock. His touch makes me wild, but he suddenly withdraws his hand, and I whimper.

"I just need a little more time," he tells me, and then he's sketching again. "Patience, Maggie."

"Pfft, like you're one to talk. You're the least patient man I know!"

He ignores me and moves his eyes back to the paper on his lap.

And fuck me sideways, but this whole thing is making me hotter. I have to bite down on my lip to keep myself from begging for it. Because apparently, I want to beg when I'm tied up.

Sem must notice how much I need release. It's blatantly

obvious. But he just smirks at me and continues to sketch. It goes on for ages. It could be minutes or hours, but by the time Sem's done, I'm sure just one touch from him will make me come.

"Are you finally fucking done?" I ask, irritated and needy.

Sem peeks up at me and shakes his head in disbelief. "It was twenty minutes, Maggie."

"Felt like two hundred years. Now show me my portrait."

Sem looks embarrassed for a minute before turning the paper toward me, and I see myself sketched on it. And it's fucking good. Like, he's super talented.

"Sem," I breathe, my eyes wide. "You're really, really good. This is amazing."

He shifts on the bed, and I want to reach out and touch him but can't.

"Can I keep it?" I ask.

"If you want it."

"I do. I fucking want it."

I want you.

Where did that thought come from?

Sem's Adam's apple bobs, and he sets the paper on the end table and then touches my knee gently.

"Thank you for posing for me."

"Anytime," I say, and I mean that literally. This was hot. I'd do this again in a heartbeat. Especially if he ties me up again. "Now, what do I get for it?"

"What do you want?"

"I want to come, Sem. Look at my balls. They're blue. That's a veritable health emergency."

"Don't know what that means," he says as he reaches down and spreads my legs a little, lifting my balls into his hand and rolling them in his palm.

My eyes flutter shut because if he keeps doing that, I'm going to embarrass myself.

"I have another position we could try," he says, and I nod frantically. Because fuck the positions, I just want to have sex with him. I want to feel him stretching me out, want to feel him inside me. "You think you can take me?"

"I always do," I breathe. "I just need to prep. Do you have..."

Sem reaches over and pulls out a condom and a packet of lube. The same exact kind I have at my house. Ah, so Sem's been paying attention. Of course, he has. He doesn't seem to miss much when it comes to me.

"You can untie me, and I can do it," I say, tugging on my restraints, but Sem just cocks his head.

"Nah. Can I do it?"

My body trembles at that because, *holy shit*. "Um...if you want."

He spreads my legs slowly and pushes one of my knees up to my chest, glancing down at my hole.

"What do I do?" he asks.

"Just stretch me out. And make sure to get a lot of lube in there."

He swallows and then squirts a bit of lube on his finger, massaging my hole gently before I hiss impatiently, "Just put your fucking finger in, Sem!"

He ignores me, choosing to tease me instead, and then finally...fucking finally...he inserts the first finger.

"Jesus fuck," I mutter as he slowly slides it all the way to his knuckle.

"What now?"

"Move it around. I..." I gasp when he does what I ask,

hitting that spot inside me. "Oh fuck. Another. Just stick another inside of me."

Sem, of course, doesn't do it right away. He just takes his sweet goddamn time until I'm panting.

And then the second finger is inside of me, scissoring me open.

"You're so tight," he mutters. "So little." I exhale shakily, and he adds, "I want to teach you self-defense."

"Damnit, Sem. *That's* what you're thinking about right now?" I hiss as he continues to stretch me.

"I want to teach you to shoot a gun, Maggie. I want you to be safe."

"Whatever you want. I don't care. Just do me already."

Sem adds a third finger, and I arch my back slightly.

"Come camping with me for the Fourth of July."

"Will it hurry you up if I agree to it?" I bite out, and he chuckles.

"Yeah."

"Then fine. I'll go camping with you. Now stick your dick in me. I'm *dying*."

"Will you moan for me if I do?" Sem asks, and I shake my head.

"Never."

Sem wets his lips. "Bet I can make you moan."

I bite the inside of my cheek and shake my head again because I've lost the ability to talk. All this anticipation has fried my brain.

He rips open the condom package with his teeth and rolls it onto his leaking cock.

Then those strong hands lift my legs and place them on his shoulders. He grips my hips and places himself *right there*.

"Hurry," I plead, and Sem turns his head slightly, biting

down gently on my ankle. "So impatient. Maybe I should make you wait a little longer."

"Don't be an asshole. I've waited a hundred hours for this. I'm dying of old age!" I bite out as he shifts his hips forward. A relieved exhale leaves my throat as he breaches me, and then he slowly, *slowly*, enters me. Until I'm fully impaled on him.

My hands flex as I scramble for purchase, but I'm helpless beneath him. I'm entirely immobile and completely at his will and I can see in his eyes that he likes it. Me tied up. Helpless. Begging for it.

He pulls out and thrusts back in, and I huff, trying to keep my whimpers and moans at bay. I'm already so close, and he hasn't even really done anything. But that torture I had to endure earlier, of watching him sketch me, has made me all kinds of crazy.

"Make all the fucking sounds. I want to hear you," he says, leaning forward, nearly bending me in half.

And part of me wants to give in, but what's life without a bit of challenge?

"No," I whisper, and he clenches his jaw as he pumps in and out of me in short bursts that make my back arch. He's rubbing against the spot inside of me again, and I'm pretty sure I'm going to come without anyone even touching my dick.

That seems to be a thing when I'm with Sem.

He places his big hands on the mattress on either side of my face and leans down farther. My legs slip off his shoulders and link around his waist as he tunnels in and out of me.

"Look at you," he says, tilting his face and running his nose up my cheek, breathing deeply. "So fucking tight for me.

You like having your ass full of my big cock? Tell me how much you want me to come in your tight hole."

Oh, sweet Jesus.

"No dirty talk," I manage to choke out, but Sem just quirks that mouth up a little realizing how much I like it. Goddammit.

"Nah. You're taking it so good, Maggie. Like a good little cock slut." His hard thrusts emphasize each word. "*My. Little. Slut.*"

God, this man is killing me.

I bite down on my lower lip and close my eyes, which just makes it worse because my senses become heightened. I can feel his warm breath hit my neck as he pummels me into the mattress. I feel the slick sweat sliding between our bodies and his heartbeat thundering in his chest.

"Your pretty little ass was made for my cock. It's begging for it. Will you beg me for it too, Maggie?"

A whimper escapes me as he rolls his hips up and hits that spot just right.

"*Yes! More, please. Fuck.*"

"That's my good boy," he grunts, and I moan uncontrollably at those words.

As soon as that sound echoes around the small room, he picks up the pace, licking the rim of my ear and growling, "I want to hear you come. Say my name, Maggie. *Say it.*"

Welp, I think I've lost this game already. Might as well really go for it.

His face hovers over mine, and our eyes meet as he watches me come undone. And I don't hold back, I pant and whine and moan while my balls draw up into me, and I spurt my release all over our chests. And because I'm a little bit of a sucker for him, I moan his name as I do it.

Sem.

His name on my lips drives him over the edge. He bucks his hips frantically, groaning as he bites down on my neck roughly, unloading into the condom.

I suck in air at the delicious pain radiating through my skin as he pries his teeth from me and presses his forehead to mine.

"I win," he pants.

"Yeah, and what do you win?"

"Next time, you let go. No more holding back. I want to hear you scream."

"A little morbid," I manage to say, even though I am weirdly looking forward to that.

"Nah," he says and then reaches up, grabs a knife from the end table, and cuts me loose. The fact that Sem was hovering over me with a sharp blade in his hand and I didn't even flinch, makes me realize that I'm obviously in need of some clinical help.

Either that or I really fucking like the guy.

He quickly wipes me up with the edge of the sheet and then pulls me into him. My back presses against his chest as Sem rests his face on the top of my head.

"You took me so good," he says softly, and my chest inflates because, yeah, I did.

"That's because you prepped me well."

He spreads his large hand across my stomach and throws a heavy leg over my thigh. "I'm doing that from now on."

"You've got it," I say and feel my eyes start to close. Because for some reason, with Sem, I feel safe. I know nothing can harm me when I'm with him. He won't let it.

When we both wake up from dozing a few hours later, my stomach rumbles loudly, and Sem tightens his hold on me.

"You're hungry," he says, his voice a little rough from sleep.

"Duh," I say, looking over my shoulder at him and smiling softly. "Want to grab dinner? I'll order ahead so we can just pick it up."

"And come back here?" he asks.

"Sure, I'm easy."

"Yeah, you are," he says, and I poke his chest.

"Watch it."

I poke him again, and he flicks my hand away.

"I'm stronger than you, Maggie. I'd watch out."

Of course, that triggers me. So, I launch myself at him, straddling his waist, my entire naked body plastered against his.

"You might be stronger, but I'm determined."

He huffs a laugh and then tries to pry me off of him, but I cling like Velcro.

"Maybe I should tie *you* up," I say, nipping at his neck. "Use those serial killer ties you have hidden in your drawer. See how you like it."

Sem tries to wrench me off of him, but I just tighten my grip.

"Don't sound like you hated it. You were begging for it."

I bite down on his neck roughly, and Sem arches his hips, trying to buck me off.

"You're going to have to wear me now," I tease. "You'll never get rid of me."

Sem bucks again and then rolls over, so I'm trapped underneath him. My cock twitches against his, and he huffs in annoyance.

"Get off, Maggie," he mutters.

"Nope. You made your bed. You've gotta lie in it now, motherfucker."

Sem chuckles at my obstinate tone and rolls onto his back again, and I just stick to him.

"You're obnoxious. Stop sucking on my neck."

My lips move from his skin with a pop. "You love it, you horny bastard," I say and then hold on tighter when he stands up, those thick legs pulling us both up easily.

Sem meanders to the small kitchen and opens the fridge, pulling out a beer.

"I could do this all day," he says, popping the cap off. It clinks onto the counter, and he leans against the wall, resting his head against the cabinets and taking a long swig. I climb up him a few more inches and lock my ankles together behind him.

My stomach grumbles, and Sem eyes me.

"If you get off of me, we could get dressed and go eat."

I debate the merits of that. I really do, but I ultimately decide to stay right where I am.

"Make me."

He takes another long swig of his beer and then pushes off the wall.

"Might as well shower then," he says and walks us into the bathroom, which is actually a decent size for an RV.

As he turns on the water, I say, "You know I hated camping when I was a kid. My dad put me in Boy Scouts. Can you imagine? *Me*. In Boy Scouts. Camping in tents. Digging holes to poop in. The only good thing about it was all the other boys. That's when I knew for sure I was gay. Guess it backfired on my dad a little."

Sem smirks as he tests the water before stepping inside with me still clinging to him.

"Anyways, my point is, I could totally camp in this. I mean, this is like glamping. There's running water. And a fridge and a toilet. This is amazing," I say as Sem unhooks the showerhead and runs it over my head. Water slips between us, and then he moves it over his head until we're drenched.

"You're going to eventually slip off of me," he says, and I shake my head as he grabs a bar of soap and rubs it over my back and ass. He spends a little too much time on my hole, and I retaliate by giving him another hickey.

A familiar smell permeates the air, and I look down at the soap in his hand.

"Is that my soap?

Sem blushes, and he shrugs. "Smells like you. I like it."

Oh, my heart.

"Lean back a little," he grumbles, trying to change the subject, and I let him. I press my back against the wall so he can wash my chest. And he spends a lot of time there, too, tracing my belly button and rubbing his thumbs over my nipples.

My spent cock twitches between us, and I can tell he notices because he smirks.

"Not a word, Sem. Now give me the soap. It's my turn," I say and swipe the bar of soap from him and run it over his broad chest. His eyes watch my hands move over his abs and pecs, and then he grabs the shower head and rinses us off.

My fingers lock behind his neck as he moves out of the shower and when he reaches for a towel, I unhook my ankles from around his waist and slide my feet to the floor.

"I could have clung on longer."

He snorts. "Keep telling yourself that."

"I could've," I say, taking the towel from his hands and

drying myself off. "But I *am* ravenous. And low blood sugar is a thing."

Sem grabs a pair of shorts and a tank top and pulls them on, sans underwear which is way hotter than it has any right to be.

He hands me my clothes, I quickly tug them on, and then he lifts me up once again and carries me out of the RV and into his truck. When we're inside the cab, I'm pulled into the middle seat as he buckles me in. It's where I belong anyways. I don't want to sit so far away from him.

Who would have thought that my feelings for him could change so dramatically in mere weeks? It feels like yesterday that we were daring each other to fuck and now I want to snuggle into him. To be close to him.

He mentioned me inflicting some kind of voodoo spell on him, but right now it feels like the opposite. I feel like he's bewitched me and I'm not even upset about it.

As we drive out of the RV park, me tucked under his arm, I place an online order for the food. My hands trace his legs, teasing him as I run my fingers up the skin of his thighs. He doesn't stop me. He just allows my hands explore.

We're pulling up to the burger joint a few minutes later, and I shiver when Sem helps me out of the truck. He adjusts his hard length, tucking it under his waistband, and then peers down at me.

"Why are you so cold?"

"It's breezy and I'm like half your size, so I shiver. You know, like a normal human?"

Sem reaches around me into the truck, grabs a sweatshirt from the small back seat, and tugs it over my head. It's so large it covers my shorts and almost hits my knees.

"Fuck, that's..." he rubs a hand over his jaw and fiddles

with the hoodie strings, tugging me closer. "You look like you're not wearing any pants."

"It's not my fault you're gigantic," I say, rolling up the sleeves and then the bottom of the sweatshirt a little. "I bet you're imagining me wearing only this and bending over for you, aren't you, straight boy."

Sem tugs me closer and leans down, "And you'd let me, too."

My breath hitches because, yeah, I so would.

"I want to carry you inside."

I want that too, but we have to act a little normal in public. People wouldn't understand this thing we've been doing. I don't even understand it. I just know that I *like* it.

"Probably not a good idea," I say and then reach down, place my hand in his, and tug him into the busy joint. The way his rough palm slides against mine makes my stomach do somersaults. I half expect him to let go of me as we move through the crowd of people, but he just holds on as we make our way to the takeout counter. A group of people are waiting for their food, and only then does Sem release me. He pulls me to his side as we wait for my name to be called, and I discreetly press my nose into his side and inhale.

Damn, he smells way too good.

Sem's fingers are playing with my earlobe when a familiar voice causes me to turn my head.

"Hey, Magnus!"

I stiffen when I see Colin moving through the crowd. Without thinking, I move slightly away from Sem.

Don't ask me why I do. I just fucking move and hate myself a little when I do it.

"Hi, Colin," I say as he makes his way to my side. He looks

good tonight, wearing loose track pants and a short-sleeved shirt showing his lean musculature.

Not as good as Sem, but still.

"Hi, Sem," Colin says, meeting Sem's gaze and then looking back at me with a soft smile on his face. "I missed you in yoga this morning. I looked for you, but August said you were busy."

"Oh, yeah, I had a thing with my family. Had to miss class," I tell him, and Colin nods, reaching out and tugging lightly on my oversized sweatshirt.

"You look cute in this."

"Thanks," I say, feeling myself blush, not from the compliment but because Sem can hear this entire thing.

Fuck me sideways. This is not how I wanted the night to go.

Colin's eyes latch onto my neck, and he turns to look up at Sem. I brush my hand against the red bite mark lingering there, and I feel my cheeks heat.

"Oh..." Colin says, his eyes lingering a little too long on Sem's neck now.

Shit on a stick.

I peer up and see the small purple bruises lining his skin. Well, this is embarrassing.

"Are you two..." Colin begins, but I just shake my head quickly.

"Oh. Nope. No, just friends."

Sem huffs in annoyance, runs a hand through his hair, and looks away, his jaw clenching.

"Oh, well, in that case, I wanted to...I was going to text you about meeting up this week but got busy with other things. But now that you're here...do you want to go out sometime soon?"

"Oh," I say, shuffling on my feet. Sem's stiff behind me, his arms folded across his chest as he silently watches this entire thing unfold.

I rub at my neck. "Okay, yeah, why don't you text me, and we can see what works."

Colin's smile widens, and he leans over and presses an air kiss next to my cheek.

"Okay, see you soon then. I have to get home to Daniel," he says, lifting a take-out bag in his hand. "Apparently, he's starving."

I force out a small laugh as Colin turns to Sem. "Bye, Sem. Nice to see you again."

"Fuck off," Sem mutters, and Colin actually stumbles as he walks away. Probably unsure if he'd heard him correctly. Colin even looks over his shoulder, his brow furrowed at the two of us. But I just smile at him, waving once more, as if to say, *Nothing to see here. You must have been hearing things.*

Once Colin disappears, I turn to Sem and say in my sternest teacher voice, "You can't say things like that to people. You are so rude sometimes."

"So are you. Making plans in front of me with *him*."

I open my mouth to reply but then shut it. Because it *was* a little rude. And a bit heartless, if I'm being honest. Sem had just been inside of me, and I'd acted like I was embarrassed by him.

"Okay. You're right. I'm really sorry. I was just caught off guard by him showing up, and I didn't know if you wanted me to *out* you, that's all. Jesus. Let's just get our food and go eat. Maybe once we're less hungry, we'll be nicer to each other."

"I'm always fucking nice to you."

Damn, but he's right. "Well, then at least once we eat, we can talk like...adults."

Sem clenches his jaw and shakes his head. "Whatever."

I bristle at his tone but don't have time to say anything else because my name is called loudly by the person behind the counter. I swipe the bag from the worker and hand Sem the cups.

"I want iced tea, please," I tell him, and he grumbles under his breath but gets it for me anyway, and then we are on our way back to the truck, Sem carrying everything in his large hands.

Despite me being a total prick, he still helps me inside the cab. But this time, instead of sliding me to the middle seat next to him, he buckles me into the passenger seat and my heart drops a little.

Fuck, he's pissed.

I'd be pissed too if he did that to me. I acted ashamed to be with him, which isn't even the case.

It's not the case at all.

God, I fucked up and the truth is, I don't even know why I did it.

When he pulls away from the curb, I peek over at him. He's clenching tightly to the steering wheel and keeping his gaze laser-focused on the road. I can feel the tension rolling off of him the entire drive and he won't even look at me. I'm so used to him watching me all the time that when he doesn't, it's unsettling.

"Where are we going?" I ask softly, not wanting to wake the angry giant.

"I know a place."

"Not back to your RV?" I ask, and he shakes his head once.

Fuck, he doesn't even want me to go back to his place. I

wonder, for a moment, if this is the end of whatever this is between us. I wouldn't blame him if it was.

For some reason, the thought makes me sadder than I expected. Am I actually starting to have feelings for the big guy?

Twenty minutes later, Sem parks the truck at the top of a steep hill overlooking the entire city. It's stunning, and as I look around, I forget for just a moment that he's pissed at me.

"How did you find this place?" I ask, craning my neck to the left and right, taking in the city's twinkling lights in the distance.

"Exploring," he bites out, grabbing the bag of food and jumping down from the truck. I half expect him to slam the door and leave me to make my own way out, but he turns to me and holds out his arm.

I scoot over to the driver's side, wrapping my legs around his waist and clinging to him as he walks us to the back of the truck and pulls the tailgate down.

"We're not alone," I tell him as he sets me on the truck bed. My legs dangle off the end, and I glance to my right and see a van parked nearby. The windows are fogged, and I can only guess what's going on inside.

"Yeah, people come up here to fuck."

My eyes widen at that. "For reals?"

"Yep."

I bite down on my lip and ask, "Have you come up here to fuck?"

For some reason, the thought of him with someone else really irritates me. I'm not sure I want him to answer me truthfully.

"Maybe."

I stare with narrowed eyes at him as he launches himself

up next to me and begins sorting through the food boxes. He eats like this is his last meal. I don't know how he even consumes so much food. Because it sure as hell doesn't show anywhere on his body. He's sculpted.

I reach out and press my hand to his arm, and he stills for a moment before continuing to dig through the bag.

"What's wrong, Sem?" I ask as he hands me my burger. "Why are you still upset? I know how I acted was wrong. I panicked. I said I was sorry and I really meant it."

"It's fine. I'm just hungry."

I roll my eyes at that because I don't think that's it at all. He's keeping something from me, and I'm determined to figure out what's really going on.

"So, you're not still pissed at me for earlier?"

"Nah."

"So, you weren't jealous?" I force myself to ask because I want to know. *Need to know.*

Sem side-eyes me. "Jealous of what?"

"Colin."

Sem turns to stare at me and then takes a large bite of his hamburger. He doesn't even swallow it down before speaking. "You can be with whoever you want."

"Is that so?" I ask and then pop a french fry into my mouth. "Hm, then maybe I *should* go on that date with him."

Sem's silent and just chews his food, his eyes staring at the city lights in the distance. And the silence is driving me crazy. Usually, we're bickering or talking. We're never just quiet.

"For reals, Sem? You really wouldn't mind?"

God, now I'm fishing for answers. Desperate much?

"Mind what?"

"Me, dating Colin. Going on dates with him. Like the holding hands, kissing kind of dates."

"Why the fuck would I? He's your dream guy, right? Who am I to stand in the way of that?"

I set my box of food on the truck bed and turn toward him. "Sem."

"Hm."

"Look at me."

Sem turns his face toward me, and I reach out, grabbing onto the back of his neck and pulling him closer to me. His blue eyes flash a little, and then flick down to my lips. I wet them and say, "You're telling me that after months of stalking me...."

"I don't stalk...."

"Riiiight... ok, so after months of following me around *by accident* and *haphazardly* finding yourself all up in my shit..." I smirk playfully. "You would be fine with me just walking away? Letting another man date me, letting another man fuck me?"

Sem swallows and diverts his gaze from mine.

"He's the one you want."

"What do you want? Do *you* want me, Sem?" I ask softly.

He closes his eyes. "Fuck."

"Tell me, please."

He slides his tongue over his teeth and then pulls away from me, his food discarded next to him.

"I do. But fuck, I'm confused...I don't know what the fuck I'm doing..." he finally utters after a long, drawn-out silence.

"Right back 'atcha."

"...or what I'd even label myself as. All I know is that from the moment I laid eyes on you in that hospital..." My heartbeat increases as I watch him run a hand across his strong jaw. "I wanted to know you."

"Tell me why," I demand softly.

"Because you're...different. I've never met another guy like you before."

"Is that why you followed me around for ages?"

He shrugs. "Maybe, and I wasn't following you. I was... observing. For my drawings."

I nudge him with my elbow. "*Observing*, okay. Whatever. Just admit it. You're in *lurve* with me. You want to marry me. Have my babies."

Sem scoffs and grabs his food, shoving the rest of the burger into his mouth and chewing. I laugh lightly at his awkwardness and then lean back, popping another fry into my mouth.

"Well, to be fair, I've never seen anyone as big as you before that night. You kind of scared me at first. All wild-eyed and intense."

He scowls at that. "Why the hell were you afraid of me? I'd never hurt you."

"Well, I know that now," I say, sighing. "But at the time, you looked like a madman." I side-eye him and add, "You still sometimes look like one. A hot, sexy one, but a total psycho nonetheless."

"Yeah. I only look like that when people mess with you. When I see you get hurt my brain cracks a little, and I go a bit nuts. I just want you to be safe."

My heart flutters in my chest, and I rub it.

"Sem, I want you to understand me. *Clearly*. I won't go out with Colin if it upsets you," I say softly, and Sem freezes. "I know what we're doing is just casual or maybe just a game between...friends, but we started it together, didn't we? I won't see anyone else while we're...doing whatever this is."

He sits with that for a moment, before saying, "Nah,

Maggie. I want you to be... You need to do what's best for you, yeah? I don't want to stand in your way or hold you back."

My heart sinks slightly, and I force my face to show no emotion. Because if he looks at me, really looks, he'll see how disappointed I am right now.

At this moment, I don't want Colin.

I want *him*.

I want him to fight for this. For me.

God, my mind is a mess.

"Okay," I say softly. "If that's really what you want."

Sem grunts something and then stuffs his wrappers back into the bag and scoots father back into the truck bed. I glance back and see him, legs stretched out in front of him, the back of his head pressed against the window, and his eyes closed.

He looks...sad.

And I can't help it. I'm physically unable to stay away. I move back to be with him, crawling onto his lap, my back against his chest, and tuck my head under his chin. For a moment, I wonder if he will remove me from him. Holding my breath, I wait, but instead of pushing me away, his hands wrap around my waist, holding me against him. His face nuzzles into my hair, and he inhales deeply.

"What are you doing to me?" he whispers.

"I don't know," I reply.

"You're confusing the fuck out of me. I feel like I'm losing my mind."

"I'm sorry."

We sit like that for a while, the two of us listening to the wind blow through the brush covering the hill and to the silent squeak of the van across the way as it rocks gently.

Sometimes silence is needed. Sometimes words aren't necessary.

I shiver and curl up into him further. "I'm sorry you're confused, Sem. Do you want me to...do you want me to leave you alone? Give you some time to think?"

His arms tighten around me. "Fuck no."

I huff a small laugh and lean my head back against his shoulder. "Okay. Let me know if that changes."

"It won't."

I sigh and then decide to break the tension by saying, "Okay, now to bring attention to the elephant in the room. Someone in that van has amazing stamina."

"Seems like it." Sem stuffs his hands into my sweatshirt pockets as he shifts me on his lap. Then he leans down and slowly runs his nose across the skin of my neck. His lips brush against my pulse, and he breathes against it.

"I'm sitting here trying not to smell you, but damn, it's hard."

I tremble slightly, although this time it's not from the cold. I love how candid he is and how he always seems to state the obvious. There's very little guessing with Sem.

"It's my soap."

"No, it's you."

"Oh, my heart," I whisper. "You can smell me anytime you want."

We sit like that for a minute, just Sem breathing me in, his fingers tracing shapes on my skin when I ask, "Sem...."

"Yeah?"

"Can I ask you a question?"

"Yeah."

"You're a fantastic artist, really talented. Why don't you do something with it?"

"Nah. It's a hobby. I just like doing it for fun. I prefer working with my hands. Building shit. That's enough for me."

"You're very gifted. Will you make me something one day?"

"What do you want me to make you?"

I tap on my lips and shrug. "First, tell me what kind of mediums you work with? I know you can draw and you work with wood because you made all those cabinets in your RV. What else can you do?"

"Some welding. Luke's better at it than me, though."

I lean back against him and glance up at the stars twinkling above us. "How about you make me something and surprise me? I'm sure that talented brain can come up with something."

Sem grunts in agreement, and I bite back a smile.

"Hey, you think those kids in that van will get arrested?"

"Nah. Maybe. Dunno."

"You ever had sex in public?" I ask, and Sem shifts me on his lap.

"A few times. You?"

I shake my head. "Nope. Not really my thing."

"How do you know if you've never tried it?"

He's right. I won't know unless I try. "Fine, how about this? One day you and I can get it on somewhere public."

"How about now."

"Oh my god, no, not now," I laugh. "I'm not in the mood to be arrested tonight."

"Life isn't worth living unless you've ended up in jail at least once for doing something fun."

"That's not good advice, Sem. And are you telling me you have a record?" I ask, looking at him, bringing our lips entirely too close. He parts his own, and it takes everything within me not to run my tongue along them.

Because if I kissed him, this wouldn't be casual for me anymore. It'd be so much more.

"Will you tell me why you went to jail?" I ask and lean my head back slightly to remove myself from temptation.

Sem exhales and leans his head back against the window. "Nothing big. I was a minor at the time. Got picked up for breaking and entering. Stole some shit. Stupid kid stuff."

"Shocker," I say, then ask, "Have you stolen anything from my apartment?"

Sem looks away from me, and I poke at him. "You have, haven't you? What did you take? My underwear? Do you smell it each night before you go to bed?"

Sem bites down on his lip, and I poke him again. "Tell me, you creepy man."

"I'm not creepy," he grumbles, and I turn around fully, so I'm straddling his hips.

"You are if you stole my panties."

"You don't wear panties."

I raise an eyebrow. "Don't I? Maybe you haven't discovered my stash. Haven't snooped hard enough, big man."

I'm giggling as Sem looks down at my crotch and then meets my eyes.

"Tell me what you stole!" I say, reaching up to tickle him, but he just huffs.

"I'm not ticklish."

"Impossible! Everyone's ticklish."

"I'm not," he replies blandly as I try to find a place on his body that will make him squirm. But he just sits there stoically as my hands roam across his neck, under his arms, and then down toward his waist.

"Keep going, and you'll end up on your back," Sem warns, but of course, I don't listen.

Suddenly I'm flipped onto my back, my wrists restrained above my head while one of his hands slowly moves toward my side. I watch it lower in slow motion, and my heart beats quickly in my chest with the anticipation of what's about to happen.

"Sem, don't you dare. I will scream! Then you will be arrested. The cops will come and take you away. I'll have to write to you in jail and send you an allowance for bags of Cheetos." I'm squirming underneath him, but he's trapped me with his muscular legs. "We'll disturb van-people's sex marathon. That's not a nice thing to do, and I'm a very nice person! I won an award for that in elementary school! My mom still has it somewhere."

"What the fuck are you talking about, Maggie? You're trying to confuse me with all those words."

"I swear, I'm not!" I giggle.

He seems to consider it and then shakes his head, "Nah, you asked for it," Sem says, those fingers dangerously close to my skin.

"I did *not* ask for it. I'm the victim here. Don't you dare tickle me. Please," I plead with a huff of laughter, but Sem doesn't listen.

Of course, he doesn't.

CHAPTER SEVEN

SEM

I drive us back to my RV, the sound of Maggie's laugh ringing in my ears. I tickled him until he was nearly crying, and then I let him go because I'd taught him enough of a lesson. Not that he ever learns. He just loves to provoke me.

I glance over and see his small body curled up next to me, his eyes closed. I didn't even ask if he wanted to stay the night with me. I just made the decision for us because I want him with *me* tonight. In *my* bed. For as long as he'll stay.

Because we both know he's going to end up with Colin.

Perfect, fucking Colin.

Although to be fair, I had a chance to tell Maggie what I wanted. I could have asked him to call it off for me, but I just couldn't do it. He deserves better than me. I'm not book-smart. Half the time, when Maggie prattles on about something he's interested in, I just nod and wonder what the fuck he's talking about.

Nah, he's better off with someone who can understand all that shit. Someone smarter and more sophisticated than me. Someone he has more in common with.

And the other issue is that I'm not even really sure if I'm gay. Maybe I'm bisexual? I've always noticed that some other men were attractive, but not really in a sexual way. I never felt the urge to have sex with a man before. When I saw Maggie for the first time, though, it was like something just clicked in my brain. I wanted him. I needed him. What does that even mean? Where does that leave us?

I can't keep fucking around with Maggie only to make him miserable in the end. He'd never truly be happy with me.

So, if he wants it, I'll let him have a chance with Colin. Even though it makes me sick to my stomach.

Honestly, the thought of him with someone else...curled up against someone else...smiling at someone else makes me a bit ragey.

Goddammit.

I park the truck, and instead of walking to Maggie's side, I just grab his hips and bring him right to me. He slides across the seat with a squeak, then he's in my arms, and I'm carrying him into the bedroom. I undress him slowly, letting my eyes take their fill. This may be one of the last times I can look at him like this.

"You okay?" he asks, his hands in my hair as I kneel before him, helping him out of his shorts. I want to kiss his skin and lick my way across his chest, but I don't. That's not what this is.

Right?

"Fine," I say roughly and stand up quickly.

Maggie yawns and then flops backward onto the bed, his small frame barely taking up any space. Fuck, he looks good in my bed. I'll sketch this tomorrow when he leaves for work.

Grabbing the back of my shirt, I pull it over my head and kick off my shorts before crawling over next to him. I press myself right up against his back, and he sighs happily as if it's all that he's been waiting for.

For me to cuddle with him.

He reaches for his phone and sets his alarm, and while he does it, I spread my hand across his thin stomach, tracing my thumb over his ribs and rest my chin on the top of his head.

"You're very warm. Nice and cozy," he says groggily. I watch as he opens an app on his phone, and immediately a jumble of words appears on the screen. "I'm going to read for a bit. Is that okay?"

I nod, biting the inside of my cheek, as I'm once again reminded how damn smart he is. A college grad going for a teaching credential. What the hell is he even doing messing around with someone like me? When I was sixteen, I was expelled from high school and ended up in a continuation program. Barely graduated from that too. I have a juvenile record, and there's a good chance that sometime soon I'll end up with a criminal record just for doing something stupid. I'm a total fuck up compared to him.

I clear my throat, trying to squash the negative thoughts. "What're you reading?"

"Oh," he says, looking back at me and smiling shyly. "A gay dystopian romance. It's fire. Seriously. People need to write more of this stuff because it's life."

What the fuck does dystopian mean? He must read the confusion on my face because he says, "You know what that means?" When I don't answer, he says, "Dystopian is like the end times. The world is destroyed. That kind of thing. Someone recommended this book to me, and I've been dying to start it. It's been sitting on my TBR list for days."

I squint at the phone and try to make sense of it all but end up just feeling like more of an idiot.

Maggie watches me for a second and then asks, "You know, I've never asked. Do you like to read?"

That question catches me off guard, and I stiffen against him. He barely tolerates me as it is. If he knew...."

"Does it matter if I fucking read?"

Goddammit, I sound defensive.

Probably because I am.

"Well, no. Some people hate it and that's fine. I'm just curious as to why."

I feel my face turn red, and I turn my eyes away from his and choke out, "Nah. I don't like to read."

"Ok. Any reason why? What do you hate most about reading?" he asks, fully turning his attention to me.

I swallow and keep my gaze diverted. I want to sink into the floor and disappear. But I can't lie to him. He should know who he's been hanging around with. I'm literally the opposite of Colin, who reads for a living.

"What I hate most is...fuck...I just...I can't read, okay?" I whisper the last part so softly I can barely hear it.

Maggie stills and then shakes his head. "I'm sorry, *what?*"

"You heard me. And I mean...I *can* read, but the words are all jumbled. Backward and upside down. And it takes me two hundred hours to read something simple."

"Oh...so...do you have dyslexia?"

I shrug and then say, "Yeah. So, I just don't read if I can help it. It's frustrating and gives me headaches."

"I'm sorry, Sem. I didn't know. Thank you for telling me,"

he says as he places his hand on my chest. The contact feels warm and good against my skin. He bites down on his lip, glances at his book, and then back at me. "Want me to read to you?"

"What?" That was *not* what I was expecting him to say.

"I can read to you. Do you like listening to stories?"

I nod and find that I have a lump in my throat. "Yeah. I do."

"Okay then. Buckle up, big guy, because this is going to be amazing."

When I wake to the sound of his alarm ringing obnoxiously on his phone, the first thing I think is that it feels right. Him here with me. Last night, he read to me until he dozed off in the middle of a slightly boring scene. I don't blame him. I was snoozing for some of that as well. But I do have to admit that the sex scenes were pretty damn good. They gave me some ideas for things I want to do to him.

Maggie groans, his voice slightly hoarse from reading for so long. God, my fucking chest aches. Not once did he make me feel like shit for not being able to read well.

Unlike all the people who made fun of me growing up.

Stupid Sem.

A memory flashes through my mind of my older brother Liam breaking one kid's nose for shouting that at me when I was in sixth grade. Luke also made his rounds, knocking out the bullies, until eighth grade when I shot up twelve inches and could take care of myself.

Now, no one messes with me. But that doesn't mean I don't feel like shit about my inability to do simple everyday things, like reading small sentences or figuring out elementary math problems.

I pull Maggie closer to me, and he sighs, switching his alarm off and grabbing onto my hand. He presses it right over his heart, and I swear to god, I can't move. I can feel his heart beating against my palm, and I want to keep him tucked against me forever.

I can't, though, can I?

I blink rapidly at those thoughts and then lean down and brush a soft kiss against his ear.

"Wake up, Maggie."

He grumbles and burrows a little further under the covers.

"Maggie, baby, time to get up."

"Don't wanna," he mutters adorably.

"You're going to be late for work. I still have to drive you home."

"Ugh," he mutters and then drags my hand from his chest to his hard morning wood. "Give me an incentive, Sem."

Which is no hardship for me.

So, I do.

I stroke him languidly until he comes in my hand, with a low moan on his lips.

Then, when he's finally up and dressed, his hair rumpled, a pillow crease indented on his right cheek, I tug my hoodie over his shivering body and carry him to my truck. He immediately moves to the middle seat, buckles in, and tucks himself against me.

When we arrive at his apartment, he lifts his head and presses a kiss on my jaw. "Thank you," he says. I'm beginning to live for the small press of his soft lips against my skin. "I'll call you when I'm done with work."

"Okay," I reply, and I help him hop out of my truck.

Maggie looks up at me with sleepy eyes. "You don't have to walk me to my door, Sem. I can manage."

"I know, but I'm gonna."

He sighs in acceptance and presses himself against my chest. I just give in to the urge to pick him up of the ground. He wraps his arms around my neck, his legs locked against my back as I carry him to his door. I love that he allows me to lug him around. I won't stop doing it until he tells me to.

Maggie huffs sleepily and then slides down my body. He wraps his arms around my waist, pulling me in for a hug, and my heart squeezes inside of my chest.

I crush him to me and then force myself to let him go.

With a small wave, he disappears behind his door.

I fight the impulse to pick the lock and go inside. I always want to be near him. But I force myself back to my truck and drive to work instead.

The day drags on, and when it's finally time to leave, I head home to shower and then settle down with my paper and pencil to get these images out of my head. Because visions of Maggie last night have assaulted me all day, and I cannot get them out of my head.

His body curled up in my lap.

His hand in mine.

His legs tangled with mine in bed.

And for the first time since meeting him, I include myself in my drawings.

MAGNUS

When I get home from work that evening and enter the apartment, I half expect to see Sem sitting there waiting for me. A crushing wave of disappointment crashes over me when I realize that my apartment is empty.

"Shit," I mutter. "Get it together. That's not what this is."

I glance down at my phone, hoping that he's texted me, but the screen only contains texts from Colin.

Oh crap, he wants to go out with me Thursday. I don't even really want to go, but my mind flashes back to Sem last night, telling me to go for it. I war with myself for a few minutes before reluctantly sending a message back to Colin and agreeing to dinner and a movie.

I stare at the words, and when the anxiety begins to bubble up within me, I turn off my phone, setting it face down on the counter, and tug on the ends of my hair in frustration.

This feels wrong. In my gut, it feels wrong and I don't want to go through with it anymore.

I lift up my phone again to cancel when I see that August is calling.

"Hey," I say, slightly concerned because I just saw August at work, and he *never* calls me.

His deep voice echoes in my ear and he sounds upset. "I need your help, Mags."

My heart triples in speed, worry prickling my skin. "Ok, what's up?"

"I need you to come with me to pick up Emery."

"What? Why?"

"Because that asshole just called me, and he's drunk as shit."

"It's only five o'clock...."

"Do not even get me started. I don't know if I can look at him without killing him. I need you there to make sure I don't dump him into the ocean."

The vehemence dripping from August's voice makes me pause because August likes everyone. I know he and Emery have never really gotten along but I'm surprised at how much he seems to hate his soon-to-be stepbrother.

"Okay, yeah. I can do that. Come get me, and we'll go together. I'll make sure you have an alibi if you do decide on homicide."

I consider calling Sem but decide to keep him out of it. August can take care of himself and me if need be.

I think.

August arrives shortly after we hang up, and I slide into the passenger seat of his SUV.

"So, he really called you?" I ask, curious why Emery would call August when he seems to go out of his way to avoid my best friend.

"Don't ask me what goes through that messed up head of his. I was as surprised as you," he says and runs a hand through his hair. "My mom *cannot* find out about this, okay? She always sees the best in everyone, and I don't need him dragging her into his shit right before her wedding."

"My lips are sealed," I say and lean back in my seat, watching as we move into a more crime-ridden part of town. The streetlights are dim, many of the storefront signs are broken, and there are steel bars across all the windows.

"Jesus, where is he hanging out?" I ask, glancing around nervously.

I feel if Sem found out where I was, he'd freak out. He's turning out to be incredibly protective of me.

Perhaps he's always been, and I just never noticed.

"I should have brought Sem with us," I mutter, and August scoffs, parallel parking in a tight space on the dark street.

"Oh, don't be so dramatic. I can protect you just fine. Nothing's going to happen anyways."

I look at him skeptically because he's well-built and strong, but he's also too nice. I have a feeling if someone came at me, he'd try to reason with them before actually throwing a punch. Whereas, Sem would always throw a punch and then ask questions later.

Actually, he wouldn't bother to ask any questions.

"Do not look at me like that," August grumbles and then wrenches the door open, and I scurry out, following him inside a shady bar on the opposite side of the street.

Curious eyes trail us as we enter the dimly lit space. The air is humid and smells like stale beer and cigarettes. A seventies rock ballad plays over the sound system and my sneakers stick to the tacky floor when I walk.

I lean into August and mutter, "Your step-brother better appreciate this because I am way too pretty to have my body murdered and thrown in some back-alley dumpster."

August just rolls his eyes and chuckles.

"Oh, come on," I breathe. "The bartender looks like she eats nails for breakfast and I'm pretty sure there's a dead guy over there." I gesture to the corner of the bar.

August glances around. "Ok, point taken, just don't piss off the bartender..." he says and then his face pinches and his eyes narrow. "Oh fuck, that's not a dead guy, that's Emery."

August grabs onto my arm, seemingly oblivious to my safety concerns, and pulls me forward. We approach Emery, his torso sprawled out over the bar, his tattooed arms resting on the sticky surface, and his hands cradling a glass of clear liquid.

"This little shit yours?" the brawny woman behind the bar asks.

"Yep. Mine," August says, and Emery turns his head and blinks up at August with his dark brown eyes. His chin-length hair falls across his face, and he blows at it.

"Nah, not his," he mumbles and then tries to reach up and pat the side of August's face, but August just pushes his hand away.

"Get him out of here. He's a sloppy drunk and an asshole," the woman says and then she holds out her hand, silently asking for payment for the however many drinks Emery managed to consume.

August sighs unhappily, pressing his credit card into her awaiting palm.

"Thanks, brother," Emery slurs and tries to stand but falls forward into August's chest.

"I'm not your brother," August grinds out as he struggles to keep Emery standing.

"Soon though," Emery says, his large brown eyes meeting August's. "Such a shame."

August grunts and then shifts Emery in his arms as the lady slaps August's credit card onto the bar top.

"Leave me a big tip. This asshole was disrespectful. I kept him from getting killed despite wanting to watch him get a few teeth knocked loose."

August looks at me, and I nod, swiping his card from the counter and scrawling a large tip on the slip of paper.

"Thanks boys," she says, and August shifts Emery in his arms.

"You have a low? High?" he asks, and I remember that

Emery is a type 1 diabetic. Apparently, a very irresponsible one.

"I'm fine," he drawls sloppily.

"Good. Now walk, asshole."

"My legs're tired," Emery attempts to say, leaning against August's chest like a ragdoll. A slight snore escapes his nose.

"I think he's asleep," I say, and August sighs heavily.

"Fuck my life."

Then August bends down, and a moment later, Emery is swept off the floor and into his arms.

"Oh my god," I say as people turn to stare. "I didn't know you were this strong." I reach out and squeeze his bicep. "Why didn't you tell me?"

"Don't insult me," August grunts, and he moves as quickly as he can toward the door with a full-grown man in his arms. Emery is not small. He's thinner than August, but he's just as tall. August will hurt his back again doing this, but there's no stopping him. Despite having a justified dislike of Emery, August is incredibly loyal. He'd never just leave Emery somewhere where he could get hurt.

When we make it to his SUV, I quickly unlock the doors and peek inside. You know, just in case there's a serial killer lurking in the backseat, and then watch as August settles Emery in.

The movement startles Emery awake, and he looks at August with hooded eyes, reaching out and sloppily touching his cheek. "Look at you. The hero. The golden boy. Everyone's favorite."

"Shut up," August replies and buckles him in. "Get in, Mags, before I do something I shouldn't."

I nod and hop into the passenger seat as August starts the

engine. Peering over my shoulder, I see Emery watching August before closing his eyes and nodding off.

"God, I hate him. He's such a punk," August mutters and then glances over at me. "You okay?"

"Yeah. I'm fine. I didn't do much."

"You just being around helps keep me level-headed. Thanks."

"Anytime, friend. You know that."

We drive for a few minutes, and I ask, "What are you going to do with him?"

"Shit, I dunno. I can't bring him home. Can I stay with him at your place? Make sure he doesn't choke on his own vomit? Die of low blood sugar?"

"Yeah, of course. I can…I'll just stay over at Sem's."

August nods, turning the SUV around and driving toward my apartment on the opposite side of the city. The entire time we drive, Emery dozes, his mouth hanging open, his chin on his chest, and his hair covering his face. When we finally arrive at my place, August hefts Emery into his arms and carries him up the stairs without breaking a sweat. I'm seriously impressed and make sure to tell him so. August just glowers at me as he sets Emery on my bed.

"He smells like a brewery. I need to shower." August sniffs his shirt and then glances at my bed. "I'll wash your sheets tomorrow, I promise," he says, and I shake my head.

"No worries. Really. You know where the blankets are. Call me if you need anything. I can be here in a few minutes. Sem doesn't live far from here."

August looks down at Emery, sprawled out on the bed like a starfish, and sighs. "Yeah, man. I will."

I grab my car keys and pack a small bag of things I'll need for work tomorrow, and then I'm out the door. It only takes me five minutes to drive to Sem's place, and I suddenly feel my stomach clench with nerves. Knocking on his door uninvited late at night is not what we're about.

Does he even want me here with him?

Am I crossing some sort of invisible boundary that we've never discussed?

Jesus, I need therapy to sort through all of this. This whole thing is messing with my mind.

I shake my head and then force myself to move because I'm not going to sleep in my car tonight.

My knuckles rap lightly on the door, and a moment later, it swings open, revealing a shirtless Sem who's wearing low-slung sweatpants. Smears of charcoal adorn his cheeks and hands, his hair slightly mussed. He looks so damn hot that I have to look away for a second.

"Maggie," he says, his eyes wide with surprise, and then he's stepping back, letting me move inside. "You okay?"

"Yeah, August and Emery are at my place...long story. Can I stay here tonight? You know, if you don't mind?"

Sem's Adam's apple bobs, and he nods. He turns around quickly, swiping a stack of papers from the table and stuffing them into a drawer. I catch just a glimpse of long lines and smears of black.

Damn, I want to see what he's working on.

"Were those more drawings?" I ask with a raised eyebrow, peering around him at the half-open drawer.

He clears his throat, reaching back and slamming it shut. "Yeah."

"Can I see?"

The tips of his ears are pink. "Nah, Maggie. Not right now."

He runs a hand through his hair, and I move toward him, reaching up and brushing my hand against his cheek.

"Okay, no worries. But you know I'd love to see what you've drawn. You're amazing."

"One day," he says.

I rub a thumb over his jaw. "Look at you. You're a mess."

"Yeah, got in the zone for a bit," he replies, and I grab onto his hand and pull him into the bathroom. He leans against the counter, those thighs spread open in front of him, and I force myself to reach over and grab a washrag instead of just crawling up onto him. Wrapping myself around him is becoming a bit of an addiction.

I step between his legs and wet the rag, brushing the damp end over his cheeks and his arms, washing his skin clean.

While I do this, his hands move to my waist and squeeze gently. I glance up to his face and his eyes are dark and intense as he stares into mine.

I clear my throat. "We should get ready for bed," I say and press my palms onto his hard chest.

"We should," he says, and I huff out a nervous breath. I don't know what's wrong with me, but the things I'm feeling are too new to really process. "We have more of the book to read."

"We do," he says and then slides his hand up to the back of my neck and tugs me closer to him. My breath catches in my throat as he lowers his head, running his nose from my jaw to my temple.

"Fuck, I want you," he mumbles. "It's all I can think about. Why is that, Maggie?"

"Dunno," I manage to say as my heart pounds in my chest. I reach down and link my fingers under the waistband of his sweats. My fingers brush against the head of his cock, and he trembles slightly against me.

"Fuck," he mutters, and then I'm hefted into his arms, and he's striding toward the bedroom, my legs wrapped around his waist, my tongue licking the lobe of his ear.

When he gently, almost reverently, sets me down on the bed, my heart stutters in my chest and I feel dizzy. I bite my lip hard to keep my emotions off my face. I know that these feelings for Sem are futile. This isn't going anywhere. He doesn't know what he wants. I can't risk my heart on a man that's not even sure he wants a relationship with another man. This is just sex. It has to be.

I lay back on the bed as his blue eyes move across my body, and he lets out a shaky exhale.

"How do you want me?" I ask, playing with the end of my shirt and pulling it up slightly, exposing my naval.

He doesn't move for a full minute, just breathes, his bare chest heaving as he stands and watches me touch myself.

And then suddenly he's on me, his body over mine as he yanks my shirt up to my chin and presses his face against my belly. His hands grip my sides as he inhales my skin.

"Why the fuck do you smell like peaches?" he asks, and then he's ripping the clothes from my body.

After that, we don't talk again for ages.

CHAPTER EIGHT

"Sem, are you listening to me?" I ask, pausing where I am in the book and listening to the breathing on the other end of the phone. It's clipped and unsteady, and I roll my eyes.

"Are you serious right now?" I say and then allow a small smile to split my lips.

Two days have passed since my sleepover at Sem's, where he fucked me into oblivion. To be honest, I needed time to recover after that, because he didn't fuck me slowly like the previous times. Nope. He completely lost whatever self-control he had over himself and pounded into me so hard we literally shook the entire RV. I'd lost my voice the next day.

My ass is still sore.

While I needed time to let my poor hole heal, I do miss having him around. I shouldn't, but I do. I've over-analyzed these blooming feelings and have come to the conclusion that I *like* Sem. I *really* like Sem. The real question is how much does he like me back? Will this lead anywhere or is he just in it for the fun of the game, the competition, and the thrill? Is this just a fleeting moment for him? A fling with a man before he goes back to dating women?

It sure as fuck doesn't feel like a game or a fling to me anymore.

Since Sem hasn't shown up the past two nights, I've resorted to calling him each night and reading to him before bed. I can tell he likes the book because sometimes he'll interrupt me occasionally and ask questions, and once, he even laughed.

"What?" Sem breathes on the other end of the line.

"Are you..." I lower my voice even though I'm all alone in my apartment. "Are you jerking off right now?"

He huffs. "Nah."

I can hear rustling, and I move the phone from my ear and hit the camera button. It rings a moment before Sem answers. I can see his flushed cheeks, his blown-out pupils. I can tell he's not wearing a shirt, and I wonder excitedly if he's not wearing any pants either. God, a naked Sem is a glorious sight.

"You are *such* a liar," I say with a small laugh. "What's wrong with you? I'm in the middle of a good part. We've been waiting for this...."

"Sorry," he interrupts, "I know, but your voice is so hot. And I'm fucking horny all the time now."

"Sem." I blush happily. "Why didn't you just come over? I could have taken care of that for you."

"Can't. I was too rough last time."

"Um, *no*. It was perfect," I say, my cock thickening just thinking about how he thrust into me, our bodies writhing together.

"You could barely walk the next morning."

"And that, my friend, is a good fucking. Don't let anyone tell you differently."

He watches me and then shakes his head. "Nah, Maggie. Gotta give you a break. Can't control myself around you."

I sigh in mock annoyance, and Sem says, "Show it to me."

I play dumb. "Show you what?"

He grunts in annoyance. "I want to see your cock. Take it out. I love looking at it."

"You do not," I reply with a scoff and then turn over and reach down my pants, cupping myself.

"Oh fuck. You're touching it, aren't you?" he asks, his eyes darkening with lust. "*Show me*," he growls.

"Nope."

"*Maggie*," he grumbles.

"Should have come over. You're missing out on all this."

He exhales, and then I can see his arm working below the camera, making my mouth water. Oh, to suck on that thing. Probably couldn't fit much of it in my mouth, but damn I'd try. I'm nothing if not enthusiastic.

"Look at you, so fucking pretty," he mutters, and his arm moves faster out of the frame.

"Am I? Tell me more," I say, loving the compliments because while I've always known I'm a slut for sex, I'm also a slut for praise, apparently. Especially coming from Sem. I realize his opinion of me matters.

Sem wets his lips and then, "I love fucking you. Love how you can take all of me and you can take it hard. You don't know how amazing that is."

I can't help it. I'm totally getting myself off to this.

"You're so tight, so small and soft, but you're not delicate. I can let loose and not feel like I'm going to break you. Goddammit, I just want to stay inside of you. All the fucking time."

Now my fist is working harder, and I'm staring into his hooded eyes.

"Jesus, Maggie, look what you do to me?" He angles the camera down, showing me his dripping cock.

"Sem." I groan, and Sem moves the camera back to his face.

"Sometimes when you talk, the things you say. Shit, you're so fucking smart, and funny too."

"Yeah?" I breathe, as my cheeks heat.

"The sound of your voice. I could get off on that voice alone. I have."

Oh, Jesus.

I slam my eyes shut, and it's over embarrassingly quick. I shoot all over stomach and when I peel my eyelids open, Sem's barely breathing, his gaze boring into me.

"Come over," he pants. "I won't fuck you. I can keep my hands to myself. I think."

"And that's an incentive? How about you come here. I'm too tired, and my entire body hurts. Today, the kids were wild. Please don't ask me to move from my bed, especially after *that*."

Sem's eyebrows lower in concern. "What happened at work?"

"Oh god," I groan, reaching over and wiping myself clean with a tissue. "We went to Adventure City today, and I swear, keeping five and six-year-olds from dying is like a full-time job. One literally ran into the street when I looked away for one second. Another ate dirt."

Sem smiles a little at that. "And you want how many kids?"

I sigh and throw an arm over my face and sigh. "I'd settle for six. You want any?"

Sem shifts on his bed, turning onto his side. "Never really thought about it."

"You're really good with them, Sem. I saw you at the park. You'd make a great dad one day."

Sem pulls his bottom lip into his mouth but doesn't say anything.

"Think Caleb and Whit will ever have kids?" I ask.

"Nah. I dunno. Maybe. Ma wants grandkids. But Liam and Anne aren't trying, and Luke...well, he could have kids somewhere he doesn't even know about."

I imagine miniature Sems running around, and I feel my stomach clench in longing.

Do not even go there.

"My parents have mentioned grandkids a few times, but God, I don't know if I want my kids around them. They're so closed-minded. I wouldn't want them making comments, and then my kids ending up confused or feeling judged."

Sem brings the phone closer to his face, his eyes narrowed. "If we had kids, they wouldn't set foot in your parents' house. And if they did want to see them, we'd monitor every visit."

My heart flutters at his use of *we*, but I don't mention it. I just tuck that memory away for later consumption and overanalyzation.

"Yeah, I think you're right," I sigh and then say, "Hey, enough about that. Now that you're less horny and can actually focus on what I'm saying, want me to keep reading? We're literally at a turning point in the book. I think they're going to finally have sex."

"Sure," he says, and I turn my camera off and pull up the book on my phone. And then I start reading. Pretty soon, my voice is trailing off, and my eyelids close. Darkness consumes me, and minutes later, I'm dead to the world.

Sometime later, I'm awoken by the bed dipping behind me. A large hand slips across my stomach, pulling me flush against a familiar body.

"Sem," I whisper and then snuggle into him. "Finally."

"Tried. I couldn't stay away," he mutters.

"Good."

Then I let myself dream.

"What are you going to do?" August asks the next day at lunch when I stare despondently at Colin's text. As nice as he is and as much as I pined after him for months, I don't really want to go on that date with him anymore. I cannot believe how much my tastes have changed in the past few weeks. Colin went from being my ideal dream guy to someone I would maybe want to call a friend.

Sem has managed to reverse my idea of a dream guy in a matter of weeks. He's a sneaky bastard. I should have known this would happen with the way he slips around spaces, lurking and snooping. He managed to wheedle his way into my heart and now I'm envisioning all sorts of things.

Like a future.

With him.

"I don't know," I mutter. "I can't cancel, can I?"

"You definitely can."

"But Sem told me not to. He's like pushing me toward Colin but then pulling me back to him. I'm so confused. Last night he broke into my apartment after I fell asleep and just held me."

August shrugs his shoulders. "Okay, one, that's fucking

crazy, and two, don't look at me for answers. I've got no idea how Sem's brain works."

I look around the room and softly say, "He's still struggling with his sexuality. That's a recipe for disaster, right? I mean, we haven't even kissed yet and I don't know what's holding us back anymore. Does he not want to kiss me? Like, is sex with a man somehow okay, but kissing is too gay for him?"

"I have no clue, man. And you've been having sex with him for weeks but haven't even kissed? That's pretty messed up."

"Ugh, I know. I don't know what I'm doing with him, but...I don't like it when he stays away. I miss him when he's gone. I shouldn't, but I do."

"No shit," August says, rubbing at his cheek. "Sounds like a mindfuck on both ends."

I press my face into my hands and shake my head. "Oh, why did I get involved with him in the first place? I knew it was a bad idea, and I did it anyway. God, tell me what to do."

"Prayer won't help you now."

I glower at my best friend and then place my forehead on the table. "I should just go out with Colin, huh? I mean, there's no future with Sem, right? We are not compatible, at all."

"You want a future with him?" August asks, and I shrug.

I swallow and feel my eyes sting a little. "I don't know. I like him. More than I thought I would. He's surprising in the best kinds of ways."

August pats me on the back and then grabs half my sandwich, shoving it into his mouth. "Sounds like you have to figure shit out."

"God, don't I know it."

My phone pings again, and I see Colin's name on the

screen, so I just turn my phone off. I don't know what to do about this.

I worry myself sick about it until I get home from work later that evening and find Sem in my kitchen, his hair pulled back, and his jeans slung low on his hips.

Like he belongs there.

And instantly, I'm hard.

This is becoming a problem.

I clear my throat and ask, "Is that an apron?"

Sem glances over his shoulder and sweeps his eyes over me. "Hey, Maggie."

I adjust myself and move toward him. "Are you cooking?"

"Yeah."

"I didn't know you could do that."

Sem arches an eyebrow at me, grabs a beer and takes a long swig. "And why wouldn't I know how to cook?"

"I dunno. You just look like you barbeque or something."

"I love barbequing, but my mom made sure we each knew how to cook too. Told us we weren't going to grow up to be useless assholes."

"Sounds about right," I say and then lean a little closer to the stove. "So, what are you making?"

"Nothing fancy," he says and then nudges me away. "Back up. Stop trying to micromanage."

"I do not micromanage. All I want to do is *see*."

Sem nudges me back a little further, and I huff in annoyance. "Fine. Whatever. I'll stay out of your hair."

Sem chuckles and continues to cook, and I can't help but perch on the kitchen table and watch him. Because damn, he looks good. My dick definitely takes notice too.

"Next time, please be naked under the apron."

"Such a dirty, fucking mind."

"You have no idea," I mutter, and Sem shoots me a look that means we'll be exploring that later. I am so there for it.

My phone pings, and I feel my stomach drop again. I need to have this conversation with Sem. Like yesterday.

"Sem…" I say, my voice fading as he turns to look at me with those blue eyes I'm growing to love.

His eyebrows lower at my wary tone. "What? What's that look for?"

Before I can stop myself, I blurt, "IhaveadatewithColinon-Thursday."

My words run together, and then I slap a hand over my mouth because I feel guilty for even making plans with Colin in the first place.

Sem's fists clench by his sides, and he says slowly, "Do you?"

"I do. I'm sorry, but you told me to, and so I made plans with him last week. I just wanted to tell you. I don't do well with keeping secrets."

Sem cracks his neck and then nods once, turning back to the stove. His shoulders are stiff, and I can see his jaw working as he grinds his teeth together.

"You're mad," I say, and Sem doesn't reply, just stirs something in a pot.

"You can tell me if you're mad. It's fine."

Sem cracks his neck again, and I sigh heavily. This is going nowhere. This guy is *not* going to talk to me about his feelings. He barely talks, period. I have a feeling he expresses his emotions by blowing things up.

Or shooting them.

Which is not really on par with how I do things. I like open discussions and dialogue.

"You can do whatever the fuck you want, Maggie," he finally says, and I deflate.

"Yeah, Sem, that's what you've been saying, but what about what *you* want?" I ask, and Sem turns off the stove and twists to face me. His arms cross over his chest, and he glowers at me.

"Doesn't matter what I want."

"And why would it not matter?"

"Because I'm not an option for you."

Anger wells up within me, and I'm back to wanting to strangle him. How dare he. What the hell is all this to him then? Is he fucking with me?

"Screw you," I say through clenched teeth as I stand up. "You're not an option? Who made that determination?"

"I did."

"And *why* aren't you an option? Can you tell me that? Can you give me one good reason?"

Sem swallows down some more beer and grabs some plates from the cupboard, and I want to smash them onto the floor. I'm having a tantrum, apparently. Haven't grown out of that stage yet.

"Tell me, Sem, before I break every plate in this house."

He raises his eyebrows. "Nah, you wouldn't do that. You love these plates. Bought them off Etsy."

"Oh, wouldn't I?" I raise an eyebrow and feel like I'm slowly slipping off the edge of sanity. He must pick up on that vibe because he sighs heavily and then rubs a hand down his face.

"Listen, Maggie. The truth is...It's because I'm not...I'm not *enough* for you."

"What the hell does that even mean?"

"It means what it means."

This man is going to give me an ulcer.

"You have to tell me what it *means*, Sem. Just saying some cliché phrase like that doesn't mean it has meaning."

Sem looks confused, and I point at him and then at myself. "Why are *you* not enough for *me*?"

"Just leave it."

"*I will not.*"

He rolls his neck, then moves toward me with a towel in his hand. He pulls at it, and I eye it nervously.

"What are you doing?" I ask as he stops in front of me menacingly. Something dangerous flashes through those blue eyes, and I swallow roughly.

He runs a finger down my cheek, and then he pushes me gently backward until I'm sitting in a chair.

"I'm going to tie you up now."

"Um, *no,* you're not. We are having an adult conversation here. You were just going to open up and tell me why you think you're not enough for me. We were going to express ourselves openly and honestly."

He reaches into his pocket and pulls out two more restraints, and I seriously question my judgment. Because apparently, I've been fucking some kind of psychopath.

But I knew that already, didn't I, and I did it anyway.

"Do you have a shovel somewhere? Some lye as well? Large pieces of plastic to wrap up bloody bodies?" I ask with a little too much snark.

Sem reaches for my hand, but I yank it away.

"Like hell you're tying me up," I huff and quickly lift up my legs and kick them against his chest. The sudden movement surprises him, and he stumbles backward, giving me enough time to slide off the chair and run.

I yank open the door to the apartment and rush out, my

heart beating frantically in my chest as a laugh bubbles out of me.

Oh my god. I'm just as crazy as him. It's verified at this very moment.

Thundering footsteps move up behind me as I scurry down the stairs, but I don't look back, just pump my legs harder. But I know it's futile; he'll catch me eventually. It's inevitable with how much taller he is than me. I zig-zag around the outside of the complex, trying to evade his swiping hands, but eventually, he manages to grab me.

An arm snakes around my waist, and I'm yanked into his arms.

"Sem!" I squeal, drawing the eyes of a few people who live around here. I wave and smile at them because I don't want them to call the cops on us. This is just some harmless fun.

"We're all good!" I call out. "My husband can't get it up unless he feels like a predator, if you know what I mean," I add with a giant smile and a wink.

The people, who have stopped and are now staring, begin whispering to each other as I'm flailing in Sem's arms and completely rethinking my life choices. Sem doesn't say a word, just grunts and throws me over his shoulder.

"Goddamn, you and Caleb are always pulling this shit," I hiss as I slap at his lower back.

But of course, it doesn't matter what I do because he doesn't put me down. He just smacks my ass roughly and marches me back into the apartment, kicking the door open with such force that I know I'll be patching a hole in the wall tomorrow. And by that, I mean, calling a handyman to do it because, really, what do I know about drywall?

"Put me down," I demand, and Sem throws me onto the bed. He literally launches me onto it from across the room.

I bounce twice and my breath leaves my body for just a moment. Glancing up, I see Sem glowering at me.

Jesus, maybe he's really mad.

Well, fuck him too. Trying to tie me up to evade an actual serious conversation.

"Why are you not enough?" I ask again, not giving up. I need to know so I can have some closure when this all ends.

"Drop it."

"No."

"*Drop. It.*"

"Make me."

Sem growls as he pounces on me. His hands roughly capture my wrists and tug them over my head. His face is right over mine and I lick my lips in anticipation.

Because, fuck me, I want him to kiss me.

His wild gaze moves from my eyes to my mouth, and he swallows roughly.

"Hey. Sem. Eyes on me."

Those blue irises meet mine, and I hold his gaze. "I need you to understand this. You're enough, Sem. You're *enough*." I say softly, and he blinks once before his mouth crashes down onto mine. And just like I expected, Sem kisses like he does almost everything else. Wildly and aggressive.

He bites down on my lower lip, sucking it between his teeth before licking into my open, panting mouth. His fingers clench against my wrists before one hand moves to my face, grasping onto my jaw and moving me just the way he wants. His fingers dig into my skin, and I arch beneath him. Fuck, this is the best damn kiss of my life.

My breath comes out unsteadily, my heartbeat thundering in my ears, as he feeds on my mouth. And then his hips arch, and I feel his hard cock brushing against mine.

Oh god, I haven't dry humped in ages. I missed this.

His hand threads through my hair, and he tilts my head more, fucking his tongue into my mouth as we rut against each other.

We don't come up for air for ages.

When he finally rips his mouth from mine, my lips are sore, my cheeks red from beard burn.

He glances down at me and then groans. "Look at you."

I feel my cheeks redden even more, and then my stomach grumbles, interrupting the moment.

"Ignore that."

"Nah."

"I just want to keep doing this," I say, trying to press my lips to his, but when he doesn't give me what I want, I pout. "Fine. Whatever. Torture me. Seems to be your favorite pastime."

Sem smiles softly, presses his forehead to mine, and then he's rolling onto his back, my body clinging to his, and he stands up, walking us both to the kitchen.

"You need to eat," he says, grabbing the lukewarm food from the stove, scooping me up a serving, and placing it in the microwave. He fumbles with the buttons, but I'm not paying any attention to what's happening. I'm too busy nipping at his jaw, licking up to his ear, and sliding my tongue around the rim.

"Stop that," he mutters, and then he's leaning me against the fridge and pressing his lips to mine again.

The beeping of the microwave finally forces him to wrench his mouth from mine, and I whimper.

"Don't want to eat anymore. Food is dumb. Never want to eat again," I say, pushing my tongue into his mouth as he fumbles with the microwave door. He reaches inside as I bite down on his bottom lip and a sudden crash has me looking groggily over his shoulder. The spaghetti is splattered across the counter, the bowl broken into pieces, but I don't even care. At this moment, an earthquake could be rattling the foundation, and I'd be oblivious.

I'm drunk on Sem.

"Later. I'll eat later," I whisper, thread my fingers through his hair, and bring his mouth back to mine.

This. This is enough for me.

CHAPTER NINE

Kissing Sem changed our entire dynamic. It opened doors that I didn't know were even closed. The moment our mouths met, something inside the two of us unraveled.

Sem's hands are always on me now, exploring, running up and down my bare skin. As soon as I arrive home from work, he's on me, picking me up, his hands sliding my shirt off, his tongue in my mouth.

I fucking love it. I live for it, how addicted he is to me.

And I'm equally obsessed. I strip him naked each night and spend hours tracing the lines of his skin with my mouth and fingers.

Initially, August was concerned because I showed up to work post-kiss smiling like a lunatic. It didn't help that my lips were swollen from overuse and my cheeks were rubbed red from his stubble. I'm sure I looked wrecked. But all he needed to do was look in my eyes to see that it was done in the most delicious way.

I reassured August I was perfectly fine. More than fine. I was *happy*. He had stared at me worriedly but then nodded and let it go.

He respects that I'm an adult and can manage my own life. I will live with the decision to keep doing what I'm doing with Sem because it feels right.

Needless to say, I canceled my date with Colin that night. I didn't even think twice about it. Sem had been curled up behind me asleep as I texted the rejection message. As soon as I'd sent it, relief filled me.

If I was going to be with Sem, I would be with him and only him.

Colin took my message with obvious grace. I didn't tell him *why* I couldn't meet him for our date, and he didn't ask. He just rolled with it, good-natured as always. When I saw him at yoga the following morning, he just sent me a small smile during class and then texted me after, asking if we could still be friends.

Yeah. Friends, I could do.

"Sit still," Sem says, his eyes narrowing as I squirm on the RV table.

I bite down on my lower lip and wiggle a little more in my seat because Sem sketching me again is like some kind of aphrodisiac. The previous drawing he did of me is currently sitting on my desk in my apartment, and let me just tell you, I've gotten off to thoughts of that night multiple times. I'm going to frame that drawing and hang it on my wall, jerk off to it when Sem's not around.

"It's too hard…you know how I get."

I slide my shirt up a little, exposing more of my stomach, and Sem bites down on his lip.

"Do I have to tie you up again?" Sem asks, and I roll my eyes.

"Um...yes. You so should. Yes."

Sem sighs and then leans back against the sofa and sets the sketch beside him.

"Come here," he says, and I'm up in a flash, straddling his thighs, my hands clutching at his shirt as I press my lips to his.

Finally.

Posing is torture.

Sem tilts his head and licks into my mouth when a loud pounding resonates within the small space, and my entire body stiffens.

"Open up, asshole!" a familiar voice says, and Sem tilts his head back and groans.

"Go the fuck away!" he shouts at his brother Luke who's banging on the door.

"Come and make me. You've been neglecting me. I'm feeling sorry for myself," Luke replies loudly and then pounds on the door again.

"Oh my god," I say and try to remove myself from his lap, but Sem's hands tighten on my hips.

"Don't you fucking dare," he mutters, and I shake my head in disbelief.

"Sem, your brother is right outside. He knows we're in here. We can't just ignore him to make out."

"Of course we can."

"Who the hell are you in there with?" Luke asks loudly, and then I hear the RV begin to rock slightly.

"Um, no, we can't. He's feral," I mutter.

"I'm going to bury him alive," Sem mutters, and when I try to move off his lap again, Sem holds me against him.

"Sem," I giggle at how irritated he looks right now. "He's going to burn this place down if you don't answer the door. You need to answer it. He'll crawl right in through the windows if you don't."

Sem stares at me for a second and then sighs, "Fine. I'll get rid of him."

Luke shouts, "I can hear you, asshole! You can't get rid of me!"

Sem closes his eyes in annoyance, but a slight smile pulls up the corner of his mouth. It's obvious that he loves his brother. More than I love mine. It's rare to have that kind of fondness between siblings.

"This will only take a minute," he says, and I stare at him because there is no way Luke is leaving in a minute. If I've learned anything about the van Beek boys, it's that they do whatever they want whenever they want.

Sem opens the door, Luke pushes his way inside, and his eyes immediately land on me. He smiles widely.

"I knew it!" Luke shouts and then turns around and punches Sem in the stomach before wrapping his arm around his neck and pulling him down, ruffling his hair.

"Get off me!" Sem grumbles, the two of them wrestling, knocking into things until Luke finally lets Sem go.

The two of them are flushed and breathing heavily, but both wear manic grins on their faces. And for a small second, I wish I had this kind of relationship with my brothers. But I don't. We've never really gotten along. They've always seen me as 'other' and have gone out of their way to avoid me or make me feel less than. I only ever hear from them through texts, and they never make a point to visit me. Not that I really want them to. They can stay far, far away.

"You guys need a hobby," I say to both of them, my hands on my hips.

"Seems like my little brother already has one," Luke says, his eyes sliding up and down my body.

"He's not a hobby. Don't fucking look at him," Sem growls and moves to stand in front of me.

Luke just chuckles and flops down into a chair. "No need to get possessive. I'm just here to collect you both."

"For what?" Sem grumbles as I peek around his broad body to glance at Luke.

"If you weren't so busy fucking this guy, you'd have seen the texts I sent you this week."

Sem reaches behind him and moves me back in place, and I grumble my discontent. He can't just leash me like this. I'm not a puppy.

I duck under his arm and scurry across the RV to where Luke sits. Luke pats his leg as if to tell me to sit on it, and Sem practically roars as he picks me up and cradles me in his arms.

"Fuck off," he tells his brother.

I swat at Sem's arms. "Put me down. We can't do this around other people." He has to realize this isn't normal, that people will think we're weird. But then again, Sem isn't really normal, is he? And Luke isn't either. And, well, what am I? What is normal anyway?

"Like fuck we can't."

Luke starts laughing so hard that tears stream down his face. "My little brother acting all possessive over a guy. Who would have thought? Ma is going to die with happiness."

Sem grunts, shifting me in his arms, and I sigh in resignation. He's not going to put me down, so I just wrap my legs around his waist and tuck my face into his neck.

"At least sit down," I tell Sem softly. "Makes it a tad less weird, yeah?"

Sem thinks on that a minute before moving to the sofa and settling down, shifting me on his lap, so I'm facing forward. I glance up at Luke, who looks all too pleased with what he's witnessing.

"I knew you were eventually going to end up together, with how he watched you," Luke says. "He was like half in love the minute he saw you standing in the hospital in your flower pajamas. Talked about you for *days* after that."

"Shut up, Luke. What the hell do you want?" Sem says, cutting him off.

"Oh no, please do go on," I say, eyeing Luke. "I'd love to know what he said."

Sem squeezes me against him, and I giggle.

"Ah, Mags, the things I could tell you..." Luke eyes his brother and then says, "I'll tell you later, yeah? When Sem's not around."

Sem grumbles, and I bite my lips to keep myself from laughing.

"Just tell us what you want, Luke," Sem says.

"Ah, well, you'd know why I'm here if you ever looked at that phone of yours."

"I did look. And I ignored your messages."

"Asshole. I should just leave you here and go on by myself then."

"What the hell are you talking about?" Sem grunts.

"Monster Jam! I've been bugging you about buying tickets for days, but you never responded. So, I had to go ahead without you."

"Shit," Sem says, looking genuinely disappointed. "Did I miss out?"

"What the hell is Monster Jam?" I ask, but they both ignore me.

"Nah, bro. You got lucky. Liam and Anne had to cancel last minute, so I have two extra tickets to Monster Jam if you want to join."

Sem tenses beneath me, and then his face breaks out in a wide smile. "Fuck yeah. We're in."

I glance at the two smiling brothers and arch an eyebrow, "Um, seriously, guys, what the hell is Monster Jam?"

"Oh, tiny, just you wait," Luke replies. "You are going to *love* it."

"Oh my god," I say, looking around the crowded stadium. "Why did you say I could wear this, Sem? Why did you let me out of the house looking like this?"

Sem glances down at my tight black shorts and sequined pink half-shirt and then bites his lip. "Because you look good like that."

"Yes, I know I do, but Sem, I do *not* fit in here. You could have warned me so I could have toned it down a little. I'm not dressed appropriately and some people are staring," I whisper, tugging my shirt down over my belly button. This is like my worst nightmare. I stand out like a sore thumb. A dainty rose in a sea of flannel and mullets. It's all I can see for miles.

"Fuck 'em," Sem says, reaching out and drawing me into his side. "You can wear what you want, whenever you want. If anyone looks at you the wrong way, I'll take care of it."

Luke steps up, wrapping an arm around his brother's neck and glancing down at me. "Don't worry, little dude. We've got your back. No one will say a thing. Most of these people don't care about you. They're too busy thinking about themselves. Truth."

I look up at these two big men that I've gotten to know and grown to care about and feel lucky that I have people on my side. It's nice to finally feel accepted for who I am. I smile at Sem and bump his hip with mine. "Thanks for being awesome."

He grins back down at me, his eyes warm and bright. Fuck, he's just so damn beautiful.

In the distance, I catch a glimpse Caleb and Whit approaching, their fingers linked together as they stop in front of us. Caleb's wearing a pair of torn jeans and a loose tank that shows off his arms and part of his chest, while Whit is dressed in his usual fitted black pants and long-sleeved Henley.

These two could not be any different if they tried. But somehow, they just work.

"I've been waiting for this all year," Caleb says excitedly and then turns to Whit, "You ready for this, babe? You are going to have so much fun."

Whit eyes him and then sighs, "Doubtful."

"Ah," Caleb says, nuzzling into his neck. "You're such a grump today."

"I'm not a grump."

"You so are, but I'll make it up to you later, yeah?"

Whit closes his eyes and sighs, pushing Caleb away from him gently, and then stroking his hand across Caleb's cheek.

"Fine."

Caleb beams at him.

"Alright, let's go, you guys. No more making out. Makes me feel like a fifth wheel," Luke says, handing us each of our tickets and making our way through the noisy crowd. Sem tucks me into his side as he elbows people out of the way. When we finally make our way up a thousand stairs to the nosebleed seats, I glance down at the dirt arena in front of us and take it all in.

"So...let me get this right. We just sit here while big trucks drive around and smoosh things?" I ask, and Luke laughs.

"Yeah, tiny. That's basically it."

"And that's fun?"

"It's so fucking fun," Luke replies, and Sem tugs me down into a folding seat next to him. Sem barely fits into his. His hips touch both sides of the armrests.

"Here," Sem says and hands me a pair of noise-cancelling headphones.

I hold them up and look over at him. "What are these for?"

"You'll need 'em."

I glance over at Luke, who has a pair in his lap while he pulls a bag of food out from nowhere. Whit's fussing with Caleb, trying to put the headphones on his head, but Caleb's thwarting him by nipping at his fingers.

Those two are too cute, I think, as a sudden roar makes me jump in my seat. Sem grabs the headphones and stuffs them over my ears. Okay, now I know why I need them. The thunderous rumble of the trucks filing out into the dirt arena is so loud it rattles the stadium. If I didn't have these things on, my ears would probably be bleeding. Tinnitus is no joke.

I glance over at Sem, who is watching me, waiting for my reaction, so I just offer him a small smile as music starts playing in the background. Okay, not going to lie. This is kind of pumping me up. I turn toward the arena once more and watch as the crowd goes wild. A movement to my right diverts my eyes, and I see Luke and Caleb cupping their hands over their mouths and shouting. Both of them stand up suddenly, pumping their fists in the air. Next to them, Whit has his eyes closed as he sighs heavily.

One enormous red monster truck revs its engine and spins around and around in the arena, kicking up dirt, and I can't tear my eyes away. Sem reaches over and cups my hand in his and I can't help myself. I lean up and press my lips gently against his. For everyone to see.

"That was amazing," I say, bouncing on my feet, reaching out, and grabbing onto Sem's hand. His fingers flex against mine, as he tugs me a little closer. He held my hand the entire time we sat there watching the trucks do tricks down below. And once, he even leaned over and pressed a kiss to my temple.

He seemed completely unconcerned with what anyone thought about us being together, so I told myself to just let it go. I was going to enjoy my night with him.

Would this be considered a date?

Were we dating now?

"Who knew that watching monster trucks crush cars could be so exhilarating? And that one purple truck that flipped over and broke apart...I was really rooting for her."

"I'm glad you liked it," Sem smiles as we make our way down the stairs to the large lobby. Whit and Caleb trail behind us, Caleb's head on Whit's shoulder.

"Fuck, I'm starving," Luke says, rushing up to us, rubbing at his stomach. "We grabbing food or what?"

"Didn't you just eat the entire time we were there?" I ask, and Luke shrugs.

"I could always eat. I'm a growing boy."

Sem looks over at me, and I nod. "Okay, yeah, I guess we could grab a bite."

Then I lean into Sem a little and say, "I have to use the bathroom before we go."

Sem nods and presses his hand to the small of my back, leading me through the crowd toward the men's restroom. He watches me walk inside, leaning against the hallway wall to wait for me.

I do my business quickly, avoiding some stares from curious men, but no one bothers me. But then again, there's always one.

As I'm washing my hands, I hear it.

Of course. Someone just had to go and ruin this night for me.

"What the fuck you doing here, boy?" a man says gruffly. He's tall and wide with a scraggly beard nearly obscuring his mouth and a tattered t-shirt stretched over his round belly. He smells like beer even from where I stand a few feet away, and I wrinkle my nose at the stench.

"Taking a piss. What did you think I was doing in the restroom?" I reply with as much snark as I can muster. I dry my hands quickly and try to move around him because leaving is the best way to de-escalate this situation. But he reaches out his dirty hand, and shoves me in the chest. I stumble back and plop down on my ass. The floor feels moist and sticky under me and I cringe, my heart thundering in my chest.

"You don't belong here, you fucking dirty queer," he slurs.

A few people are staring, some looking disgusted at...God, maybe they are looking at *me* in disgust and not the bigot swaying on his feet. No one moves to help me so I pull myself up and try again to duck under his thick arm to get to the door, but he latches onto me roughly once more.

I try to yank my arm away, but his grip tightens on me, his fingers digging into my skin, and now I'm afraid.

"It's fucking unnatural," the man spits, and some of it lands on my hand.

Some of the onlookers are filing out the door now, leaving me alone to deal with this dickbag. But then a stall door bangs open, and another man approaches, looking at the two of us and assessing the situation.

"Shut your ignorant mouth," the unknown man says sternly, his eyes narrowed on dickbag. I don't know him, but he's standing up for me. Okay, so maybe not everyone here sucks.

"You okay?" he asks me.

And I shake my head, swallowing roughly.

"You with him...you a queer too?" the smelly man asks, and before anyone can say another word, I'm dropped from his grasp and he's thrown back against the tile wall.

He hits it with an audible grunt, and Sem is there, looking like an avenging god, clutching onto the man's neck with both hands. His thick fingers flex so tightly that the man's face turns purple.

The man who stood up for me nods and then leaves. But we're drawing a new crowd now and some have their phones out, filming everything.

"Oh my god," I breathe as Luke casually strides in next to Sem, leaning against the wall like this is some kind of movie matinee. And not a violent shakedown.

"Bro, come on. Squeeze a little tighter," Luke says, looking at his nails. Sem grunts, and the muscles of his arms strain as he literally lifts the man up, his feet dangling off the ground. My eyes widen at the raw power of it. I'm impressed, intrigued, a little repulsed and, if I'm being honest, a lot turned on.

"Open that ugly mouth a little. Let me get his tongue," Luke says casually and then grabs onto the man's chin, tugging it down. "Think I can rip it out with just my fingers? 'Cause, I think I can."

"Do it," Sem grunts, and the man looks like he's going to pass out. The veins in his eyes burst as he gasps for breath. "He touched what's mine."

The man begins to tremble, his eyes widening, and I can't do anything but stand there and stare. Because Sem just claimed me while choking a man to death.

And I like it.

What the hell is wrong with me?

"Oh shit," Luke says with a scoff as he glances down. "Piss yourself, man? Really? Do you have no shame?"

Sem looks at the man's wet pants and releases him so quickly that the man slumps onto the ground, choking and pawing at his neck.

"Disgusting," Sem spits as the man coughs and wheezes.

Luke pushes off the wall and steps next to Sem. "How about we bring him back to the yard and show him how a hydraulic press works. Never done it with a body before."

Oh my god.

"You guys, we're *not* doing that," I finally manage to say, but neither looks at me. Their sole focus is on the man in front of them. They don't even notice the people watching this all unfold with morbid fascination. I get it. I totally do. It's weirdly hot and sickening and scary.

I cannot look away.

"Or we could put his hands in the shredder for touching what doesn't belong to him," Sem suggests, like they're talking about their favorite video game. "Never done that either. Would probably hurt."

"Um. No. Nope," I say sternly and then grab onto Sem, forcing him to look at me. "Sem. We're not doing anything of the sort. No one is getting pressed or shredded, not even dickbag here. We're leaving."

Luke looks disappointed for a second and then sighs, "You sure?"

"Yeah. I am. He's not worth it."

"Okay. Whatever you want, tiny."

He moves to wash his hands, and people slide out of his way. Sem grabs onto my hand and presses a drawn-out kiss to my forehead. He rubs his thumb over my cheek and then turns, squatting down to make sure he meets the man's eyes. "Hope you learned a lesson, asshole. You keep your filthy hands to yourself and those ugly words inside. Now apologize to him."

The man shoots me an angry glare and seems to be considering not doing it, but then he manages to grumble, "Sorry."

"Louder," Sem shouts, and I jump slightly.

The man swallows nervously, licking his lips, and shouts, "Sorry."

Satisfied with that, Sem stands up and strides over to me, scooping me up. He tucks me into his chest as he moves out of the bathroom. He strides past the onlookers, not even waiting for his brother or cousin. People stare at us as we pass, but I don't care. I tuck my face into his neck and let them look. They can think whatever they want.

I don't care.

When we get to his truck, he sets me gently inside and closes the door softly. He moves around to the driver's side, but he doesn't get in. I see his chest heaving and then a loud crash rocks the cab. I glance up to see Sem clenching his fist, his knuckles cracked.

"Oh my god," I breathe as he roars and punches the door again.

He runs his bloody hand through his hair, his body trembling. His eyes are wild as he tugs on his hair and paces outside the truck for a few minutes.

I take a deep breath, tuck my hands under my thighs, and wait. Because what else do I do in this situation? It's obvious he needs space. A few moments to process it all.

"Sem?" I breathe when he finally gets in the truck. I crawl over to him and straddle his thighs. I reach up and gently touch his face. "What did you do? Why'd you do that?"

He clenches his good fist and grits out, "Why the fuck do you think…" He squeezes his eyes shut. "You know what? I'm going to go back in there and murder him."

He moves to exit the vehicle, but I squeeze him to me.

"No, no, you aren't. He's not worth it. And I'm fine. Look at me, I'm okay. I'm used to it…sort of. It's fine."

He grabs onto my chin roughly and forces me to look at him. "It's not fine. Don't ever think that. None of that was fine."

My eyes sting, filling with tears, and I press a soft kiss to his mouth. But he doesn't kiss me back; he sits there completely stiff until I move off of him with a resigned sigh.

When I'm buckled up, he revs the truck engine and peels out of the parking lot. I grab onto his thigh to keep my balance, but he doesn't tuck me into his side like he usually does. He grips onto the steering wheel tightly as he maneuvers the streets and freeways home.

I gently touch the bloody hand resting on his lap. "You need ice for this."

"I'm fine."

It doesn't look fine, but what do I know? I've never punched a car before. But it seems like it hurts. Could it be broken?

When we finally make it back to my apartment, Sem's still vibrating with anger. He tries to carry me up the stairs, but I refuse because of his injured hand. Instead, I walk with him to the door and open it with shaking fingers. I turn around when I'm finally inside, expecting to see Sem right behind me, but he's not. He's standing in the doorway, his fists clenched by his sides, his chest rising and falling.

"Sem, what...what are you doing? Come in. Please. You need to ice your hand. You're hurt."

He shakes his head, some of his hair falling across his cheeks. "No. I need to go."

My eyebrows rise, and I move toward him. "What? Why? Stay. Let me take care of you."

He presses his good hand against the doorframe and breathes deeply. "If I stay, I may hurt you. I'm too pissed off."

"No. You won't." I say, and he visibly trembles.

"I will. I need to...smash something. Break it." He squeezes his eyes shut. "I can't believe I let him hurt you like that. Say those hateful things to you. I brought you there and I didn't protect you. It's my fucking fault."

"Sem, no. Please don't do this. It's okay. It's not your fault."

"It's not fucking okay," his voice breaks. "I...fuck...I need to go...."

"No, don't leave. Not like this. Not when you're so angry. I'll worry. Just...use me, Sem. *Use me*. I can take it. Take it out on me, please."

His eyes soften and he looks broken, his Adam's apple

bobbing in his neck, and I move closer to him to hold him to me, but he steps away.

"No...baby, that's the one thing I could never do," and then he's backing away from me, his footsteps thundering down the stairs. And I'm left gaping at his retreating figure.

Something I never realized until today is that Sem feels very deeply. It's hidden beneath the quiet stoicism and the wild impulsivity but seeing how he reacted tonight...there's much more to him than I realized. It feels like I'm constantly peeling back the layers of him, discovering new things. How much more complex could this man be?

I need a lifetime to learn to this man.

I remain in the doorway for a few minutes, staring at the empty hallway, unsure of what to do. Should I chase after him? Do I let him have his space? I lean against the doorframe and press a hand against my aching chest.

In all the time I've known him, I've never seen Sem so broken up about something before. What happened to me tonight upset him so bad and it feels like my fault.

Oh god, if he hurts himself more tonight, it will be all my fucking fault.

"Shit," I whisper, and just when I feel like my heart can't break anymore, my head snaps up at the sound of footsteps punching up the stairs. Suddenly Sem is in the doorway again, his hands on me, lifting me up, and his mouth on mine. His cheeks are wet, and I grab onto his face, wiping the dampness away with my thumbs.

"Sem," I breathe.

"Maggie. Tie me up," he grinds out, kicking the door shut and striding quickly to the bedroom.

"*What?*" I gasp.

"I don't wanna hurt you, but I need you," he pants as he sets me down and pulls his shirt off.

Then he's lying on the bed, his wrists above his head. "Tie me up. Hurry before I change my mind."

With no time to consider his request, I quickly grab two of my work ties from my closet. Holding onto one wrist, I secure it to the metal headboard and then reach over and do the same to the other, making sure to take care with his bruised hand.

"Okay," I say, breathless, looking down at Sem sprawled across my bed. "You good now?"

Sem yanks his arms, and the headboard rattles, but the ties stay secure.

His nostrils flare in surprise. "What the fuck, Maggie."

An unexpected, choked giggle slips from my mouth. "I may have been shit at it, but I *was* a Boy Scout, remember? I earned that knot badge."

His eyes narrow, and his chest expands. "Fuck. *Come here.* I want you."

I arch an eyebrow at him and feel something shift between us. "Oh, no, Sem. I'm in charge now. What did you think would happen when you asked me to tie you up?"

He exhales shakily, and I feel power surge through me. This big, strong man tied up and at my mercy. I can do whatever I want with him.

I run a finger down his chest, and he trembles beneath me.

"Will you let me do whatever I want, Sem?"

He watches me a moment, fire in those blue eyes, and when he nods, my entire body lights up at his concession.

"You're gonna let me take care of you and then you'll feel so much better when this is over." I slide my finger through his happy trail trailing towards the bulge in his pants. "Now, let's see. You were so brave earlier, so protective. What should your reward be?"

Sem licks his lips, and I pull my shirt over my head and drop it onto the floor. Running my hand slowly up his inner thigh, I gently squeeze his hard length beneath his jeans.

"Maybe, I'll play with you a little. Would you let me do that?"

Sem arches his hips, and I bite my lip to hold back a smile. He's begging for it in his own silent way.

"Patience," I say, and he grunts in annoyance. "Such a shitty word, isn't it?"

Then I slowly tug his pants down, discovering he's not wearing any underwear. Oh, sweet lord, this man is driving me crazy. His hard cock is jutting up in the air, and I stroke it a few times, relishing the way he pants for it. And when he's properly worked up, I pause to kick off my shorts and underwear, then straddle his stomach and lean down, pressing my lips to his.

He lifts his head off the pillow, chasing my mouth, but I remove it too quickly and begin a slow, torturous decline down his neck, chest, and stomach until I'm *right there*.

I grab onto his cock, press it against his stomach, and slowly lick my way from base to tip.

Sem exhales shakily, his cobalt eyes never leaving mine. Is he memorizing this? Will he draw this later?

Fuck, I hope so.

I swirl my tongue, teasing his slit, and when I pop the head into my mouth and suck, his breath stutters.

Oh, he has no idea what I'm going to do to him. I love sucking cock and I'm about to make this so damn good for him.

Breathing deeply through my nose, I take him in as far as possible as he moans loudly.

I do it again, and he throws his head back, muttering sharp curses. The tendon in his neck bulges against his skin as I drag my lips right to the tip and begin my slow torture. He's writhing, undulating his hips beneath me. His arms strain against the restraints, the muscles bulging beneath his skin. He wrenches against the ties so often that the headboard rattles against the wall. I wouldn't be surprised if he ripped it right off the frame.

I drag my tongue up him with a low hum and then let him slip from my mouth. He watches me with damp, trembling lips.

Pressing a kiss to his hip, I reach over and grab the lube off the bedside table.

Because I'd be an idiot not to take advantage of this situation.

Lifting up one of his heavy thighs, I press it up against his torso, exposing all of him to me, and nearly come right then. Damn, this man is hot, literally everywhere.

Uncapping the lube, I squeeze some onto my fingers. Sem's eyes widen as realization sets in, but he doesn't protest.

"Think you can take this?" I ask, swirling a finger around his hole.

He breathes deeply, and I pull him back into my mouth.

"Fuck. Fuck. Fuck," he mutters as the tip of my finger slips inside. Sem's above me, yanking on the restraints again, trying to get loose, and cursing me. He's so far down my throat that I'm gagging on him as my finger sinks knuckle deep inside of him.

But I don't let up; I fuck him with my finger and my mouth until he's nearly sobbing.

I insert a second finger and suck his balls into my mouth one by one and his eyes roll back into his head. I watch in awe because this has been a fantasy of mine for days. Weeks. Probably even months if I'm being honest with myself.

I scissor my fingers, exploring him, and then move my mouth back to his hard cock. He's close. I can feel how his ass clenches around my fingers, how he's chanting my name on broken breaths.

Then he's shaking his head, thrashing above me as I work a third finger in and start to peg that sensitive area inside him over and over. He's down my throat. My eyes water, drool pooling between us, and he's warning me, begging me, but I don't let up. I just swallow around him as he unloads straight into my stomach.

He finally goes limp, his arms hanging loosely from the restraints.

I lean my cheek against his hip, his semi-hard cock still in my mouth. I'm a mess, completely wrecked, but I don't care. I just gently suck on him a bit more until he asks me to stop.

I glance up at him, my fingers still inside of him. "Better?"

"Shit," he huffs, and I smile softly. "Untie me."

"Nope," I say and slowly remove my fingers from him.

"Come on, Maggie. Untie me. I feel...I feel better."

I shake my head, determined to get my way this time. "I'm not done with you yet, Sem."

I reach into my drawer and pull out the small plug I'd purchased for him when we first started this. You know, just in case I ever won a bet.

I show it to him, letting him get a good look, and then lean forward and press it against his lips.

He narrows his eyes at me but parts his mouth anyway. I

slip it inside, and the sight is so erotic I'm reaching down and tugging at my aching cock.

I'm so close and ready for release, but I need to do this first. I remove the plug from his mouth and rub lube onto its smooth surface before lifting Sem's leg again and teasing his entrance with it.

"Think you can suck my cock without choking on it?" I ask as I move the plug slowly inside of him.

His eyes widen at the intrusion, but he doesn't tell me to stop. So, I keep pressing forward.

Sem grunts. "It's small enough. I think it would be an easy fit."

I roll my eyes and let the plug slip inside a little farther.

"It's normal-sized. I've told you this, and you said it was perfect," I reply and then smile when those tight rings open up for me and take the rest of the plug. As the end settles right against his cheeks, I lean back and take a long look at it. Goddammit, that's hot.

"You look good with something in your ass," I say, and he flushes.

"How does it feel?"

He rolls his lips between his teeth. "Weird but I like it."

"Hmm," I say and then crawl up his chest.

"Now," I say, pressing the tip of my cock to his mouth. "Let's see how good you are at taking it in the mouth. Bet you gag, big man."

"Fuck off," he says and lifts his head up, swallowing me whole.

And, of course, he wins this round.

But then again, are there really any losers in this scenario?

No, no, there are not.

CHAPTER TEN

"Are you seriously still wearing that?" I ask, reaching down and pressing a hand against the plug still in Sem's ass. I'd released his arms from their restraints some time ago, and we've just been lounging around in bed. It's late, and I'm going to be exhausted tomorrow, but I don't care. I just want to stay awake with him for as long as possible.

"Yeah," he says, nuzzling his face against my hair.

"Why?" I ask with a small laugh.

"One day, you're going to fuck me. I should probably get used to something up my ass."

I sputter at that. "Um...I'm sorry, what?"

"Unless you don't want to," he replies, looking shy. "I'm not sure how that works, actually."

"Oh, um, well, everyone is different. We all have our preferences. I've just never...." I begin, and Sem leans his head back in shock.

"Seriously?"

"Yeah. You know, I've just always been a bottom. It's just what stuck, I guess."

Sem wets his lips. "So, I'll be your first?"

"Yeah," I say with a small smile. "You like that, huh?'

"Yeah. I do. A lot. You've been all of my firsts, so…."

"So, it's only fair. By doing this, we will level the playing field."

I reach down and touch the plug again, and Sem rolls onto his back.

"Enough with touching it."

"Sorry, it's just unexpected. Didn't think you'd ever let me do that to you. But you were so there for it."

"Yeah, well, I'd do pretty much anything for you, Maggie."

I tuck myself against his chest and sigh, inhaling him. I nip at his skin and then lick it. "I know that."

He sighs, his hands on my lower back, and then he stands up and brings us into the shower. I should chastise him for being so careless. His hand is still swollen but he iced it and told me he'd go get it checked by a doctor tomorrow, so I let it go. According to Whit, the van Beek men commonly get injured by doing reckless things. I guess I'll just have to get used to it, especially if I plan to stick around. And I do.

After showering, I crawl on top of Sem and tuck myself against him. One of his large hands splays across my back, and he massages up my spine.

"God, your hands are fabulous," I mutter, my lips brushing against his skin. "I really, really hope you didn't break that one."

"It's fine. I've had worse."

I lift my head and narrow my eyes at him. "Is that so? Do tell."

"Not much to tell. Just broke a few body parts growing up doing stupid shit. This is nothing."

He flexes his injured hand to show me that it's okay. I grab onto it and press my mouth to his knuckles, kissing them softly.

His eyelids flutter, and he sighs.

"Maggie," he says, and I nuzzle against his jaw.

"Yeah?"

"Can we...would you want to..."

I lean up a little farther so I can see his face. He works his lips between his teeth, and I trace one with my finger.

"I'm dying of suspense."

He huffs and then meets my gaze. "I want to go on a date with you."

My entire body freezes, and his cheeks turn pink. "We don't have to...."

"Absolutely not. Do not take that back," I grunt, sitting up and straddling his chest. "Ask me again."

I'm practically bouncing with excitement as Sem grabs onto my bare ass and runs his thumbs across my skin.

"Will you go on a date with me?" he asks with a shy smile.

I pretend to think about it and then lean down and kiss him. "Of course, Sem. I'd *love* to go on a date with you. Took you long enough."

He looks surprised at my response, and so I just kiss him again. God, this man is cute.

"Where are we going to go? Do I need to dress up? Are you going to wear a suit and tie? Oh god, please wear a tie."

My mind is running wild, and Sem just watches me, the corner of his mouth hitching up. "Can you give me some ideas? Never been on a date before."

"You lie."

"Nah, just never had to go on one before. Usually got what I wanted without it."

"You slut. Did you break into people's apartments and wait in their beds with your dick out? Did they just sit on it?" I laugh and dig my fingers into his neck, trying to tickle him, but he just blinks up at me.

"Nah. You're the only one who sat on it when I asked."

"You did not ask. You dared me to."

He shrugs and squeezes my hips. "Worked, didn't it?"

A sigh escapes me, and I lay back down on top of him.

"Yes. Yes, it did. And fine, we can plan it together. Our first date," I say, becoming more and more excited the longer I think about it.

My fingers tug on his nipple, and he grabs onto my hand and folds it into his palm.

"Enough."

I glance up at him and smirk. "Fine, but tell me this. Are you going to put out after our date? Because if not, that might be a deal-breaker for me. I'm totally in this for the monster cock."

He grabs onto the back of my neck and shifts me until my lips are hovering over his.

"You teasing me?"

"Maybe. I mean, I would never say no to your dick, but honestly, I just love it when your cheeks get all pink, and you get all shy," I smirk and nip at his chin. "But I'm not teasing about this. I want to go on that date with you. You should have asked me ages ago."

"Would you have said yes?"

"Yeah, Sem. I would have."

"Even when I was stalking you?"

"Aha!" I shout, pointing at his face. "You admit it. Finally!"

Sem rolls his eyes, and then I'm on my back, his large, naked body sprawled across mine and he's shutting me up with a deep kiss. I guess I'll let it go...for now.

I glance at the doorway and then at my phone. Sem should be here any minute, and I cannot wait. It's the day of our date and I'm giddy with excitement. I haven't felt this way in... well, in forever.

A real date. With Sem.

Who would have thought? But it feels absolutely right.

A knock on the door has me breathing deeply and tugging the door open. Standing before me in the hallway is Sem looking absolutely delicious.

"Oh my god," I whisper, letting my eyes sweep over him. If there is one thing I never thought I'd see, it's Sem all dressed up.

I'm instantly hard because, damn, he wears it so well. I adjust myself slightly as I take in the white button-up shirt that strains against his chest. The sleeves are rolled up, showcasing his muscular forearms. Over his shirt are a grey tie and a stylish dark green vest. His legs sport fitted black jeans, and over one arm is a grey suit jacket. His hair is perfectly pulled back in a neat ponytail. He looks like a dream.

"I'm overdressed," he says, his cheeks darkening as he takes in my casual shorts and t-shirt.

"Um. *Hell no*. You are perfect. Let me just push my eyeballs back into my head and then I'll go change."

I run into the bedroom and begin shuffling through my closet.

Glancing over my shoulder, I see Sem leaning against the

doorframe and bite back a groan because I'd rather just stay here and peel those clothes off of him. One by one.

"Stop looking at me like that," he grumbles, pressing his hand against his crotch.

"Not my fault you look like sex. We could market you. I'd be a millionaire. Men and women would line up just to stare at you. We'd sell little rags people could use to wipe up their drool. God, I'm a genius."

He rolls his lips between his teeth, and I tug my shirt over my head. I quickly shrug on a retro button-up shirt and pull on some dress pants. Next is my bowtie and suspenders, and when I'm done, I turn to Sem and hold out my hands.

"Ta-Da!"

Sem moves toward me and tugs on my T-Rex bowtie.

"Why the fuck are you so damn cute?"

"God made me this way," I snark and then grab onto his hand and link my fingers through his. "Now, where are we going, big man? I've been dying to figure it out. Even called Luke for some clues."

"You did not," Sem grumbles.

"I did. But he wouldn't tell me. Said it was a secret. Though he did tell me something."

Sem glances down at me, and I smirk up at him.

"What did he say?"

I mime zipping my lips, and Sem snorts. "Probably don't want to know anyway."

Then he picks me up and carries me to his truck, where he sets me inside. I buckle my seatbelt and then cozy up to him as he drives us into the city.

"So...are we going somewhere fancy?" I ask, my fingers running up and down his thigh. "I think we are since you're dressed like this."

Sem grabs onto my hand, and I notice that the knuckles are healing well.

"Patience. You'll see soon enough."

"Perhaps, I could give you an incentive to tell me sooner?" I say, glancing up at him. "I can be very persuasive."

He glances down at me and links our hands together. "Patience, Maggie."

I roll my eyes but smile as I lean against him and casually smell him. I have no shame, apparently.

Thirty minutes later, we pull up to an expensive restaurant, and I gasp.

"For reals?" I say, unbuckling and leaning forward. In the distance, I can make out the sun setting over the expanse of the ocean, reflecting orange and yellow stripes over the water. "This place is ridiculously expensive, Sem. You can't be serious. You need to sell your firstborn to eat here."

He pushes open the truck door and holds his arms out. "Yeah, well, it's our first date, so...."

"I love it," I gasp as he picks me up and sets me gently on the ground. I grab onto his hand, pulling him forward. "How did you get a reservation?"

Sem shrugs like this is no big deal. "Made it a while ago."

My eyes widen at that. "You did not."

"I did."

"When?"

He swallows as he looks down at me. "Does it matter?"

"Um, no." I stand on my tiptoes as I grab onto his tie and tug his mouth down to mine. "You, Sem van Beek, are full of surprises. Now feed me. I'm hungry."

We spend the next two hours curled up next to each other, lazily grazing through the multiple dishes we ordered. At first, I'd wondered if Sem wanted to be a little more discreet about being seen on a date with another man, but he'd just slid into the booth next to me and wrapped his arm around my shoulder.

It was game over for me after that.

I held nothing back.

I flirted my way through dinner, making sure to keep my hands on him at all times. And my heart fluttered in my chest when he blushed at the waitress who told us we make a cute couple.

Fuck yeah, we do.

"You look like you're sucking cock eating that," Sem grumbles, watching me lick chocolate off a spoon.

I do it again slower and flutter my eyelashes at him.

"How about I suck yours later?" I say, and he shifts in his seat. "Stuff that big piece of meat right into my mouth."

"You're teasing me again," he says, and I suck my thumb into my mouth, licking some cream from it.

"I find that I quite like teasing you, Sem. Now, after this, what's the plan? Have any more tricks up your sleeves, or are we going home so I can strip you out of that suit and eat your ass."

He takes a long gulp of water and glances away, the tips of his ears pink.

"Stop saying shit like that, Maggie. I'm not going to be able to get up from the table."

I snicker and reach over, touching his hard cock. "Shame. Should I get you off right now? We'd be doing it for the greater good. We wouldn't want to scare off any customers with that monster."

He glances down at his crotch and then meets my eyes. "You're an asshole. I'm going to get you back for this later. Maybe tie you up and tickle you."

I gasp at that, removing my hand from him and taking a long sip of water. Because damn, I know I'm affecting him, but he's doing the same to me. I'm almost feverish. Who knew dating Sem would be so much fun?

Fuck all my previous ideas of what my dream guy should be.

The man right next to me is where it's at. He's everything I want.

I just hope he feels the same way about me.

Eventually, we pay the bill, and then he grabs my hand and pulls me outside, picking me up and pressing a filthy kiss to my lips. A couple moves past, eyeing us, but I don't care. Take a good look, people. This man is mine.

Sem presses a final kiss to my mouth and then lets me slip from his arms. I grab onto his hand, and we walk side-by-side down the boardwalk. When we make it to the sand, we slip off our shoes and sink our toes into the water.

"This reminds me of all those days ago when you took me out in the water," I tell Sem. "You looked so hot out there riding the waves."

"Yeah, well, you looked hot in that swimsuit. It was very... bright and tiny. Could see you from all the way out in the ocean."

"You could not," I laugh. "And I know you liked that swimsuit because you bit my ass."

Sem smirks at me. "It is bite-sized."

I nudge him and laugh.

He reaches down and presses his hand against my ass, and squeezes. His palm nearly cups an entire cheek, and I roll my eyes.

"Fine, you're just abnormally large in every way. Happy now? Where I'm small, you're gigantic."

He pulls me into him and fiddles with my bowtie. "But that's okay, right? We work, don't we?"

"Oh, Sem. You have no idea how well we work. We fit together like puzzle pieces."

And then I pull him down for a long and dirty kiss.

CHAPTER ELEVEN

"You ready to go?" Sem says with a smile, opening his RV door open for me. He grabs onto my duffle bag and sets it on the floor. The two of us are on our way to meet his family for their annual Fourth of July camping trip. We'll be spending tonight at his parents' and then making the trip into the mountains tomorrow morning.

The past week has been bliss. Ever since our date, I've let myself start to plan. For a future with him. Our future.

"As ready as I'll ever be," I say, pressing my face into his chest and pulling him into a hug. "Whit already called me to warn me."

Sem leans back slightly, one hand on the back of my neck, the other on my hip.

"Warn you about what?"

I bite my lip and smirk up at him. "About what it will be like with your family."

Sem scoffs and then bends down, pressing a languid and obscene kiss to my mouth.

When he finally pulls away, I have hooded eyes and an erection. Wonderful. Just what I need for an hour-long drive through traffic on a Friday night.

"Whit's a crybaby. You'll fit right in. I bet you even join in."

"Maybe I will," I shrug and then move to the front of the RV, settling into the oversized passenger side chair.

Sem moves into the driver's side, adjusting the steering wheel and turning the motorhome on with a loud rumble.

Leaning over, I plug my phone into the stereo. "Made us a playlist for the drive. I asked Caleb what kind of music you like, and let me say I'm not surprised. Stereotypical country boy, huh?"

Sem smiles over at me as the music pumps through the speakers. "Never said I was anything else."

"No, no, you did not."

"That a bad thing?"

"Nope," I say, popping the P. "I happen to have a thing for your brand of country boy."

He bites his lip and side-eyes me before pulling out of the RV park. We pull onto the freeway, and I relay the conversation I had with Whit earlier. Apparently, tonight there will be explosives. A truck-load full. I bite back a grin thinking of how exasperated Whit sounded when he told me to make sure I have a first aid kit on me at all times.

Sem just smirks and says, "No one's died yet."

Not entirely reassuring, but I have to admit, I'm bouncing in my seat a little, thinking about watching stuff get blown up.

I glance over at Sem expertly navigating the large motorhome through the crowded freeways, and I find that I'm so impressed with him. He draws beautifully, he an expert builder, he's hardworking and has a good job. He might not be traditionally book-smart like Whit or my friends from college, but he's a fucking prodigy in ways that make my chest swell with pride.

If he was mine, I'd show him off all the time.

He deserves it.

"Why are you looking at me like that?" Sem asks, peeking over at me.

I close my gaping mouth and sniff. I'm not ready to tell him what I was really thinking so I smirk and say, "You're hot. I'm horny. Think I can give you road head?"

Sem huffs with a smile. "Stop saying stupid shit, Maggie."

"How is it stupid? I'm small enough. I could fit right there between your legs, and we both know I'm very good with my mouth."

He glances down at his lap and shifts in his seat. "Nah, too dangerous. Wouldn't risk you like that."

I sigh dramatically, biting back a smile. "Fine, big guy. But you'll let me go down on you while you drive one day. Just you wait."

We make it to Sem's parent's house later than planned because of traffic. Oh, the joys of living in the city, I think as Sem navigates the motorhome down a long gravel driveway. In the distance, I can make out an older two-story house sitting in the middle of a large plot of land. On one side is a large garage and on the other is an array of four-wheel vehicles.

"Are you going to take me out in your Jeep?" I ask Sem.

"If you want to."

"Oh, I so do. Will you let me drive it?" I ask, looking through the windshield and catching sight of Sem's mom and dad on the porch. Caleb and Whit meander outside and lean against the railing.

"Sure. If your feet can reach the pedals."

I reach over and poke Sem, and he chuckles.

"Is that your older brother?" I ask, unbuckling and pointing to a man I don't recognize.

"Yeah. That's Liam, and the woman next to him is his wife, Anne," Sem says and then stands up, grabbing my hand. He pulls me into him, running his cheek against the top of my head.

"Fuck, that was torture," he mutters, his hands splayed across my back.

"What was?" I ask.

"Thinking of you between my legs the entire trip."

I snicker and nip at his chest. "Serves you right. A man has no right to be this sexy. I've been hard all day."

He glances down at my crotch and huffs. "Later. We'll take care of that later. If we stay in here any longer, they'll come for us."

I glance out the windshield and then slip my hand into his.

"Can we hold hands in front of them?"

Sem swallows and nods. "Yeah, they all know how I feel about you."

"Oh, do they now?" I ask, propping my chin on my fist. "Pray tell."

"Later, Maggie."

I roll my eyes, hating the suspense, but let him lead me out of the RV anyways.

"Look who it is! Fucker finally came home," Liam says as we approach them. All eyes turn toward me, and then they all swivel down to where Sem's holding my hand.

"Can see why you stayed away," Liam says, and his wife, Anne, smacks him on the back of his head. She's shorter than him, so she has to really reach up there to get a good swat in. I like her already.

"Shut up," she says and then walks over to me, pulling me into a tight hug.

"I've heard so much about you. Sem hasn't shut up about you since he first laid eyes on you. This guy never speaks, and then it was *blah, blah, blah. Magnus this, Magnus that.*"

I blush and pat her back as she pulls away from me. Her eyes twinkle, and she glances up at Sem.

"He says you're his muse," she whispers, and Sem's cheeks pinken.

"I told you that in secret," he grumbles and then reaches over and picks her up into a tight bear hug.

She laughs as he crushes her under his arms, and then Sem's mom, Del, approaches. We've met once. She'd given me her number and insisted I call if Sem caused me any trouble.

I'd never used it.

Looking back, I think I secretly liked how he followed me around.

"Hi, hon," she says and pulls me into her arms. "So good to see you again." Then she lowers her voice and softly says, "He's so happy," and I melt a little.

Because yeah, I think he is.

"Alright, enough of this," Luke announces, coming around the corner, with a large box cradled in his arms. "I've waited all day for you to get here, Sem. You took your sweet ass time. Ready to go blow shit up?"

Whit sighs heavily next to Caleb, who is leaning against his chest. "You are not going with them," he mutters, and Caleb turns his head and presses his lips to Whit's.

"Come on, babe. We've already discussed this. Live a little."

"I live plenty with you and die a little each time you come home hurt."

Caleb's eyes turn to mush, and he nuzzles into Whit's neck. "Babe. I'll be fine. I promise. It'll be fun. These are the illegal kind, everyone knows they're the best."

"And that's supposed to inspire confidence?" Whit mutters.

I bite back a giggle and look at Sem whose head is bent, shuffling through the box in Luke's arms. "This all you bought? That's not enough, man."

Whit huffs and grumbles, "It looks like plenty to me."

"Fuck no. Do you have any faith in me?" Luke says. "I have an entire truck's worth. We have probably enough for a few hours. Unless the cops come. Then we'll have to finish off the rest tomorrow."

"Oh my god," Whit breathes, and I have to lock my knees to stop myself from rolling.

Liam slaps Sem on the back as he strides around them. "Let's go, assholes! No time to waste. The night is still young. I'll drive with you, baby bro."

Luke jogs after Liam as they make their way down the driveway toward an idling truck. As I squint in the fading evening light, I can see it piled high with fireworks.

"Be safe," Anne calls to her retreating husband and then disappears back into the house with Del.

Sem turns to me, grabbing onto the back of my neck and squeezing lightly.

I glance up at him, and he brushes a knuckle against my cheek. "Ready to go?"

I bite my bottom lip and nod, tucking my hand into Sem's and walking with him toward the garage on the other end of the property.

"What's in here?" I ask.

"The ATVs. We'll take those out there. Gotta get far enough away from the house. Ma almost killed us last time a projectile blew out a window."

"That did not really happen," I gasp.

"Yeah, it did. She was pissed."

Footsteps approach from behind, and I can hear Whit saying to Caleb, "You're not driving. I am."

I tilt my head toward Sem and ask, "Can I drive?"

"If you want."

"Oh, I so want."

"You know how?"

"No, but I am very teachable."

Sem and I approach the garage, and he leans down and pulls the metal door open. It rolls up with a clash, and then Sem pulls a set of keys from the wall, tossing a pair to Caleb.

"Race you there," Sem tells Caleb, who chuckles and slides onto the back of an ATV.

"Nah, you go on ahead. Whit's driving. You know how he gets."

Whit straddles the ATV, and Caleb presses his body against his. "Yes, because I'll be driving there *safely*. You might have nine lives, Caleb, but you've used eight of them already."

"Babe," Caleb mutters and licks at his neck.

Okay, enough of that, I think as I turn my gaze back to Sem, who is patting the seat of the ATV.

"Come on, Maggie. Get that tiny ass over here."

I slide on in front of him, and he pulls me into his hard muscular chest, pressing a kiss to my neck.

"Let me get it out of here, and then you can drive it, yeah?"

"Okay, yeah."

He places the key in the ignition and turns it. The ATV roars to life, and Sem expertly maneuvers it out of the garage. He stops it, and it idles.

"Alright," he says, slowly instructing me how to shift it into first and get it moving. I do exactly as he says, and it lurches forward. I would have gone flying off if it wasn't for Sem, clutching me tightly with his thighs.

"Shit!" he shouts as he grabs onto my hands and helps me slow it down.

He's breathing heavily as Caleb and Whit slowly drive by.

"Suckers!" Caleb shouts as they pass, and Sem flips him off before taking my hands off the bars.

"Alright, Maggie. Not so crazy, yeah? I'd like to make it to the fireworks show alive."

I arch an eyebrow at him. "Oh, you want to make it there alive so you can then proceed to blow yourself up?"

He shakes his head at me and then helps me put it in gear and lightly gives it some gas. His hands rest on top of mine, and I honestly don't mind it. I like being close to him in every way.

"Faster," I say as we pass Whit and Caleb, who are still plugging along.

Sem bites down on my earlobe and then revs the engine, and I squeal as we take off into the darkness.

"Oh my god. Slow down!" I squeal as we bounce over ruts and our tires spin. Sem's hands clutch mine tightly over the handlebars, and he chuckles darkly in my ear.

Fuck, this is fun. I need to get me one of these.

An explosion lights up the sky, and I glance up.

"Oh my god," I say as Sem slows the ATV down. In the distance, I can see Luke and Liam lighting off fireworks.

"They couldn't wait?" I ask.

"They have no patience. Seems like you'll fit in just fine here," Sem says.

I nudge him with my elbow as Sem helps me maneuver the ATV a safe distance away. Then he picks me up off the seat, pressing a hand to the back of my neck and leading me forward.

"So, are the cops really going to show up?" I ask as a few more burst from the ground and explode in the sky.

Sem shrugs. "Possibly."

"Oh my god."

I'm starting to realize that Whit wasn't joking, especially as Liam and Luke start laughing maniacally in the distance.

"They're planning something, aren't they?" I ask.

Sem grins down at me. "Probably."

A headlight lights up the ground behind us, and I turn around as Whit and Caleb leisurely approach on their ATV.

"Oh, hell yes," Caleb says excitedly. "Did Luke get the jumbo skyrockets? Because I've been dying to see how those explode."

"I'm glad I grabbed the first aid kit," Whit replies dryly as Caleb smacks a kiss on Whit's cheek and bounds off.

Sem watches his cousin's retreating figure and then turns his gaze to Whit, holding out his fist. They bump it, and then he nods toward where Luke, Liam, and Caleb are talking animatedly.

"Hurry the fuck up, Sem!" Liam shouts.

"I should probably go out there. You coming?" Sem asks me. I look at the rockets and then back at Whit.

"How about you go and I'll stay with Whit for a bit. I'd like to see how dangerous this is from afar."

Sem's eyebrows bunch, and then he nods. "I'll keep you safe."

I run a hand over his chest and fist his shirt, tugging him down.

"I know. You always do." I press a kiss to his mouth and then demand, "Don't you fucking die or burn off any important body parts. Like your fingers, or your pretty face, or your dick."

He licks his lips and exhales deeply. "You got it, Maggie."

When I let go of his shirt, he strides away, and Whit moves to stand next to me.

"You made the right choice. It's safest back here."

"I'm starting to see that." I nudge him lightly with my elbow. "You're dying a little inside, aren't you?"

He sighs. "Yes. I usually do when I'm out here."

"They'll be okay, right?" I ask.

"God, I hope so." We stand in silence for a moment, and then he side-eyes me. "So, you and Sem, huh?"

"Yeah."

"That was...unexpected."

"I know. I didn't see it coming. But then again, I didn't see you and Caleb coming either. Sometimes things just...happen."

Whit tucks his dark hair behind his ear and nods. "That it does."

Then the ground suddenly quakes beneath us, and Whit shakes his head, his face paling slightly. "Oh, Jesus."

In the distance, Sem jabs a giant rocket into the ground. Luke pulls out a....

"Is that...is that a flamethrower?" I ask, but Whit just taps his fingers nervously on his folded arms and sighs.

The wick begins to ignite, and then all four of them shout, running away as fast as they can, their eyes wild with glee. And to be honest, my heart drops a little because they don't move nearly far back enough when the rocket launches into the air and explodes into a burst of color.

"I need a drink," Whit mutters next to me. "Ten maybe. Perhaps if I'm passed out, I won't have to bear witness to this...."

"I think I know what you mean," I say, eyeing him.

He looks down at me with a small smile. "Glad you're here, Magnus. At least now I have someone to share this insanity with."

"Heh. Me too," I reply as another explosion shakes the ground. I swallow roughly as I see Luke spinning the flamethrower in his hand and pretending to holster it like he's a cowboy and then frown when I see Sem standing much too close to it.

"Be honest. On a scale of one to ten, how hurt will they get."

Whit shakes out his arms and then sighs. "Twenty. But there's no stopping them. It's best to just let them do what they want and...pray."

"Oh my God, Sem," I gasp, watching as Sem makes his way toward me, blood dripping down his face, and I reach out and grab onto his chin, tilting it to see the damage.

Luke and Liam stride up behind us, grinning like fiends. A burn covers part of Luke's wrist, and Liam has singed off part of his hair. Caleb looks primarily intact, except for a scraped knee from tripping on a rock as he ran away from a wayward firework.

Whit's already fussing with him, shooting him withering looks. Caleb just sits back and lets Whit tend to his wound, enjoying the pampering far too much.

Sem looks down at me with a giant smile, and I roll my eyes.

"It was cool, right?" he asks. "You have to admit it was."

"Yes, until you blew yourself up. What is wrong with you?" I ask, holding up the gauze that Whit had wordlessly handed me as soon as we saw the disaster that was about to strike.

"Hey, nothing's wrong with him!" Luke shouts. "That was epic. Worth every penny."

"Oh my god," Whit grumbles, and Caleb and Sem chuckle.

I press the clean gauze to Sem's open face wound and then poke him in the chest.

"That was reckless...."

He grabs onto my hand and pulls me up against him. "Yeah, but it was cool. Admit it."

I huff, and then a small smile breaks across my face. "Fine. It was cool *at times*, but never again, Sem."

"Nah, I can't promise that."

"Fine, then at least don't use a flamethrower next time. How was that a good idea?"

"It was Sem's idea," Luke yells as he jumps into his truck with Liam. They speed past us, dust flying up around their tires as they disappear into the darkness.

"Your idea, huh?"

Sem rolls his lips between his teeth and smirks.

Jesus, this man is going to be the death of me.

Sem's wound is bleeding profusely when we finally arrive

home, and I glare at him. Blood drips down his temple and disappears beneath the fabric of his shirt.

"You didn't hold the gauze to the wound?"

He shrugs. "I was driving."

"Seriously, we need to clean that. Right now. You're going to have a scar."

"That going to bug you, if I have a scar on my face?"

I envision it and then shake my head. "Of course not. It will be annoyingly sexy."

When Sem smirks, I hold out my finger. "Do not get any more ideas into that head of yours. No more scars. No more getting hurt."

We make our way inside the house and see Sem's mom fussing over Luke while his dad fist bumps his son. His dad's hand is promptly smacked away, and then his mom's eyes meet Sem's, and she frowns.

"I'm glad none of you ruined our vacation by being idiots," she says sharply. "If I had to spend the Fourth of July in the hospital, I would have disowned you all...except Whit. I would have kept him. And Magnus. I'll keep you too."

"Sorry, Ma," Sem mutters, and then fist bumps his dad as he walks to the sink and wets a paper towel, handing it to me.

"I'm sorry. What's this?" I ask, holding the paper towel in my hand. Smudges of dirt line it from Sem's hands as I hold it between my two fingers.

"To clean the..." he motions to his face, and I raise an eyebrow at him.

"No, absolutely not. We're getting the first aid kit, and we're cleaning the shit out of that. I'm not patting it with this dirty paper towel. What is wrong with you? You'll get an infection."

His mom looks at me with a small smile, and I grin back. Then promptly let it fall as I point to a chair.

"Now, sit."

Sem does as he's told. After I patch him up and the rest of the guys are put back together, we move to the firepit outside, which Sem's dad has started using the flamethrower.

Of course, that's where they all get it. Apparently, the firebug apples don't fall far from the pyro tree.

It's much too hot to sit close to the flames, so we all drag the chairs farther away and lower ourselves into them. I try to sit in my own, but Sem just wraps an arm around my waist and pulls me into his lap.

At least I'm not the only one. Anne's on Liam's lap, fussing with his singed hair, and Caleb's on Whit's, looking blissed out. Luke's all alone, but he doesn't seem to mind. He's just sipping on a beer, picking a little at the gauze that wraps around the burn on his wrist.

"So, you guys packed your gear?" Luke asks, and Sem and Caleb nod.

"What gear?" I ask, looking back at Sem.

"Climbing gear."

"I'm sorry. You climb? Like mountains?"

"Yeah, tiny. You will too."

Before I can protest, because I've never climbed a thing in my entire life, except for Sem of course, Luke asks, "And the guns?"

"Yeah, bro. Got them all. Dad even has extra guns packed for Whit and Maggie," Sem replies, and Whit shakes his head as Caleb whispers something into his ear.

"He hates guns," Sem says, and I lean back further into him, letting him wrap his arms around my waist and holding me tightly against him. "But you'll try it, right? You said you would."

"Yeah, as long as it's nothing too dangerous. I don't want to actually die by a gunshot wound."

"Nah," he says as he presses a kiss to my neck, and I sigh contentedly at the feeling of his lips against my skin.

"So, how long have you two been together?" Anne asks me, and my eyes swivel to her. Everyone's looking at us now, and Sem grunts behind me.

"I'm not...I don't know if we've discussed...." I begin, but Sem just presses a finger to my mouth, shutting me up.

"He's mine."

Anne watches us with amusement and then says, "I know that, Sem. We've all known that for months, but how long have you two been...together. I need all the details."

My face burns as everyone watches us and I roll my lips between my teeth. Sem shifts beneath me.

"For a while."

"Ah," Anne says, and Sem's mom smiles widely at us.

"Is it serious?" Del asks and then adds, "I've been dying for grandbabies...."

"Del," Sem's dad chastises, and she huffs in annoyance.

I peek over at Sem, who's fiddling with the end of my shorts, and he surprises me by saying, "Maggie wants at least six kids."

Everyone's silent for a moment until Del whispers, "Praise the Lord."

I glare at Sem because we have not discussed what this is between us, and yet a small part of me is thrilled that maybe he wants more than whatever this is we're doing.

Jesus, I'm already half in love with the guy.

Luke swats his leg. "Enough of this serious shit. Everyone's getting fucked. Caleb, Mag, Anne. They're all happy as pie about it. Now that that's cleared up, can we move on to other important matters, like how Caleb just admitted to me mere minutes ago that he was, in fact, not a drug dealer in middle school. That the weed I bought off of him was, in fact, *not weed.*"

Caleb smiles widely and fist bumps Sem, who's chuckling.

"What was it then?" I ask.

Luke meets my gaze. "Oregano."

"You seriously told him it was pot?" I ask Caleb with a laugh.

"Yeah," Liam says. "He did. And this loser believed him."

"I was thirteen," Luke grumbles. "Didn't know any better."

My eyebrows rise. "And you smoked it?"

"I did. Got high as a kite too," Luke replies.

Whit huffs as he slides a hand up Caleb's shirt. "You cannot get high off oregano. That's not a thing, Luke."

"How would you know? You ever tried it, Whit?" Luke quips, and Sem laughs again, taking a long sip of beer.

Oh my god. These people are seriously ridiculous. No wonder Sem turned out the way he did. They're like free-range, gun-toting criminals. It's the Upside Down out here.

The following morning, we wake up a little too late. I have zero incentive to move when Sem is curled up behind me, his hand tucked down my pants cupping my junk. I just lie there and rub against him until he blinks those blue eyes open.

"Best way to wake up," he grunts and then grabs a condom and slips inside of me. He takes his time, working me up and over the edge, and when we're both spent, lying in our mess, he nudges me.

"We better get moving."

"Meh," I mutter, and so he picks me up, carries me into the shower, and washes me clean.

After that, we lazily pack and drive the three hours up the mountain. It's cooler up here amongst the trees than the dry heat at the lower elevations, and it's a bit of a relief. I tend to wilt a bit in the summer heat so the cool breeze currently floating through our shaded campsite is entirely welcome.

I glance over my shoulder and see Sem bending over, and I can't help but check out his ass. Because, let me tell you, after our shower, he leaned over, and I slid that plug right between his cheeks. If he moves the right way, I can see the outline of it.

"Boo," Luke says in my ear, and I jump. The camping chair I was trying to unfold clatters to the ground.

"What is wrong with you? Do you enjoy frightening people?" I grumble, and Luke chuckles as he bends down and quickly unfolds the chair for me.

"Nah, just you. I like watching you jump. So, tiny, you going to come climbing with us once we're done setting up?"

I look over at Sem and shrug. "I don't know. Do you think I should? I've never done it before. What are the chances that I fall to my death?"

Luke pats my head, and I glower at him. "Nah. No dying today. Don't worry. I've gotchu. Sem would murder me if anything happened to you. Plus, I want to be the best man at your wedding."

"I don't know if we're...we haven't discussed that."

Luke scoffs. "Yeah, no need to discuss. You're getting married. Truth."

I suck my bottom lip into my mouth and then peek over at Sem, who is watching me converse with Luke.

I offer him a small wave, and he moves toward us.

"What's he saying to you?" Sem asks, pulling me into his side.

Luke points a thumb at his chest. "Just asking to be the best man at your wedding."

Sem fiddles with my earlobe. "Stop flirting with him first, and then maybe I'll consider you over Liam."

Luke gasps in faux shock and then smiles widely. "Fuck you, you jealous bastard. I'm not flirting with Mags. Stop being so insecure."

Sem glowers at his brother and then puts his hand on my lower back, leading me away from him.

"I wasn't flirting," I tell Sem, who only shrugs.

"I know."

"And he wasn't flirting with me."

Sem glances down at me. "I know."

I stop him and then reach up, tilting his head down until his gaze meets mine.

"I can still feel you inside of me. I can still taste you. Hear you. You've invaded all of my senses, Sem. I don't want anyone else but you. You have to know that."

Sem swallows and looks away, blinking rapidly. And then picks me up and presses his mouth to mine.

"You looked so hot climbing today," Sem says as he plays with my hair. I'm sprawled out on the mattress inside the RV. My arms feel like limp noodles, and my fingers ache from climbing only halfway up the rock face. Now I know why Sem is so muscular. He does shit like climb up entire mountains for fun. That's no joke.

"So did you."

"Nah, you looked like you belonged there. You were a natural. Like a little spider monkey. I knew you would be with the way you climb all over me," Sem replies, pulling his shirt over his head and pulling me into his bare chest. I let myself stare at it for a little too long, and Sem notices because he flexes, forcing his abs to pop out.

Showoff.

"I would have never tried climbing if it wasn't for you. So, thank you. I find myself constantly pushed out of my comfort zones when I'm with you."

Sem presses his face into my hair. "That a bad thing?"

"Nope. Not at all. I love it."

Sem sighs and then nibbles on my ear.

"Is there anything you can't do?" I ask.

"Read."

I glower up at him. "Who gives a crap about that. I can do that for you. You're plenty talented in other ways. You draw, you can build things out of nothing with your bare hands, you can surf, scale mountains...."

He licks his way across my neck.

"...cheat death. You are like a Marvel character. Who needs Thor when I have you?"

Sem glances down at me and presses a soft kiss to the tip of my nose.

"You're out of my league," he mutters.

"Um, no. That's entirely untrue. You are so far out of mine I'm holding on for dear life."

Sem's eyebrows bunch. "Nah, Maggie. For real. You are. You could have anyone...."

"I don't want anyone. I think we've established that."

"Have we?"

"Um. Yes. We have. I've told you so."

Sem looks unsure, so I bring my rubbery, sore arm up and stroke across his cheek.

"I haven't been with anyone since you, nor do I want to be with anyone else."

"Same."

"Good, so how about this," I begin, tapping against his full bottom lip. "How about you and I label what this is between us."

"What do you mean?"

"I mean...let's be boyfriends."

Sem rears back a little, his eyes wide, and for a second, I wonder if he's disgusted with the idea. My heart stops, but then he utters, "Boyfriends?"

"Yeah. Is that too much for you? I know you haven't really come to terms with your sexuality...."

He shakes his head. "Nah, I think I'm bi. I mean, I must be."

"Is that so?"

He nods.

"Hm, okay, so since that's kind of sorted, what's the problem?"

"Why would you..." He clears his throat. "Why would you want to be my boyfriend?"

I narrow my eyes at him. "Are you serious?"

When he just nods, I clasp his hands with mine, threading our fingers together.

"Do I need to tell you all the ways I think you're exceptional?"

"Maybe," he says shyly, and I thread my fingers through his

hair and pull his face closer to mine. Good lord, this man is adorable.

"Fine, I'll tell you what makes you extraordinary and I'll tell you every single day until you believe them yourself. Shall I start now?"

Sem wets his lips and nods.

Oh, my heart.

CHAPTER TWELVE

The next morning, we go to a local shooting range, and I watch Sem and Luke unload their rifles at the wooden targets in the distance with excessive enthusiasm.

"Freedom, baby!" Luke shouts, his cackles echoing between the bouts of gunfire.

Sem grins widely next to him as shells litter the ground.

It should not be hot, but it is so hot.

My boyfriend is a maniac and I love it.

Sem takes his time to explain everything to me when it's my turn, and when I finally take aim and hit the target, Sem looks mighty proud.

I puff up a little.

"This is turning you on, huh?" I ask with a raised eyebrow.

Sem just subtly adjusts himself in his pants.

After lunch, Del ushers us outside for a hike. Luke, Liam, and Caleb are roughhousing as they jog down the trailhead and are almost out of sight as I glance down at my Converse.

"I was not prepared for this," I say.

"Want me to carry you?" Sem asks, stepping up next to me and grasping the back of my neck. He squeezes it lightly, and I stare at him with a small smile.

"Absolutely not," I reply and then look over at Del, who's approaching from the right.

She lifts her hands and motions for Sem to move along.

"Go on, Sem. No need to hang back here. I'd like to chat with your man," Del says, and Sem looks down at me, brushing a finger over my cheek. He seems reluctant to leave me alone.

"I'll be fine. I said I wasn't prepared for this, not that I can't do it."

He looks unsure, but after another second, he nods and jogs forward, slapping his brothers on the back as he rushes past. I watch that round ass and muscular legs for a little too long, then turn with flushed cheeks to face Sem's mother, who's watching me with twinkling eyes.

"I'm glad you could make it this weekend," Del tells me as we make our way slowly down the path. I can feel every bit of rock against the soles of my feet. I'm going to be sore tomorrow. "Sem was so excited when you agreed to join us. He even called and told me."

My mind conjures up images of what Sem was doing to me the day I agreed to go camping with him, and my cheeks burn hotter. "Yeah, I'm glad I could make it. It's been a lot of fun."

Del looks at me with a kind, open face and then leans toward me. "I know you and Sem got off to a rocky start."

"Yes, well, it was an unconventional beginning, I admit," I begin, clearing my throat. "But the more time I spent with him, the more I got to know what an exceptional man he is."

Del reaches out and squeezes my arm lightly. "He is wonderful, isn't he? Though, he struggles to see it."

My brow furrows at that. "I know. It blows my mind. I mean, he's incredibly talented. He has to know that. I've seen his drawings and his woodworking. He's amazing."

Del beams at me. "It's true." And then her smile fades. "But, you should know he had a tough time as a kid. He was bullied a lot growing up. He's not traditionally smart like his brother Liam. He struggled so much in school. Broke my heart."

"He was bullied?" I ask with raised eyebrows. The way he'd reacted to my father and brother, the man in the bathroom, it all makes so much more sense now.

"Yes, it was pretty consistent until he grew taller than them all. Liam and Luke were fierce protectors, but they couldn't shelter him from it all. And then, when he got older, he tried to compensate for his inadequacies by being incredibly reckless. Got himself into a lot of trouble and got kicked out of school. Had to finish high school in a continuation program."

"I never knew."

"He's probably embarrassed to share it. He always talks about how smart you are."

"I'm not that smart."

"To him, you are. He thinks you're brilliant. And I worry…."

I lean toward her, needing her to spit it out. "What?"

"I worry that he feels inadequate around you. Like he doesn't deserve you."

Our earlier conversations filter back into my mind, and I inhale shakily. Oh my god, the things I'd said to him about my dream guy.

"I had no idea he felt that way, but I promise I won't ever

let him feel like that. I'll tell him how amazing he is every day until he believes it."

I press a hand against my aching chest and look forward. I see Sem glancing back at me, looking worried. I just wave at him and force out a smile, and he relaxes instantly.

"He's very protective of you," Del remarks, and I nod, swallowing the lump in my throat.

"Yeah, he is."

"He's careless at times and a little wild, but he's loyal. *Incredibly loyal*. He will never, ever do anything to hurt you."

"I know." My heart expands in my chest, and I inhale shakily.

"Once he makes up his mind about something, he has difficulty letting go..." Del stops walking and grabs onto my hands. "Magnus, tell me you'll love him like he deserves. He has such a tender heart. I hate seeing it broken."

My eyes are stinging, and I swallow roughly. "I'll do my best. I promise."

I can see Sem jogging toward us out of the corner of my eye, and Del quickly lets go of my hands.

"What's wrong?" Sem asks, his eyes moving from my watery eyes to his mom. "What did you say, Ma?"

Del looks a little sheepish. "Nothing you need to know about."

Sem crouches down and looks at me. "What did she say, Maggie?"

"Nothing, Sem." I reach over and stroke a hand down his cheek, and his eyelids flutter. "I'm fine. Just got a little emotional. I'm okay."

He grumbles something under his breath, and then he points to his back. "Come on. Hop on."

I snort, swiping at my eyes. "Sem, I'm not riding on your back like a child."

He glances up at me. "I carry you all the time."

Del smiles widely at the two of us and then waves her hands at us. "Go on, Magnus. Go ahead. I don't mind walking alone for a bit. I might even turn around in a bit and head back. I need to make sure my husband isn't doing something irresponsible."

"We are not leaving your mom to walk alone," I protest, and Sem huffs still crouched in front of me.

"But you're too slow."

"This is not new information," I reply. "I was never very athletic."

"Hm, but you are flexible," Sem says with a wink and then reaches his arms out behind him, and I roll my eyes and climb on. Because he won't let me continue walking, apparently.

"I am flexible because I do yoga. You know what, Sem, you should come with me sometime. Try it out and see what you think."

He stands up and readjusts me on his back.

"Yeah, maybe I will."

I lean forward and whisper, "Then I can check out your ass. My *boyfriend's* fine ass."

He huffs and begins walking, his mom trailing behind us.

When we've put enough space between his mother and us, Sem looks over his shoulder and asks, "What did she tell you?"

I press my mouth against the side of his neck and press a soft kiss there. "She's just concerned about you. She wanted to make sure I don't end up hurting you."

"Jesus, that woman meddles."

"She just loves you and she's worried. Apparently, you're a big softie. Who knew?"

Sem grumbles something under his breath, and I lick my way up to his ear and nibble on it.

"Stop that," he grunts. "I'm getting hard."

I giggle and do it again.

"You little shit," he mutters. He starts running, his powerful body shifting underneath mine. I hold on tighter, a laugh escaping my mouth as we approach the rest of our group in the distance.

And we just barrel past them.

They holler at us as we move farther and farther away, and when I can no longer see them, Sem veers off the trail and into the woods.

"Oh, are you going to tie me up to a tree and fuck me?" I tease. "You have some of those Ted Bundy zip ties with you?"

Sem chuckles darkly, and I swallow because damn, maybe he will do that. Why does that turn me on so much?

Suddenly he stops, and his hands move away from my legs. I slide down his back, but just as my feet hit the ground, he's on me, picking me up and pressing me against the trunk of a tree. My legs wrap around his waist as his mouth descends on mine. I open for him, letting my tongue slip into his mouth as he growls against me.

When he reaches into his pocket and pulls out a condom and a small packet of lube, I arch an eyebrow at him. "Seriously, Sem? On a hike?"

"I'm always prepared."

"Were you a Boy Scout too?" I ask.

"Nah, just always horny for you."

I snort and then unbutton my pants. Whatever. No use in pretending. I'm so ready for it.

Needless to say, we make it to camp long after everyone is already back, and my ass aches, and my back stings. Tree burn is a thing.

Everyone watches us with amused glances, and my face flames because it's obvious where we disappeared to.

"Got some, huh, bro?" Luke asks loudly, slapping Sem on the back as he walks past.

Sem just tightens his hand over mine and grumbles, "None of your business, asshole."

His dad calls Sem over to help make dinner, and I grab a beer and sink down on a chair next to Whit. He eyes me with a raised eyebrow, and I roll my eyes. "Do *not* look at me like that. It's obnoxious."

He huffs. "This is how I normally look."

"No, you're judging me, but don't tell me you wouldn't have done the same thing if Caleb took you out into the woods...."

His gaze turns toward his fiancé, and a slight smile pulls at his lips. "I do have a hard time saying no to him."

A snort escapes me, "Yeah, so I've heard."

After a moment of silence, he says, "You fit in here with them."

"You think?"

"Yeah, I always knew you were a little...unusual."

I snort. "So are you, asshole."

Whit eyes me again and then says, "So are you going to share how this started with you two?"

I clear my throat and wonder if I should fib a little but then decide against it. Because really, who cares how it started. What matters is the ending, right?

"Well, Sem broke into my house and dared me to fuck him."

Whit freezes, that dark gaze of his sliding to meet mine. "You're joking."

"No, he literally showed up at my house and said I couldn't...you know. And I got all competitive. You know how I get...."

One eyebrow goes up, and he just stares at me. I squirm in my seat. Jesus, this guy has a way of making me nervous.

He should work for the FBI.

"That's weird, even for you."

"Yeah, well, it all worked out, didn't it?"

Whit glances over at Sem, who's watching us talk. A beer dangles from his hand as he leans against the side of Luke's RV, chatting with his brother. He doesn't remove his gaze from us, and I slightly shift in my seat.

"He doesn't like you talking to me," Whit says.

"Really? Why do you think that?" I ask, slightly unconvinced.

"Does he know we were together for a while?" Whit asks.

"Yeah."

"And he seems possessive of you...."

"Well, yes, he is, but he'll have to get used to us talking because you're marrying Caleb. And I plan on sticking around for a while, so...."

Whit takes a sip of his water and then lowers his voice and leans toward me a little. "I've been meaning to ask you..." He clears his throat and then asks, "Would you stand up on my side for the wedding?"

My eyes widen at that because I was not expecting that at all. "Are you serious? Like the best man?"

He huffs. "Don't get so excited...."

"Oh, Whit, I already am. I'm going to be your best man!"

Whit taps his fingers on his thigh. "Please, keep it down. It's not that big of a deal."

I bounce a little in my seat and then lean toward him, "Ooh. What are your colors? Have you discussed that? Flower arrangements? Where's the venue?"

Whit's rubbing at his chest, looking nervous.

"Ooh, can I throw you a wedding shower? Please, please?" I grab onto his arm and squeeze. "I happen to be fabulous at party planning."

He glances down at where our bodies connect, and I quickly pull my hand away. "Sorry. I got a little too excited about this. I am very happy for you two."

"It's okay. And perhaps you should speak to Caleb and his aunt about the wedding. They know all the details."

"Oh my god, I cannot wait. Who else is in it?"

"Luke, Liam, and Sem," Whit begins and then adds, "I only have you."

"Oh, Whit," I say softly, resisting the urge to reach out and touch him. "I'm sorry. Your family sucks, and you deserve so much better."

He swallows and nods. "I do, but it seems I've found another...slightly unconventional family who enjoys having me around."

"Don't be silly. They love you."

"They tolerate me," Whit mutters, and I roll my eyes.

"You're such an Eeyore. They love you, Whit. I promise. They're happy Caleb is so in love with a wonderful man. I mean, just look at him over there. He can't keep his eyes off you. It's like he wants to come bounding over here and sit on your lap."

Whit huffs, his fingers tapping nervously on the arm of the camping chair.

"He does, doesn't he?"

I giggle loudly, and out of the corner of my eye, I can see Sem moving away from the grill where his brother and dad are barbequing. A frown mars his face as he watches me laugh with Whit.

"Seems someone is jealous," Whit says and then raises an eyebrow at Sem, who stares at the two of us.

"He has literally nothing to worry about."

"Does he know that?"

"I don't know how many more times I need to tell him."

"Seems you need to go reassure him. This is still new to him," Whit tells me and then nods to where Sem's standing.

Part of me wants Sem to come to me, but I push myself up and walk toward him. His eyes watch me approach, and when I'm able to reach out and touch him, I slide my hands up under his shirt and push myself up against him.

I crane my neck up and glance at Sem, who's watching me warily.

"You have nothing to worry about," I say softly, his mother's words echoing in my mind.

Sem's gaze flits over behind me to where Whit lounges, and then his eyes flash back to meet mine.

"Seriously, Sem. Stop it." I nip at his chest, and he threads a hand through my hair. Then I'm in his arms, and his mouth is on mine, and before I can protest, he's walking us back to his RV.

He pushes open the door and I cling to him as he makes his way inside.

"What's going on, Sem?" I ask. "What's wrong?"

"I want to show you something," he says gruffly as he locks the door and deposits me on the RV table. My legs dangle above the floor, and I lean back as he disappears into the bedroom. He comes back minutes later with a stack of papers cradled in his hands.

His cheeks are red, and he shoves them at me. "Here."

"What's this?" I ask, my heart thundering. Because I *know* what they are.

Holy shit.

My eyes take in the first image staring up at me, and Sem swallows when I see my face staring back at me. It's drawn in such detail that I can even make out the smattering of freckles I have across the bridge of my nose.

"Sem," I breathe, my heart thundering in my chest. I turn to the next picture and see one of just my eyes and the bridge of my nose. The next is of me the night of the frat party weeks ago, my hands splayed across my chest, my shirt riding up my stomach, my shorts slung low on my narrow hips.

The next of me bent over for him the first time he entered me from behind.

He's captured me perfectly. In all these intricate and delicate drawings, I look beautiful.

Is this what he sees?

"Are they all of me?" I ask, moving through the rest, my heart expanding in my chest. There has to be at least fifty pages of sketches here, maybe more.

"Yeah," he says quietly, shifting nervously on his feet in front of me.

"Can I keep them?" I ask, meeting his blue gaze. Something swims in those depths that I can't read.

"Nah. I'm not ready to part with them yet."

My eyes are wet and my throat stings as I glance at another picture of me laughing, my head thrown back, my eyes shut in pure bliss.

"Why did you show them to me?"

"I want you to know...."

"Know what?"

"What you are to me."

I swallow the lump in my throat and sniffle a little. "When you came to my apartment that first time and we...had sex... why did you do that?"

"Because I wanted you. And I didn't know any other way to have you. I knew you were too good for me, but I went for it anyway."

"And the other times?"

"Because I was...fuck, I was addicted. *To you*. Once wasn't enough for me. I feel like I will never get enough."

I swipe at my eyes, then set the drawings down and launch myself into his arms.

"I'm so glad you did," I whisper and press my lips to his.

Two weeks later

"So how is it, being boyfriends with Sem?" August asks as I sit down next to him at the picnic table. Today we're at the park with our classes, letting the kids run around outside. The heat is overbearing, and I've found solace in some shade.

"Amazing," I say with a small smile. I bite into my sandwich and sigh. "He's a very attentive guy."

August glances at me. "So, no more Colin?"

"Oh, no. Colin is old news. We're just friends. I guess I had this idea in my head of who I wanted, but it turns out I was wrong. Sem...he's...perfect. For me. He's everything I want."

August doesn't look convinced, but I ignore him. I know it's surprising, but I couldn't be happier.

"You in love with him?" he asks.

I glance at him and feel my cheeks heat. "How could I not be? I'm not sure how he feels about me, but sometimes the way he looks at me...I feel like he could. But I don't want to push him. He'll open up when he's ready."

August nods and then pulls me into a hug. "Happy for you, man."

"Me too. Hey, you going to tell me how things are going with Emery?"

August side-eyes me and shakes his head. "Nothing new to report. Just the same old. He enjoys being an annoying shit to me, and I do my best to ignore him."

"Can't ignore him forever."

"Don't remind me. My mom's already rented a cabin for us to spend a week in this January."

"And that's a problem because?"

"Because I'm going to be trapped in the mountains with him. I'm not sure I can fake it for that long. He bugs the shit out of me."

I snort and then elbow him. "I would love to be a fly on the wall for that."

August glowers at me, and I smile. "You can call me anytime, and I'll talk you off the ledge. It's only a week. You can manage."

"Not sure I can. You know what he did the other day?"

I arch an eyebrow. "Tell me."

August lowers his voice and then leans closer to me. "I found him in my room. On my laptop."

My eyes widen. "What was he doing on there?"

"He was looking at my browser history."

"Why would he do that?"

"No idea. I didn't ask. Just grabbed my laptop and tried my best to not strangle him."

"Sounds like you should delete your history then. Don't want him finding all your filthy porn sites."

August grabs my bag of chips and tears it open. "Thanks for that, friend. You're a real help."

He stuffs one into his mouth and chews as I pull him into a hug. "I'm sorry. I know you don't like him. But you're a good man. One of the best. You'll get through this."

"Not sure if I can. My mom and his dad always make excuses for him because of his past, but I think it's all just a fucking joke to him. I can't imagine it was really that bad."

I nibble on my bottom lip. "August, you know kids in foster care have it rough, right? I mean, we work with them. I don't think Emery is making it up."

August runs a hand through his hair and sighs. "Damn, you're right. I just wish I knew. But no one talks about it. Maybe if I knew what he went through I'd have some sympathy, you know?"

"Maybe one day you'll find out."

August shrugs. "Maybe. All I can hope is that once our parents marry, I'll never have to see him again."

We sit in silence for a moment, and my phone dings.

"Who is it?" August asks.

"Colin," I say and then glance up at my best friend. "Remember all those days ago when he asked me to work on that vlog with him. Apparently, the dean approved it, and he wants to know if I'm still interested in helping."

"You want to?"

I shift in my seat and glance over at the kids playing on the playground. "Kind of. I need to talk to Sem about it first."

"You think he'd stop you?"

I shake my head. "No, I don't think so. I don't want him to feel insecure about me spending time with Colin, especially since he knows how I felt about Colin before."

"Let me know how it goes."

"I will."

That evening as I sit on the kitchen table watching Sem cook for me, I internally go over what I'm going to tell Sem.

"Why you looking at me like that?" Sem asks, turning to face me.

"Look like what?" I ask.

"Like you've got something to say."

I roll my eyes. "Stop reading me."

Sem bites his lower lip. "Can't help it. I spent months memorizing you."

My feet hit the ground as I move toward him. Plucking the spoon from his hand, I set it on the counter and climb up him.

"God, I like you," I mutter, pressing a kiss to his mouth. "Let's fuck."

Sem pushes his tongue into my mouth, and we make out for a few minutes before he pulls away.

"You're trying to distract me," he says, pressing his forehead against mine and breathing heavily.

"No, I'm just horny watching you in the kitchen."

"Tell me what you want to tell me," Sem says, his hands flexing against my ass.

I sigh. "Fine, but first, I want to say that your feelings are valid, and I am open to compromise...."

"Just fucking tell me. You're making me nervous," Sem mutters, and I grab onto his chin, making sure he looks into my eyes.

"Nothing to be nervous about."

He wets his lips, and I press my thumb to his mouth.

"Colin texted me."

Sem's eyes narrow, and I can feel him shift me closer to him.

"He wants me to work with him on a series of videos. I haven't responded yet, because I want to ask you what you think about it first."

Sem breathes deeply, and then he says softly, "You do what you want, Maggie. I'm not going to hold you back."

"You aren't holding me back, but your feelings are valid, like I said."

He swallows and looks away from me. "I think you should do it."

Cocking my head, I watch him, how he inhales deeply and how his Adam's apple bobs. He doesn't like me making plans with Colin, but he'll never say it. I can tell he bottles everything up inside until one day he'll just keel over from a heart attack from the stress of it all.

"I really think you should do it, Maggie."

My heart swells in my chest with love for this man. He's always putting my needs first.

"How about," I say, pressing a kiss to his cheek, "Colin and I meet here...only when you're around."

Sem peeks over at me, his fingers flexing against me.

"Okay."

"You have to know by now that I want only you."

He swallows. "Yeah."

"How about you put dinner on hold, and I show you how much I want you."

Sem hardens beneath me, and I smirk.

He can never say no to me.

CHAPTER THIRTEEN

SEM

The glow from the computer makes my eyes water but fuck it all. I need to figure out what this stuff means.

My fingers type in the word, and I bite back a curse, deleting it and starting over.

There, now it's right.

I blink at the sentence and read it once, twice, and then three times before my brain can process it.

Fuck, I think, rubbing at my jaw. I'm such a fucking idiot.

Just watching Colin and Maggie talk to each other today made me feel small. I didn't understand anything they were talking about in their vlog. Not a damn word.

It shouldn't really matter but I'm terrified I'm not smart enough for Maggie. That he'll eventually get bored with me and leave.

I'm always telling Maggie to not let anyone make him feel

anything other than perfect, but I think I need to give myself that pep talk because I felt like shit hours ago.

"Hey," Maggie says, leaning against the wall, a blanket thrown over his slight shoulders. "What are you doing?"

I should be shutting down the browser, but I can't tear my eyes away from him.

He moves toward me, letting the blanket fall to the ground, and wraps his arms around my shoulders.

My cheeks flame as he takes in what's on the screen. I should have hidden it, but I didn't.

"Baby," he says softly, tilting my face, forcing my eyes to meet his. "This is where you sneak off to at night?"

I swallow and look away.

"Hey," he says, moving to straddle my thighs. "Hey."

His hands frame my face, and his thumbs brush against my cheeks. "Why didn't you tell me?"

"Didn't want to."

He presses a soft kiss to my mouth, and I can't help but open up to him.

"God, could you be any more perfect?" he asks, licking inside of me.

My chest swells at those words, and I let them sink into me. He's always complimenting me. I love it. I'm growing used to it. I crave it.

"You have to know I like you just the way you are...you don't need to do this. You don't need to know this stuff. It's not important. You're important. We're what's important."

He gestures at the computer screen, and I roll my lips between my teeth. "I want to learn."

"Yeah? Okay, then I can teach you. Why don't you ask me, and I can help you?"

"Don't want to bother you."

"Hey, you're not a bother. I want to be a teacher, Sem. Let me teach you. You teach me all about shooting and mountain climbing. Fuck, you teach me all kinds of things. Let me help you in return."

My eyes fucking sting. I blink rapidly. Shit. He's watching me intently, and I know he sees. He has to. I don't even know if I want to hide it anymore.

"Okay."

Maggie hums under his breath, and he presses that sweet mouth to mine, his tongue moving against mine, and I can't help but pull him in closer to me. His stiff, thin cock brushes against mine, and I gasp into his mouth. He tastes so sweet and eager. He nearly vibrates with it.

How does this never get old? I've never had so much sex in my life.

I stand up and carry him to the room, setting him gently onto the bed.

He blinks up at me, drunk on us.

Reaching down, I trace the curve of his lip and then slide my thumb into his mouth. He sucks on it fervently, his tongue doing sinful things to it. I don't even need to imagine what that mouth can do to me. I no longer need to stay up, jerking myself to thoughts of it. I've experienced it.

It was a fucking dream come true.

"Shit, Maggie, why do you always look so good."

He hums a little, reaching down and tugging on his cock, taking my finger a little farther in his mouth. And I know, I want this. Want to at least try it. Because I'm dreaming up a future with Maggie, a future I didn't think I could have, but maybe now seems possible.

"I want you to fuck me," I blurt, my voice hoarse with desire.

Maggie groans around my finger and then pops it out of his mouth.

"Oh, baby, are you sure?" he asks, and I swallow nervously.

Am I sure? Yeah, fuck yeah, I am. "Show me how to make it good for you."

He moans, reaching for my boxers and tugging them off. They pool near my ankles, and I step out of them. His hands slip up my thighs, and my muscles bunch and flex beneath his fingertips.

"Well, I'm sure it will be good no matter what, because it's *you*, Sem."

"Stop saying shit like that," I groan.

"Why? It's true. This is going to be amazing. Now tell me, which position do you want your first fuck to be in?"

I grab onto my dick and stroke it, watching his eyelids droop with lust. "I want to look at you when you're inside of me."

Maggie's eyes start to glaze and his cock twitches. He likes that. Likes that I want to see him when he's tunneling inside of me.

"Okay. I'll be on my back. That way, you can control everything."

"You sure? I don't want to crush you," I mutter, but Maggie isn't listening. He's grabbing a condom and some lube. Impatient as always.

He's on his knees on the mattress, pressing me down with his hands, and I go willingly. "On your stomach first. I'm going to prep you."

I do as he says and then glance over my shoulder. "Do I need it? I've been wearing the plugs."

"God, I know you have. It's so hot," Maggie moans and

then adds, "And yes, we need to do this. Let me get some lube up there. Want to make it good for you too."

I do as he says and try my best not to come with the feel of his fingers opening me up. I can hear him panting, liking how good I'm taking it.

"My god, Sem. Your ass is so sexy."

He leans over and bites the meat of my ass cheek. I grasp the bedframe and arch my hips back, fucking myself on his fingers.

"How often have you been wearing my plug?"

"Every day. Been waiting for this."

"God, marry me," he mutters, and my heart rate picks up speed. I'm going to have a heart attack. Did he mean it? Probably not. His fingers are knuckle deep in my ass, and he tends to ramble a lot when he's horny, spouting off shit and scrambling my brain. But hell, I like it. I really like that idea.

Maybe he'll ask me again.

We've only been together a few weeks, and before that, we were...I'm not sure what we were.

But at this moment, if really asked me, I'd say yes, no matter how crazy it seems.

"Okay, I think you're ready," he says, his cock already sheathed and ready for me.

I eye it, and he smirks at me. "Didn't want to have to wait to put it on. So I did it while I was knuckle deep in your ass. What can I say, I'm a multitasker."

I snort, and then all humor fades as he lies down on his back and watches me. This is it. I've never sat on a dick in my life, and here I am doing it for him...because I want to try everything with him. Because this means something.

Slowly, I straddle him, throwing my large thighs over his narrow hips and press my hands to his chest and run my fingers around his nipples. I use my leg muscles to keep most of my weight off of him but my entire body is vibrating with nerves, and I know he can feel it.

"You're shaking," he says, rubbing a hand up my arm. "We don't have to...."

I reach back and position him right at my hole and sink down.

"Oh my god," he groans, his back arching off the bed. I breathe deeply through my nose, accepting the sting. Fuck, that's weird, but it's not as bad as I thought it would be. And my dick certainly doesn't discriminate. It's hard, throbbing, and leaking profusely onto Maggie's chest, waiting for me to move.

"Sem," he groans, his eyes rolling back into his head when I sit on him completely. He's breathing deeply, his chest rising and falling with stuttered breaths. I trace the ribs beneath his skin as my gaze blurs.

"Are you okay?" he asks, his eyelids fluttering open and taking in my watery eyes. "That was too fast. You need to be careful, Sem. This is not a competition. This is supposed to be enjoyable."

My voice trembles. "Nah, I didn't want to wait. Wanted to feel you inside of me. Wanted all of you. Tell me you like it. Tell me you like being inside me."

Maggie's hands flex against my thighs and he smiles up at me. "I do. I so do. It's different, because I've never done this before, but I like your weight on me and you feel so good. Everything you do makes me feel good."

I press my hand against his throat, squeezing it gently, and Maggie's eyes widen and darken with lust.

I take a deep breath and then shift my whole body up,

dragging his cock through my tight channel until he's right at my entrance and then sink back down on him.

He moans my name, and that alone is almost enough to push me over the edge.

Never in my life did I think I'd be so lucky.

My hands slide through Maggie's hair as he sleeps. He's sprawled completely naked across my chest, and I sigh in contentment.

The sounds he made earlier. It was bliss just listening to them. We will do that again, even though my ass twinges at the thought.

Shit, but I *liked* it. Knowing he was inside of me, stretching me, marking me.

I want to fuck him raw next time. Want him to come inside of me. Want to feel it for days after. Want him to claim me as his.

Man, I'm so screwed. I have it so bad for him. He doesn't even know what he does to me.

Maybe I should just kidnap him and force him to marry him. Then he'll be stuck with me forever.

He sighs against me and makes adorable sleep noises.

I trace the freckles that line his nose and then let my finger move to his lips. Those lips that are slightly swollen from my teeth raking over them.

"Mm, Sem, why are you still awake?" he asks groggily.

I fucked him so good he can't even open his eyes. Damn, that pleases the caveman inside of me.

"Go to sleep," I mutter, and he shimmies up my torso, pressing his face into my neck. I can feel his breath tickle my skin as I pull the sheets up, tuck them around us, and finally let my eyes close.

Maggie's moaning my name as I rail into him the next morning. He woke up eager and hard, and when he saw me in the kitchen, clad only in an apron, he jumped on me. Nearly burned my hand on the stove. It would have been worth it because right now, his legs are over my shoulders as he writhes under me, his back plastered on top of the kitchen table.

God, he looks good like this. Needy. Flushed. Hard.

I reach out and clutch the back of his neck, pulling him in for a filthy kiss.

I love how bendy he is, how he can just fold himself in half.

He gasps as I hit that spot inside of him just right, and he clutches onto my arms tightly.

"Sem. Sem. Sem."

He's chanting my name like I'm some kind of god, and I grunt my satisfaction. He's close, I can tell. I love watching him come undone. Love the smell of him.

"You going to sketch this?" he gasps. "Going to sketch me being fucked by you?"

"Hell yeah," I mutter as I lift his hips up a little and tunnel inside of him.

"I want one of you. Of last night. When you were on me. When I was inside of you."

"Fuck," I mutter, slamming into him. So close. So damn close.

But a knock on the door causes both of us to freeze.

"You expecting company?" Maggie pants, wiggling impatiently beneath me.

"Nah," I say, pulling out slowly and sliding back in.

His eyes close, and he says, "Ignore it then."

"Best idea," I mutter as I slam back into him.

But the goddamn knocking continues.

"Go the fuck away," I roar. Jesus, I just want to come. So does Maggie. He's desperate for it. His cock is bobbing against his stomach, and I grab onto it. Love how it just fits into my palm like that. It's the perfect size.

"It's Max," a voice says, and Maggie freezes, his eyes wide in panic.

"Shit. Shit." He slaps at my arms, and I reluctantly pull out of him.

My cock aches, but it deflates a little with how upset Maggie looks right now. I hate seeing him upset.

"One second!" Maggie calls, disappearing into the bedroom.

I pull the condom off with a disappointed huff, toss it into the trash, and follow Maggie into the bedroom.

I pull on some boxers and then sit on the bed as he frantically dresses.

"Do you think they heard us?" he asks, his hands shaking slightly.

"Dunno. You are loud," I mutter, and Maggie rolls his eyes at me.

"God. I do not want to deal with any of them right now." He glances at me and then says, "Put on some pants at least. You have to hide that monster away."

I glance down at my half-hard cock and sigh. "Whatever you want."

Maggie reaches out and grasps on to my chin. "What I

want is for you to be fucking me right now, to spend the morning with *you*, but that's not possible. Not until he goes away."

He leans over and presses a kiss to my mouth before scurrying to the front door. I grab my pants from the floor and pull them on. I hurry because I don't like the thought of Maggie in there with his brother without me. I need to be there to protect him, to keep him safe.

I move into the living area and see Maggie in the kitchen, handing bottles of water to Max, and two other men who I assume are his brothers. The three of them all look similar.

And by that, I mean that they look like assholes with the same eyes, hair, and build. Clones.

I lean against the wall and cross my arm across my bare chest, flexing slightly so they know they shouldn't mess with him. I'm bigger than them. I could take them all if I wanted to.

"This the guy?" one of them says to Max, who just eyes me warily and nods.

"Yeah."

His two other brothers I've never met before, nod at me. I just narrow my eyes at them.

"Sem," Maggie says, sounding nervous. "You've already met Max. This is Matt and Mitch."

I just stare at them. They shift on their feet and then look at Maggie. I don't like how they glare at him, it makes me want to throw someone right out the window.

"So," Maggie says, clearing his throat. "What are you doing here? You never visit." He glances at each of his brothers as he fiddles with his shirt nervously.

They watch him and then turn those eyes to me. "A friend

was moving in nearby. Thought we'd stop by and take you to breakfast."

"We already ate," I say, balling my hands into fists.

"Is that what you were doing when we knocked on the door?" Mitch asks with a smirk. "Cause it sounded like someone was getting railed. Probably you, huh, Mag."

Maggie told me about his siblings one night lying in bed. His fingers were tracing patterns across my chest when he told me that Mitch is the meanest. How he goes out of his way to degrade him with words, all the while pretending like it's just a joke.

Maggie shrinks farther back, and I push off the wall and move toward him. I want to press him into me, and carry him away. Away from their ugly, hateful gazes and words.

"Back up," I mutter, pressing my chest against Maggie's back.

I lay one hand on his shoulder and the other on his hip, and he shrinks back into me.

Max, Mitch, and Matt glance at my hands on their brother, but I refuse to remove them. If they don't like it, they can leave. They weren't invited here anyway.

"I think you all should maybe go," Maggie says, his voice so small. "We have plans. I'll call you, and we can get together another time."

I narrow my eyes at his brothers, who just shrug and meander around the apartment instead of leaving. Like they own it. I hate them in this space, tainting it.

"Can't we hang a bit?" Matt asks. "We've been worried about you."

"I'm fine. As you can see."

Max leans against the wall sipping on his water. "You sure?"

"Of course," Maggie says, and then when his brother turns away, he looks up at me.

"I want them to go," he whispers. "Can you make them leave, Sem?"

But before I can move to do as he asks, Matt's glancing down at something on Maggie's desk.

"What the fuck is this?" he barks, his eyebrows drawn together in confusion.

He holds up the nude sketch I'd drawn of Maggie ages ago and waves it in the air. "Who drew this perverted shit?"

"Put that down," Maggie gasps, stepping forward and then stopping suddenly. I hate how unsure he looks.

I clench my fists against my sides and stride across the room. "I drew it. Put it the fuck down."

Matt glances at the drawing and hands it to me. I move to set it down when Mitch lets out an ugly cackle.

"I fucking knew it. All those gay clothes you wear in secret. I told you, Matt. Mags is a total fag." He slaps Matt on the shoulder and then eyes Maggie, who has gone pale. "You take it up the ass, bro? This big guy fucking you? You always were a pushover...."

I don't even think, my brain switches offline and I just let my arm swing. My fist clocks Mitch right in the jaw. A sharp pain zings up my arm as his head snaps back violently. I'm numb from the pain, adrenaline coursing through me. So I do it again, aiming for the nose this time. It cracks, and Mitch howls as blood drips down his chin.

He's stunned. They all are. They're bullies who never expect anyone to fight back.

Well, I fight the fuck back.

I'll burn down the world if Maggie asks me to.

"What the hell, man?" Matt shouts, moving to his brother and then glancing back at me in horror. "It was a joke."

"It wasn't fucking funny," I bite out. Then I swing my arm in an uppercut and knock Matt right under his chin.

His mouth snaps shut with a clack, and he stumbles back, knocking over the lamp on the end table. It crashes to the ground and shatters.

And that's when all hell breaks loose.

The three of them are on me, punching, kicking, clawing. It hurts like fuck, my body growing bruises, but I don't let up, just continue to jab my fist into their ugly fucking faces.

Blood covers my hands, my arms, my lips. I can taste it.

Copper. Metallic.

My fists are moving blindly now, knocking into them, pushing them. I'm in a rage. Those words. Their eyes. Maggie's pale face.

I'm blind to it all. I'm feral.

And then I hear it.

A snap, a cry, and a thud.

Turning around, I see Maggie clutching his cheek, blood trickling down his face. His eyes are wide as he takes me in. Oh fuck, I must have hit him by accident.

He looks horrified.

I must look like a fucking monster.

I am a monster.

I inhale shakily as his brothers move in next to him. Max rests a hand possessively on Maggie's shoulder.

"What the hell? You hit him, man. He's half your size." Max spits, his eye half swollen shut, and I step back, nearly tripping over my own feet.

Maggie shakes his brother off and moves toward me, but I

stumble backward again. His pretty face is starting to swell and bruise because of me.

I fucking *hurt him*.

"I'm..." I choke out. "I'm so sorry...."

"No," Maggie whispers, his voice breaking. "It was an accident. This is not your fault. I shouldn't have tried to grab you. I just wanted everyone to stop."

I open my mouth to speak, but I can't even breathe. My vision is going hazy. I'm gasping for breath and I'm going to fucking pass out.

Not in front of them.

Not here.

I force my legs to move, and I push past them all. Wrenching the apartment door open, I stumble outside. The air is hot, humid almost. The sun beats down on my skin, and I burn from it but my feet don't stop moving.

I don't even know how I make it home but I stumble inside and double over, my bruised hands clutched on my stomach.

They throb.

I gag violently, but nothing comes up. I'm empty inside.

Running a hand over my face with shaking fingers, I inhale deeply.

I don't even know who I am anymore.

I hurt him.

I left him with *them*.

I glance in the mirror and see my bloodstained face. I swipe at it with a trembling hand, and it smears across my skin.

I was never any good for him anyway.

I knew this but stayed anyway.

I hurt him.

He'll never trust me again.
I don't even trust myself.
He's better off without me.
I have to let him go.
I have to stay away this time.

MAGNUS

He's here. I can feel him in my apartment. He haunts the spaces like a ghost. He left me three days ago, and I haven't seen him since, but I can still feel his presence.

It's been the longest three days of my life. I've moved through the five stages of grief a hundred times since he disappeared. I'm currently back in the depression stage.

My phone rings, and I see that it's my mom texting. I don't even read it. Just delete her message and set my phone back down.

They can all go to hell. I have nothing to say to them. All of them have tried to reach out, but I don't need their shit. If I never see them again, I'm fine with that. Sem was my home, and now it's all crumbled to dust because they couldn't just mind their own fucking business.

"Hey," Colin says, tapping his hand on the table, bringing me back to the present. "Are you okay? I can come back another time. You don't seem...you just seem like you're not okay."

He glances at the yellowing bruise on my cheek, and I rub at it. It stopped throbbing yesterday, but it's a sad reminder that he's gone every time I look at it. I wish it would just disappear already.

I huff out a breath and rub at my tired eyes. "I'm sorry. I guess I'm not really in the mood to work. My mind's a mess."

Colin reaches over and squeezes my hand. "You haven't heard from him?"

"No," I whisper. "I tried calling his phone a million times but it just goes to voicemail. I drove to his lot but the RV is gone..." Ugh, I run my hands roughly through my hair and blink away the tears. "He never thought he was good enough for me. I think this tipped him over the edge. I don't think he's ever coming back. His brother said he's in Colorado."

Colin removes his hand from mine and rubs a hand over his jaw. "Shit. But he loves you, right?"

My chest clenches, and I rub at it. "We never...we never talked about that."

Colin's gaze meets mine and he leans a little closer to me. "Hey, just because you never spoke the words doesn't make them untrue. Just from watching you two in the same space a few times, I could see that he adored you. His eyes were always on you. He couldn't look away."

A sharp pain moves across my abdomen, and I close my eyes through its pain. "I thought so too, but he also left me... so there's that. You don't leave the person you love."

I think about the stack of papers left on my kitchen table three days ago. The drawings of me. I'd slept fitfully that night, tossing and turning. Then I'd heard it, the snick of the door, the soft shuffling of feet, but I'd moved too slowly. He was gone by the time I'd run into the living room. The papers scattered across the hard surface, mocking me. He never wanted to part with them, and yet there they were.

It was a sickening symbolic gesture.

And I hated him a little for it.

No matter what Colin says, no matter how much Sem adored me, he won't be coming back.

"Can I offer you some advice? From past experiences...."

I nod and stare into his kind eyes.

"Sometimes, you shouldn't wait for something to happen. Life's too short."

I raise an eyebrow at him and tilt my head. "That's cryptic. Care to expand?"

"Do you want him back?"

"Yeah." My voice comes out so small.

Colin leans back in his chair and says, "Okay, so if he doesn't come to you, you go to him. Find him and force him to listen to you."

My heart sinks at that advice. It's easier said than done. He's in an entirely different state. He didn't even tell his brothers exactly where he was going. I'd have to search the entirety of Colorado to find him. My broken heart doesn't have the patience for that. I want him back with me now. Not tomorrow. Not next week. Now.

"We'll see," I mutter, feeling terribly exhausted. My spirits have been crushed, ground to dust. I'm a mess.

"Don't give up. He's probably just upset and needs time."

"Yeah. I just..." my words trail off, and I sigh. "Thank you for coming by. I'm so sorry that I've been useless. I promise next time that I'll be more helpful with the project."

"No need to apologize. I get it. After my ex and I split, I didn't move from my bed for days. I'd say you're doing much better than me."

I manage a small smile at that, push myself up from my chair. "Hey. Before you go, I have a book for you. Found it in the library last week. I think you'll like it."

I move into my bedroom and shuffle through the pile of

clothes I haven't bothered to fold. I'll do it later when I find the energy. Right now, nothing seems to matter much.

"Where the hell are you?" I grumble, flinging a pile of clothes onto the floor.

And that's when I hear it.

"Oh," Colin says with surprise in his voice, "Sem. Hi. Magnus is in the bedroom. Let me go get...."

The book is forgotten. It can stay buried for eternity. I move so fast that I stub my toe on the edge of my bed. Pain shoots up my leg, but I ignore it as I skid into the living room. My eyes are wide as I take in Sem standing in the doorway. Damn, he looks *good*. Worn, tired, with shadows under his eyes and a few days of stubble on his face, but so fucking sexy.

Those blue eyes move from me to Colin, and his face turns ashen. Those blue depths dim slightly.

Oh fuck.

Nonononono.

"Sem," I breathe, moving toward him like he's a wild animal. My hands are out, my voice calm as he just steps backward, shaking his head frantically.

"Fuck. I shouldn't have...Fuck...I'm sorry."

Frantically, I reach out for him, but he tucks his arm behind him. The fact that he's evading me makes my heart palpitate in my chest.

"Don't you fucking dare," I grunt, reaching for him again, but he sidesteps me.

He swallows roughly. "I need to...."

He starts to move away from me, and I shout, "Don't you dare fucking run away again!" I don't care who hears me. I'm desperate for him to stay. We need to talk this out. I hate not being able to talk shit out. I just want him to *stay*.

Colin moves up behind me, and I inwardly curse him. I

want him to just leave. Sem's tortured eyes move from Colin to me, and he clears his throat as he slowly moves farther away.

"This is…. I need to…I'm sorry," he whispers, and then he's spinning away from me. His long legs carry him down the stairs, and I don't even think twice about what I need to do. I just give chase.

My bare feet slap against the ground as I trip onto the blacktop of the parking lot. They're going to be torn up after this but I don't even care.

"Sem!" I shout, pumping my legs faster, but he's quicker than me. I'm never going to catch him. He moves farther and farther away in the distance, and my eyes sting. My chest burns. I'm getting a fucking cramp in my side.

Goddammit.

Suddenly, my foot lands on something, and a sharp pain slices through the sole of my foot. I cry out loudly, skidding to a stop. Glancing down through wet eyes, I see blood seeping from my skin.

"Shit," I say, lifting up my foot and seeing a piece of glass protruding from the bottom. "FUCK!"

Suddenly, Sem's in front of me, crowding me. His face is drawn, his hair falling messily over his eyes.

"Maggie," he breathes, and then I'm pulled up into those strong arms and cradled against his chest. His walk is clipped, and then he starts to jog, bringing me back up toward my apartment. I hold on to him, clutching at his shirt, fisting it in my palm. The pain in my foot is almost forgotten as I press my face against his neck, inhaling him.

God, he smells so good. I missed him.

Don't go. Don't leave me again.

My breath comes out in choppy waves, and then I'm

sobbing as he pushes through the apartment door and gingerly sets me down on the kitchen table. I keep his shirt clenched in my fist, and he reaches up and pries it from my fingers. His touch burns as I grasp for him.

Sem's face falls, his eyes taking in my wrecked state, and he reaches out to swipe at the tears on my cheeks but then quickly pulls his hand back. He tucks it against his side, his fist flexing over and over.

He doesn't even want to touch me. How is that possible when he couldn't keep his hands off me mere days ago?

"Will you..." Sem turns to Colin and swallows roughly.

Why the fuck is he still here? Why won't he just go away? He's ruining everything.

Sem exhales shakily and says, "Will you make sure he gets this taken care of? You'll do that, right? Take care of him. For me?"

Colin nods and then says, "Why don't you stay? I can go. He wants you to stay."

"No...no, I really can't. Please."

Colin clears his throat and nods, his eyes wide. I can barely see him through the tears invading my vision.

"Don't you fucking go," I whisper through broken breaths. My throat is closing in on me, and I reach out but just grab onto air.

Sem looks away, taking a step back. "It's better this way. I shouldn't have come, I'm sorry. I just...missed you. But you're better off, Maggie. I have to go."

I swipe at my running nose and shake my head frantically. "What the hell are you talking about? Why won't you understand? It's *not* better this way. You are *not* leaving me with Colin. You can take care of me just fine. I want *you* to take care of me, Sem."

Sem's jaw works back and forth, and for a moment, I think he'll change his mind, but then he just shakes his head and takes another step back. He turns to face Colin and says softly, "Please make sure he sees a doctor for this. It looks deep."

"Don't you fucking leave," I cry, my voice breaking. "If you leave, it's over. Do you hear me? Over."

Sem looks at me with glassy eyes and runs a hand down his face. "You were always too good for me anyway. This wouldn't have lasted." And then he turns and disappears.

A small sob escapes my mouth, and I clench my chest. If my heart was broken before, I'd been fooled.

No, my heart is obliterated now.

I curl up on the table and only move when Colin carries me to my bed.

When I wake up in the middle of the night, I hobble into the kitchen and see Colin's finally gone. He'd stayed with me, bandaging up my foot and promising to take me to the doctor tomorrow. I ignored him, my face buried in a pillow, my eyes shut. I don't care about my foot or seeing a doctor. They could all go to hell.

I hiss when my heel hits the floor. It's a nice reminder that I'm alive when I feel dead inside.

Reaching up, I grab a glass of water, fill it and gulp it down, letting the water soothe my sore throat. Some dribbles down my chin, and I just let it. I'm a freaking mess and I don't know what to do.

Leaning my forehead against the fridge, I breathe deeply, fighting back the sudden wave of nausea that's hit me. I can't believe he showed up and then left me, *again*. How much different would it have been if Colin hadn't been here? Would Sem have stayed and talked?

I gag slightly and breathe through my nose. When the wave of nausea recedes, I tilt my head, and my eyes catch on a piece of paper rustling around on the kitchen table. I hop over and smooth it out.

"Let your plans be dark and impenetrable as night, and when you move, fall like a thunderbolt." -The Art of War
Don't give up.
Life's too short.
Go get him.
-Colin

CHAPTER FOURTEEN

I'm fuming. I've been in a state since Sem left for the second time. I've moved past the depressed stage and am firmly in the anger category.

He left me with fucking Colin.

I'd told him if he left that it was over...and he *left*.

The reality of this sat like a lump of lead in my stomach initially. How could he leave when it meant the end for us? But then gradually that lump transformed into a burning coal that lit something in me.

When I'd first set eyes on Colin's note, I'd crumpled up that piece of paper and tossed it in the trash. It sat there overnight, until I'd retrieved it the next morning.

Then I smoothed it out, taped it to my bathroom mirror and plotted.

If he won't come to me, then I'll fucking go to him.

Asshole.

He won't see it coming.

I question my sanity a little, but I know one thing. When I'm done with him, he won't ever leave me again.

I'll make sure of it.

"Luke," I say into the phone, my voice trembling with determination. "I need your help."

SEM

"He's better off," I mutter, moving back and forth through my RV. I've worn a path in the wood floors, but I don't even care. Nothing really matters much right now. Everything seems a little less meaningful without him.

But that's my fault, isn't it?

I made that decision.

A week ago, I'd left for Colorado. Drove straight through the night without even stopping. When I arrived, I parked the RV and slept for an entire day before waking up with an aching chest and a throbbing head.

I debated the merits of staying away, of giving him space, but then a mere two hours later, I drove back home to see him.

I've gone completely insane. If I thought it was bad before knowing Maggie, it's even worse now. I've had a taste of bliss, of life, and I gave it up.

If you leave now, it's over.

I grab at my hair and tug. Pain pricks at my scalp, but I barely feel it. "Fuck."

I spin and papers flutter around me. He litters my space. Maggie's face stares up at me everywhere I look. That smile, those eyes, those lips.

I should rid myself of them, burn them all, but I can't quite bring myself to do it. I'd parted with my original drawings before I'd left and regretted it immediately. I'd missed them. They were a part of me.

So I worked almost tirelessly the past week to recreate them.

I haven't slept and I haven't eaten. I've just drawn and drawn until my hand cramps.

My eyes snag on the picture I drew today, the one of Maggie on his table, tears streaming down his face. I can't get that image out of my fucking head. It's etched there and I can't erase it. I should have never gone back to his apartment, but I had to see him. To make sure he was okay.

And then I'd left him.

With Colin.

He'd been hurt and I'd let another man take care of him.

"He's better off," I try to reassure myself, but I don't quite believe it. My heart is frayed and my stomach hurts. I find it hard to breathe. My vision goes hazy for a minute, and I blink rapidly, trying to regain control.

It's futile. I'm not in control anymore.

I'm unreachable.

Not even Luke or Liam can get me out of this hell I've walked into.

They've tried. My whole family is worried about me since I showed up two days ago, parked my RV, and hunkered down like a hermit. They watch my rig warily. They're all afraid I'm going to snap.

Too bad I already have. I'm so far past okay it should be laughable.

I need therapy for the shit crowding inside my head.

I should go back, should beg for his forgiveness. I never meant to hurt him.

Would he forgive me? Take me back?

If you leave now, it's over.

Maybe I can watch him, just keep my eye on him like I did in the beginning. I just want to make sure he's okay, that he's happy.

I move to grab my keys, mumbling to myself. "What if he's with Colin?"

The thought of it, of watching him move on with another man is...I lean over, breathing through my nose.

Doesn't matter. Just need to see him. I'll feel better once I *see him.*

I stand up and move to leave when the door bursts open and Luke and Liam charge into the RV.

I open my mouth to speak but nothing comes out. I just watch them descend.

Why do they have rope?

They're grabbing onto me without a word, the three of us grunting as they wrestle me to the ground.

"Damn, he smells," Luke grumbles, his knee on my back. "He won't like that. Gotta wash him first."

What the fuck are they talking about?

I squirm and kick, but they manage to strip me down to my boxers and tie me up. My ankles are bound and so are my wrists. And when I take a swing at them, they secure my wrists to my ankles and drag me on my ass into the shower.

"What the hell," I grunt.

"Hose him down," Liam says breathing heavily. Luke grabs the knob and turns it on. Ice cold water hits my face and I shout, trying to move, but end up on my side.

"What the fuck," I wheeze as the water changes rapidly to scorching hot. "Fuck, that burns."

Luke quickly adjusts the temp and when it sits nicely at lukewarm, he grabs the showerhead and holds it over my face and hair. I sputter and spit as Liam grabs a bar of soap and begins to wash me.

"I swear to God, bro, if I ever have to do this again, you'll owe me your firstborn," Luke grumbles.

I should retaliate, at least with my words, but my throat closes up and my eyes sting because that soap. The smell invades my senses. It smells like *him*.

So many memories filter unbidden through my mind. Of him clinging to me, of me running my hands across his body, how smooth his skin was, the way he tasted. Why did I leave? I should have never left. He didn't want me to go, and I went anyways.

Why did I do that?

What the hell is wrong with me?

I go limp in Liam's arms and let Luke rinse me off. Then a towel is placed over my head and they're quickly drying me off.

Whatever they have planned, I don't care. This whole thing is too much.

"Let me go. I need to go."

"Nah, bro. We have plans for your sorry ass," Luke says as he leans down, grabs onto my waist and hefts me into his arms. It's impressive considering my size.

My brother grunts and strains under the weight of me and then staggers out of the RV and toward his truck.

I can see my ma in the distance, her hand cupped over her eyes as she watches Luke and Liam heft me into the back of the truck. She makes no move to stop them from kidnapping me. Don't blame her. I'd be happy to be rid of my sorry ass too.

I shift, trying to get comfortable, but the ridges in the truck bed dig into my side and back.

This is what I get. I deserve it.

"Hold on, baby bro," Luke says and then pats me on the head before I hear the truck door shut. The vehicle roars to life beneath me and then I just lie there as they drive me away from my parent's house. I have no idea where they're taking me, and I don't really care.

Maybe they'll just leave me somewhere.

Maybe this will help me get out of this rut I've found myself in. And when I get out of it, I can go back to Maggie and show him that I can be the man he wants.

I should have never left him.

Not even the first time and definitely not with fucking *Colin.*

Suddenly the truck comes to a stop, and I hit my head against the side of the bed. It throbs and I blink away the pain when I hear Luke say, "You asked and we delivered, tiny."

"Oh my god. What the hell, you guys," Maggie says, and my heart picks up speed at the sound of his voice.

He's here. Why's he here?

If you leave now, it's over.

"I wanted you to bring him to me, not hog tie him and drag him out here like you're part of the cartel."

"I wouldn't say cartel, per se, more like the mafia..." Liam begins but then I hear Maggie shush him.

"We are not debating this right now. Is he hurt? Did you hurt him?"

His voice grows closer and then he peers over the side of the truck, his hazel eyes wide as he takes me in my semi-naked, tied up body. They slide across my bare skin and a slight flush covers his cheeks.

Then he points a finger at me, his gaze narrowing. "I'm pissed at you." Then he disappears from view and says sternly, "Bring him inside."

The tailgate suddenly lowers, and I'm pulled into Luke and Liam's arms. I don't even fight it, just let them carry me into the shack I'd built with Liam years ago. They set me roughly down on the twin bed inside the small space and shake out their hands.

"Need anything else?" Luke asks, not meeting my angry gaze.

I breathe deeply through my nose as Maggie moves over to them and shakes his head.

"No, the use of your creepy Unabomber shack is enough. I'm sure there's a story here, but I'll have to wait and hear it another time."

Liam chuckles and pats Maggie on the head before my two brothers wave cheerily at me and leave.

And then I'm all alone with Maggie in this small space and my lungs can't expand nearly enough. My breaths come out in small, short pants as I take him in.

God, he's so fucking pretty.

He moves toward me, his eyes roaming over my body. I notice that his hazel eyes are red-rimmed, his cheeks flushed. His gaze tracks over my naked form and he bites down on his bottom lip.

"I have a lot to say to you, Sem," he says, his voice husky. "And you're going to stay right here and listen."

He reaches into a drawer and pulls out a knife and my dick jumps. Fuck, that's hot.

Slowly, he flips the blade open and stares at it a moment.

Then he holds it over my skin, tracing a light path down my thighs to the rope holding my wrists and ankles together.

With a flick of his wrist, he slices through it and then shakes his head.

"This knife is unnaturally sharp," he mutters as I stretch out before him. My cock bobs under my boxers and Maggie's eyes flare with lust. He lowers his eyebrows and holds the knife out at me.

"Do *not* get hard right now. Not until I'm done with you. I have shit to say, and I don't need the distraction."

I glance down at my tented boxers and press my hands against it. It doesn't help. I haven't touched it in seven days. It's angry and deprived.

"Stop touching it," he huffs. Then he sets the knife down and straddles my chest. I nuzzle my face into his crotch, and he curses me. He wrestles my hands above my head, and I don't even fight it, just let him secure me to the headboard.

"God, you are infuriating. I cannot believe I even have to do this," he mutters and then rolls off of me, leaving me nearly despondent.

"Okay," he says breathless, running a hand through his hair, mussing it slightly. "Okay, now keep your mouth shut. Can you do that? I don't want to have to gag you."

I blink at him and then he nods, determination filtering through his gaze.

"I had to resort to desperate and extreme measures since you're an asshole. Your brothers, of course, were kind enough to help with my little plan. It's scary, actually, how into it they were."

I shift on the bed a little and his eyes are drawn to my crotch.

His cheeks redden and he looks away.

"Now, here's how this is going to go. I'm going to list your infractions and you're going to plead guilty. Do you agree to that?"

I swallow. What the fuck is an infraction?

"Did you or did you not leave me with Colin when I expressly asked you to stay?"

I close my eyes, regret filling my chest and give a clipped nod.

"Did you flee, even when I told you that if you did it would be the end of us?'

I blink rapidly and nod again.

"Why would you do that, Sem? Do you want this to be over?"

I exhale shakily.

"I'll take that as a no. Is that a no?"

I lick my lips and nod. "No."

He reaches out and runs a fingertip across my arm and my entire body lights up. Imagine if he actually ran his hand across my chest. I'd combust.

"I gave you every part of me and you ran away with it. You crushed my heart. But I'm willing to forgive this major transgression, if you admit fault and beg for forgiveness."

I nod and he pokes me in the ribs. "Ask for forgiveness, Sem."

I open my mouth, clear my throat and say, "Forgive me, Maggie."

He rubs at his neck and nods, his eyes a little watery. "Tell me why you need forgiveness."

I clear my throat. "Because I left you and I shouldn't have. I should have stayed. I should have stayed with you."

"Yes, yes you should have. And was me getting hurt your fault?"

I exhale shakily and fist my hands. "It was."

"Wrong answer," Maggie says, and then he reaches for the knife and straddles my thighs.

Lifting up the waistband of my boxers, he drags the knife across the fabric, watching it split like butter.

"Careful," I mutter, and he scowls at me, continuing to slowly slice the fabric.

"I am perfectly capable of cutting clothes off a....ouch," he winces, looking down at his thumb. Blood pools on the tip. "Dammit, Sem. Why do you have such sharp knives? What is the purpose of this?"

I tug against the restraints on the headboard to try and free myself, but they don't budge. I'm left to watch Maggie slide his thumb into his mouth and hop off of me, returning a minute later with a Band-Aid covering his wound.

He glances down at my half-destroyed boxers and then sighs. "I guess I should try and rip them off."

He reaches over, grips the fabric and mutters, "This is way hotter than it should be," and yanks. The fabric splits with an audible tear and then I'm left completely naked. My cock, now free, bobs against my stomach and strains toward Maggie. It knows what's up.

"Ah, much better," he says, sitting on the edge of the bed and running his eyes over me.

"Now let me ask you my question again. Sem, was me getting hurt your fault?"

I wet my lips and arch my hips just a little. "Yes."

"Do you want to be punished? Because I can do that. What will it take for you to admit that it wasn't your fault?"

"Can't change my mind."

He arches an eyebrow at me. "Oh, can't I?"

Then he slides off the bed and moves to a bag on the other side of the room and returns with a large plug.

I gulp because shit, that's big.

"I was hoping I'd have a chance to use this. I bought this in a fit of rage two days ago." he says, and I huff in anticipation as he lubes it up. "I imagined sliding it up your ass while you beg for me back but we're going improvise. Now, roll on your side," he says, and I do as he says, twisting my hips to the right and exposing myself to him.

He runs his hand across my ass cheek and spreads me, pressing the tip to my hole.

"Now relax," he says.

Slowly, *slowly* he presses it inside of me and I gasp at the sensation, humping the air and yanking on my restraints. Finally, when it can go no further and it's settled against my cheeks, he leans back and presses against it.

A light vibration starts, and I hiss.

"Hm, that's a little too low, don't you think?" he mutters and then presses down on the plug three more times until I can hear it buzzing in my ass.

A groan slips from my mouth and Maggie leans back on his heels and sighs. "Good. That's good. Now you need to tell me something. Can you do that?"

I nod, squirming on the bed.

"Do you love me, Sem?"

I meet his gaze and wet my lips. He said not to speak. Do I fucking speak? I forgot the rules. The vibration inside of me is scrambling my brain.

"You can speak," he says, and I lick my lips again.

"Yes."

He exhales shakily and rubs at his eyes, his lips wobbling. "Good because I love you too. And if you fucking leave me, *again*, Sem, I swear to god I will hunt you down. You will not escape me again. I will cling to you, and you will have to wear me. Forever. Do you understand?"

I tug on my restraints and groan. I want to get to him, but these knots are military strength.

"Say it again," I mutter and his eyes flash to me. A single tear drips down his cheek and I want to lick it from his skin.

"I love you, Sem. Even though you're one crazy, reckless son of a bitch. I love you and you are enough for me. You always have been. But I need you to believe it. *Believe me.* Can you do that?"

I nod once and try to rip my hands from my bonds, but they, of course, don't budge. Fuck.

"I'm not sure you do, so here's how this will go."

He pulls his shirt over his head and tosses it onto the floor, then he removes his pants. My cock aches to be touched by him. My entire body trembles with the need to just be close to him.

"I'm going to fuck you. Probably multiple times in multiple positions because I've missed you..." He pauses and tilts his head. "You haven't been with anyone else?"

"Fuck no."

"Good, me either. So, after all the fucking and once you've admitted that my injury was not your fault, tomorrow morning your brothers are going to stop by and we're going to drive into town and we're going to buy rings."

My heartbeat accelerates at that.

"And then we're going to pick a date and you're going to marry me. Preferably soon. Like next week. Saturday works best for me."

I squirm on the mattress, and I gasp. "Oh shit."

"And then I will spend the rest of our lives telling you how amazing you are, and you will spend the rest of your life making all this shit up to me. Preferably whilst inside of me or vice versa."

I'm dry humping the air now. God, I'm desperate.

"Okay. Yeah, okay."

Maggie looks almost shocked. "Are you serious? You're actually agreeing to this? I mean, I just decided to go for it, but I didn't think..."

"Yeah, fuck yeah. I'll marry you."

"Is this the vibrator talking? Because it came highly recommended..."

"No, no. It's...it's you. I want you. I've wanted you since the moment I laid eyes on you."

He cocks an eyebrow at me and then straddles my hips. "Okay. Good because I want you too, Sem. I mean, it's blatantly obvious. I don't know how else I can prove it to you. I've basically kidnapped you to keep you."

He reaches down and grasps onto my neck, squeezing it tightly. My eyelids droop as I arch my hips up to meet his ass.

Maggie lets it nestle between his cheeks and leans down. "Now, I'm going to let you fuck me raw and in return you're going to suck my dick. Then I'm going to untie you and we're not going to leave this bed until tomorrow morning."

"Yeah, yeah okay. Whatever you want. Please. Please."

"If you run, what will I do?"

I gasp, trying to remember. "Um...you'll chase...no, hunt! You'll hunt me down. I'll have to wear you."

He smirks at me.

"You got it, big man. Now what do you want to bet I can make you scream?"

———

My wrists burn from where the rope rubbed me raw, my ass twinges from being impaled on that plug, and my throat is sore from swallowing him down, but I wouldn't trade any of it for the world. Maggie is sprawled across my chest, his fingers tracing shapes on my skin.

Why had I ever thought that leaving was a good idea? Why had I gotten so in my head about it? I was stupid. I'd disappeared so far into my mind that I hadn't thought rationally.

He wasn't ever better off without me. We're better together. Mistakes will be made, compromises even, but it will be worth it. I know it's going to take time to learn how to be loved by this man, but just like art, it's something you perfect over time.

"I'm thinking silver bands. Matching, if possible," Maggie says, peeking up at me and pulling me from my thoughts.

I nod. He can have whatever he wants, as long as I'm included in that.

"You think this is crazy, don't you?" he asks, pinching my nipple lightly. "I mean we barely know each other."

"I know you inside and out," I mutter and thread my hands through his hair. He purrs and rubs his cheek against my chest.

"If you want, we can wait until next summer..."

"No," I grumble. "This weekend is fine."

He sighs. "Okay, so this weekend at the courthouse and maybe next summer, a large reception. That way we don't interfere with Caleb and Whit's wedding. I don't want to detract from them, you know?"

He worries his bottom lip between his teeth, and I tug him up for a kiss.

"Your family's going to think we're ridiculous, aren't they?" he asks as I nibble down his throat.

"So what? You kidnapped me and did they bat an eyelash?"

Maggie glances down at me, his lips twitching. "No, they seemed scarily invested in it, your mom too. She helped plot it all out. She supplied the rope."

I groan and move to stand up, needing a sip of water for my parched throat. Maggie clutches onto me, sticking perfectly against me, his face tucked against my neck, and his ankles hooked around my back.

I lean down and grab a water bottle and uncap it, taking a lengthy swig before handing it to Maggie.

"Thank you, fiancé." He smiles widely at me.

"Almost husband," I grumble.

"Ooh, no need to get snappy, almost husband."

He takes a long sip and then licks the water droplets from his lips. "Will you still stalk me when we're married?"

I roll my eyes. "I don't stalk."

"I beg to differ, and you admitted that you do. So there."

"Whatever. You want me to stalk you?"

"Um, yes. It's weirdly hot."

I press him against the wall and nuzzle my face against his cheek, my lips teasing his ear.

"Then I'll keep doing it. You know I'd do anything for you."

EPILOGUE

FIVE MONTHS LATER

"Why the hell is your husband watching us from the parking lot?" August says, clutching onto his books. "Can't he just come over here and say hello?"

I bite down on my bottom lip and glance up at my best friend. "It's a thing we do."

"Oh my god. Don't tell me. You are both so damn weird."

I giggle at that and then lean against his car. "So...you gonna tell me how you're doing?"

August clears his throat and shoves his books into the backseat of his car. "I'm fine."

"August, you were stuck in your car with Emery for days. In a snowstorm. And you're *fine*?"

"Yeah."

"You hate each other."

He shifts on his feet, the tips of his ear pink. "We managed."

I roll my eyes and throw up my hands. "Fine, you tell me when you're ready, okay? Because I don't buy it. This is all too weird to be true."

August side hugs me and then pushes me gently away.

"Go to your man. He's looming."

I sigh and make my way across the campus to where Sem stands. His long-sleeved shirt strains against his muscular chest and arms, his pants slung low on his narrow hips. His left hand taps against his bicep and I make out the silver ring sitting on his finger.

God, I love seeing that there.

"Hello, big man," I say, setting my bag down and hopping into his arms.

He pulls me into him and breathes against my neck.

"How long were you watching me?" I ask, leaning back and staring into his blue eyes.

"Long enough."

"You have a good day?" I ask, threading my fingers through his hair.

"Better now," he mutters and leans in for a kiss. Our mouths meet and I open for him, our tongues tangling. This has never gotten old. Not once have I ever regretted my decision to take back what I wanted.

And no one seemed to think we were crazy to do it either. His family cheered us on. My family...well, I'll let them know about Sem eventually.

When I feel like it.

August was the only one who had minor reservations. We hadn't known each other long and it was rushed. But when you know, you know.

And with Sem, I just know this is right.

I moan into his mouth, and he tilts his head to plunder deeper. Someone catcalls and we rip apart, breathing heavily.

"Okay, enough of that," I pant. "We should probably get home. I'm horny and I have work to do before bed. Miles to go, Sem. Miles to go."

He leans down and grabs onto my satchel and throws it over his shoulder as he walks me across the parking lot to his truck. He sets me inside and I scoot to the middle. It's where I belong. Next to him.

And when he starts the engine, he tucks me into his side and drives us home.

EPILOGUE

4 YEARS LATER

The bed is cold. He's not here.

I groan and sit up, rubbing at my tired eyes as I blink through the darkness.

I fumble with my robe and pull it on, moving through the small house in search of my husband. And of course, I find him, sprawled out on the ground of our youngest's room, one hand in the crib he'd built holding onto baby Lucy's hand, the other wrapped around our oldest son, Kieran.

They're all fast asleep and I clutch at my chest at the sight.

Could I have gotten any luckier?

How is this my life?

Sem took to being a dad like I knew he would. He's loyal, protective, and loving. A little bit wild, but he's the best thing that's ever happened to them and I couldn't be prouder of the man he's become.

I still have visions of more children, our house filled with the sounds of laughter. Sem's open to it. He mentions it at night sometimes when I crawl into his arms and press myself against him.

He now knows he deserves this. That he deserves me. There was never any doubt in my mind that he did. But that's the thing with relationships, isn't it? You commit to a person, love them through their growth and cheer them on. You walk with them side-by-side through their struggles and celebrate the small triumphs.

I've watched Sem come to love himself.

I'm so glad I didn't give up on him.

I grab a blanket and crawl up Sem's chest.

"Maggie," he mutters when I tuck myself against his neck. His strong arm wraps around my torso and holds me to him tightly.

"Love you," I whisper, not wanting to wake anyone.

"Love you more."

AFTERWORD

Interested to see what happens with August and Emery? That's up next! Follow me on Facebook for updates.

And if you want to see more of Sem and Maggie with their kids click here!

ACKNOWLEDGMENTS

Thank you to my editor, Angela, who made this story much better than the initial draft. You are the best and fantastic to work with!

And thank you to all the readers who bought Whit and wrote me such kind words. You're the reason I keep writing. Thank you!

ABOUT THE AUTHOR

Cora Rose loves any kind of romance and consumes way too many books each year. She currently lives in the U.S. and spends her days daydreaming about the characters inside her head.

You can reach her on Facebook or email her at CoraRose-Romance@gmail.com

ALSO BY CORA ROSE

The Unexpected Series

Whit

Sem

Emery

Luke

Lex

Colin

Diablo

The Inevitable Series

Until Him

Always Him

Standalone

Waiting for You

Unlucky 13

Exception

Printed in Great Britain
by Amazon

Printed in Great Britain
by Amazon